The Lost Generation

Endorsements

The war to end all wars didn't, but it did bring immeasurable heartache, suffering and loss on both sides of the Atlantic. *The Lost Generation* takes readers on a journey from peaceful villages to the frontlines, a place where the fate of individuals is decided not by God but by man, where faith is often replaced by a sense of hopelessness and where women awash in blood try to save those they love, those they don't know, and themselves. *The Lost Generation* is a dynamic story from the past whose message hits just as deeply in the present.

—**Ace Collins**, author of the *In the President's Service* series

This gripping and authentic tale, *The Lost Generation*, is unique in the fact that it takes you through three different couples lives who are experiencing the ravages and tragedy of World War I. From England, to Canada, to America, we see how love and faith bind, and sometimes falter, under the weight of such authentic tragedy that a world at war can bring. Hogan describes in realistic detail the gravity of such a weight, but also the beauty and strength of an everlasting faith to bind people through the most difficult of times. Many scenes brought tears to my eyes but I am thankful that the author kept it real, and brought us to a deeper understanding of how Christ is stronger than the hardest places.

—**Pepper Basham**, award-winning author
of the *Penned in Time* series

The Lost Generation by Erica Marie Hogan is a must read for those who want to pay tribute to those generations of family and friends who have served in war and defended their country from greater harm, who risked lives and the loss from loved ones. It's also a must read for those who value love as the most powerful yet overlooked attribute of mankind. Most of all, Ms. Hogan's novel laces this story of three different couples from three different countries with the loving grace of Jesus Christ in a gentle yet gripping way.

—**Elaine Stock**, author of *Always With You*

The unexpected events in this introspective novel feel authentic, and I imagine these characters as real people living during a difficult time. As I read the final chapters, I couldn't help wiping away tears.

—**Johnnie Alexander**, author of *Where Treasure Hides* and the *Misty Willow* series

The Lost Generation

Erica Marie Hogan

Elk Lake
Publishing, Inc.

Plymouth, Massachusetts

Editors: René Holt, Deb Haggerty
Cover Design: Jeff Gifford
Interior Design: Melinda Martin
PUBLISHED BY: Elk Lake Publishing, Inc., 35 Dogwood Dr., Plymouth, MA 02360

Library Cataloging Data
Names: Hogan, Erica Marie (Hogan Erica Marie)
Title: The Lost Generation; A Novel of World War I / Erica Marie Hogan, 322 p. 23cm × 15cm (9 in. × 6 in.)
Description: Elk Lake Publishing, Inc. digital eBook edition | Elk Lake Publishing, Inc. Trade paperback edition | Massachusetts: Elk Lake Publishing, Inc., 2016.
Summary: On August 5, 1914, the world changed forever. For John and Beth Young, the happiness they finally achieved was snatched out from under them. For Emma Cote, her husband Jared would do his duty, despite her feelings. For Christy Simmons, an uncertain future with the boy she loved. The lives of six people from across the British Empire to America were changed forever.
Identifiers: ISBN-13: 978-1-944430-58-0 (trade) | 978-1-944430-57-3 (POD) | 978-1-944430-59-7 (ebk.)
1. young love, 2. Nurses, 3. Red Cross, 4. Soldiers, 5. coming of age, 6. War, 7. heroism

Dedication

This book is dedicated to the casualties of World War I and their families.

Thank you for your service.

Thank you for your sacrifice.

May we always remember.

To Mom and Dad, my sister Denise, and my brother-in-law James, who have taught me and loved me through this entire process and to my ENTIRE family who've encouraged and supported me, even from so far away.

And to Papa. God called you to heaven nineteen years ago, but I've felt you here with me so many times. I know you're watching and I hope I made you proud.

Acknowledgments

This story was born through a series of little inspirations. From my father, who once lamented that, one day, no one would remember the sacrifices the generation of 1914 made for their countries, to the heartrending stories of some of those soldiers—my book, *The Lost Generation*, came alive in my imagination.

Jim Hart—you are the best agent anyone could ask for! Through the ups and downs you were there to support me and alleviate my stress. I can't even imagine how I would've done this without you. **René Holt,** you were so patient with me during the editing process—thank you! My publisher, **Deb Haggerty**, you guided me through the final stages with patience—thank you for being such a blessing and for the opportunity to share this story with the world! **Fred St. Laurent**, who phoned me and offered me the opportunity in the first place. **Jeff Gifford**, thank you for creating the most beautiful cover for my debut novel!

Pepper Basham, Elaine Stock, Johnnie Alexander, and **Ace Collins** thank you so much for taking the time out of your busy schedules to read and endorse *The Lost Generation*. Your kind words are so uplifting and such a blessing.

My ENTIRE Family—Parents, sister, grandparents, aunts, uncles, and cousins, I love all of you so much! Thank you for supporting me from day one!

Julie Lessman, who encouraged me over the years to reach for my dreams and assured me that I *would* become a published author one day.

Tracie Rogalinski—thank you for being the first outside my family to read and love this story. Your reaction to these three couples and their story was an incredible encouragement.

My work family—you've put up with me and my chatter for over three years and I'm so grateful for each of you. You challenge, teach, and support me every day and I appreciate it so much. **Becky, Diana, Brianna, Mel, Frank, Carmen, David, Susie, Amber, AnnCamille, Valerie, Janie, Tracie G., Dr. Joe, Dr. Nguyen, Dr. LeGrande, Dr. Kai**—Thank you.

The Lord has blessed me with so many wonderful people in my life over the years, it would take too long to name them all individually. I thank Him for all of them and for His everlasting love which holds me up every day, giving me the strength and inspiration to write these stories.

Prologue

1918

Blood. I'm standing in a puddle of blood.

Sweat, smoke, gas, and screams overwhelm my senses as I clutch bandages in my fists and try to figure out where to go. But there is no place to go. Because they're everywhere; all around me, begging for me to help as they die slowly before my eyes. A hand tugs on my sleeve, and I turn. I'm numb, dissolving in a puddle of my own grief, but I force myself to move forward. I once thought that being a nurse would be fulfilling, that it would give me a purpose here. That I could help. But that dream of healing the sick is fading faster than I could have imagined.

"Bandages! Nurse, I need those bandages!" a doctor bellows from across the room.

I sprint toward him, even as my mind drifts back in time to the place that brought me here. It was a simple place, a place that broached no harm and where I never would have expected to find the devastation that is now wrapped around my heart. It was a small place; a warm place where my neighbors gathered to spend a few minutes of peace, joy and socializing.

The post office. Where thousands of letters exchange hands every day. Where packages arrive to bring joy to their recipients. Where my heart was shattered into a thousand pieces.

When I was a child, I used to think telegrams were good things. But my mother feared them, more than she feared anything in her life. I didn't understand that. I didn't understand the terror of little white notes with my name typed harshly in black ink across the front. Now I do. I know the terror they hold; I understand why my mother hated them.

"Nurse!"

Against my will, I am brought back to reality. I am forced to move forward, my shoes splashing in puddles of blood and muck as I come to the doctor's side. He gives me the strangest look which I ignore. My mind is still elsewhere. On that small room back home where my world came crashing down on top of me.

The post office. I used to love it there.

STAGE 1:
DENIAL

THE LOST GENERATION

Chapter One

Lancashire, England
August 5, 1914

John would do anything to silence that rooster. He turned over, propping himself onto his elbow to stare down at his wife. Her raven hair fanned out across her pillow as she slept, one arm curled beneath the feather cushion the other circled around her curved stomach. He smiled when her full lips parted, releasing a little sigh as she slept. Beth had wanted chickens. So he'd bought her chickens. The rooster had been his mistake.

Leaning in, he kissed her forehead and then slipped out of bed. The dawning sun sent shadows dancing across the wooden floors as he tiptoed around getting dressed. Every morning he would rise, dress, and make his own coffee. He would not wake Beth unless he had to. He knew her well. If she woke, she'd be up making his breakfast rather than listening to the doctor and resting. The one redeeming quality about the rooster was it woke him before Beth.

John looked back once as he left the bedroom. Beth moaned as she turned over, her belly rocking back and forth as she settled. He closed the door quietly, holding his boots in one hand as he tiptoed down the hall to his daughter's room. He grinned when he saw Melody bouncing on her little bed. He had carved her bed out of his old fishing boat, thus preserving his childhood memories.

His daughter saw him and plunked down on her mattress, giggling.

"Daddy!" She held up pudgy arms.

"Shush." He stepped inside, laying her back down on her bed. "You shouldn't be up."

"Chickens, Daddy!" Melody pointed, kicking her legs impatiently.

"Later, sweetheart." He kissed her head, brushed back her delicate hair. "Go back to sleep and wait for Mama."

Melody pouted, lip curled under when he left. She'd be back to sleep in moments and wouldn't wake again for another two hours. By that time, Beth would be up, making breakfast and waiting for him to come home.

John walked quietly down the narrow hall and down the steps into the kitchen. It was a small house; no sitting room or indoor bath, just the kitchen and bedrooms. But it was theirs. John crossed the small kitchen in two strides and stopped in front of his pitcher and basin. He poured cold water into the bowl and then splashed his face. Grunting from the sting of the icy liquid he looked up into the mirror. Small blue eyes stared back at him, observing a lean face with high cheekbones, gaunt skin, and a long, slightly curved nose. His cheekbones were defined by week-old dark stubble and thick matching dark hair rolled over his head in messy waves. John grunted again.

Beth always says I was fearfully and wonderfully made by God. He grinned at the thought. God must have a sense of humor because he was one ugly chap.

Patting down his face with cold water and soapy lather, he prepared to shave. The sharp edge of the razor rustled against the coarse hairs, swiping them away with clean strokes. John wiped the blade against the edge of the bowl before he started again on the other side of his neck. He'd always wanted to grow a beard, but Beth didn't like it so he'd restrained himself.

Once he'd washed his face again, leaving his cheeks smooth and unmarred by the razor, John stood in front of the window as he drank his coffee. His little family had fallen into this routine when Beth had become pregnant with Melody two years ago. He'd taken a long time to realize he was not like his father and the sweet girl next door, Elizabeth Porter, was the woman he was meant to marry.

Beth had helped him, and she'd waited for him more years than any other girl would have. He'd never forgive himself for all those years of making her wait. He couldn't get them back for her, but he knew he would spend the rest of his life making up for them. If it hadn't been for her, he wouldn't be the man he was today. He wouldn't have found the faith that embodied his very being.

God always has a plan, and it's always perfect. I'm just thankful that Beth was His plan for me. John smiled.

He stepped outside, tossing the coffee grounds into the fresh soil Beth had put down for her garden the day before. John snatched his hat from the nail beside the door and headed down the walkway. As he passed, the rooster strutted back and forth in front of the coop, keeping watch over the hens inside. John eyed him, his eyebrow twitching irritably. His boot caught on an uneven stone, and he cursed.

The rooster raised his head and squawked before he continued to inspect the perimeter. John bent down, pressing on the teetering stone. The stones were old, laid there by his grandfather long before John was born. He had prayed this house would one day be his. He was thankful for having found a woman willing to share this place with him.

John stuffed his hands in his pockets and went on his way to town, whistling as he kicked the crooked gate closed. Mile upon mile of rolling hills surrounded the place John called home, spreading far across the country in bright green waves that rippled in the wind. They lived just three miles north of town down a dirt road leading into the countryside. His parents still lived just a mile from his home in the opposite direction. He did not find himself walking there very often.

He passed the great oak and turned the corner into town. People were still waking up, bringing the streets and buildings to life.

It's changed so much. John smiled, wishing Melody could have seen the town when he was a child. Too much was changing.

"Good morning, Mr. Young!" Sixteen-year-old Bobby Gray shouted from across the street, shifting his books so he could wave.

John grinned at the young man. He'd known Bobby since he was a spoiled little child and watched him grow up into a fine young man.

"Bobby." John waved back before turning into the post office. He smiled at the young lady behind the counter taking a message off the telegraph.

A newspaper sprawled out beside her, dated yesterday. John ran his hand down his face. Beth looked at the newspaper first thing every morning, searching for more news of unrest between countries, threatening to send their world into turmoil. She had asked him yesterday if he put off getting the paper so she wouldn't see the latest reports. He hadn't answered. He knew she was afraid; he could see fear in her eyes and in her manner.

"Good morning, Mr. Young." The girl stood and lifted some mail from below the counter.

John stared at her blankly for a moment. Beth would remember her name; he didn't think his wife forgot anything or anyone.

"Good morning," he muttered, giving up as she handed over his mail.

"I missed you this week," she said pleasantly. "Your mail certainly built up. I saved the past two days' newspapers for you before Freddy took them out to deliver around town."

"Thanks ... uh ..."

"Margaret."

"Margaret, right."

"Well, I'll see you in church Sunday," she said, an amused sparkle in her eye.

"Right, of course," John answered, clearing his throat as he ducked his head to hide his embarrassment. He rifled through the newspapers.

The newest—today's paper—was on the bottom of his stack. John hesitated, his fingers brushing against the edges. He was tempted to look at it, tempted to know what it said before Beth did.

Clutching the letters in one hand, he muttered a quick goodbye to Margaret before hurrying out of the post office. He made his way back through town, his eyes following Freddy as he passed out newspapers to the people on the streets. He avoided the young boy, not wanting to see the front page, dread filling his heart.

People were stopping, standing still on the streets. John looked over his shoulder, catching a glimpse of Margaret through the post office window. She, too, stood still, staring down at whatever was in her hands. One item in his grasp seemed to burn right through his skin as John realized he needed to get out of town … now!

Ever since he was a child, he had acted on instinct. Everything in life had become predictable, from when his parents wanted him around to when friends were using him to get something they wanted. John had quickly learned how to trust his gut … except with Beth. He had never known how to read her, never known what she was going to do or say next. It had been like that from the beginning. Beth saw everything. How his father had abused him; how worthless he'd been made to feel. She had seen it and done something no one else had. She'd *prayed* for him. It was with that simple faith that she won his love.

He would never forget the day they lost her father, the day trusting his gut had become a curse. George Porter had been more of a father to him than his own. He had told Beth they needed to go see her father, insisting they spend that particular day with him. When they arrived, George was already gone. Losing his father-in-law had nearly torn him apart.

John stopped, catching his breath. He hadn't even realized he had started running until he was practically standing in front of his door. He could see Beth through the kitchen window, smiling at something their daughter was chattering about. She held a glass of milk in her hand as she waddled back and forth between the kitchen table and the icebox.

He had caused her so much pain over the years. The last thing he wanted to do was change her again, to break her heart again. John sighed, looking down at the newspaper.

The one thing every person in town had been holding when the world seemed to stop was this morning's paper.

John looked up at his wife again and knew what he had to do. He could not let her face this alone, and he couldn't let her read it in the newspaper.

Slowly he unfolded the front page. The bold letters stood out right away, making his heart ricochet against his ribcage.

WAR

John stared at the headline for a moment more before looking up again. Beth wasn't in view of the window anymore. Folding the paper carefully, he strode forward, determination urging his feet along the hard path. He pushed open the door, smiling when his daughter squealed at his appearance.

"Daddy!" Melody bounced on her little bottom.

"She's been asking for you all morning," Beth announced without turning from stirring the oatmeal.

"Beth, I ..."

"Mum is coming over today," she continued. "You did remember, didn't you John? She's bringing over some of the baby things we had her store for us after Melody grew out of them."

"I remember," he said softly.

"I so look forward to having the cradle in our bedroom again. I can hardly wait!" Beth exclaimed, stroking her tummy in anticipation. John watched the movement and his heart picked up its pace. Would it be a boy or girl? What would they name him? Those had been the thoughts filling his head every day for months now. While working in the fields to provide for his family, he thought of the baby. When he helped Melody feed the chickens and let her watch him milk the cow, he would think of how the new child would change their lives in the best way.

But now, staring at his wife patting the mound beneath her apron, his heart sank. Were all of his hopes now things he wouldn't be able to share with her? The thought was unbearable.

"Beth."

Something in his voice halted her this time. She turned to him, eyes alight and a smile on her lips. But when focused on him, when she saw the stricken look in his eyes and the sadness that lurked within, her smile faded. John closed his eyes.

I promised myself I would never make her frown. I promised myself I would never be the cause of her tears. Oh, God ... help me.

"Beth," he said hoarsely, holding out the paper in a trembling hand. "It's happened."

Beth stared at his outstretched hand for a moment and then snatched the paper. John watched as her eyes examined the text and her fingers clutched tighter around the edges as she read further. He moved to the other side of the table and bent over to kiss Melody's head.

"What does it mean, John?" Beth asked, regaining his attention.

He looked up at her sadly. "I think you know, love."

Beth's full lips tightened, and she tossed the paper onto the table before turning her back. John watched her spine go rigid, one hand clutching the sink while the other pressed on her belly. He stepped up behind her and kissed the crown of her head.

"I love you, darling," he whispered, telling her the same thing he said every morning. "I've got to go to work now."

Then he turned and marched out of the house, leaving her to brood. He knew that was what she needed before she would be able to open her mind and heart to what was about to happen.

That evening, John hummed softly to his daughter as he rocked her back and forth on the edge of her little bed. He kissed her head and laid her gently on her back. Melody's eyes grew heavy, long dark lashes shuttering her sweet blue eyes.

He began to sing, his deep voice filling the room, soothing his restless little girl. Melody yawned, her little mouth forming a perfect O as she stretched her fists above her head. John chuckled, shaking his head as he continued to stroke her silky hair. It had been a long time since he'd sung to his daughter, but tonight the urge had overtaken him. Beth hadn't said a word. Her eyes merely flooded with tears as she turned her back to him.

As she has turned her back on me ever since the news. John sighed. The town was buzzing with excitement as their young men prepared to march off to war. The newspaper was filled with calls to arms. When Beth and her mother returned from town, she had mentioned the bulletins pinned to every building, enticing young men to sign up. John had already seen the young men marching into town together, prepared to go to battle with no idea of what they would be facing. He couldn't remember when their little town had been so busy; so alive.

John returned his attention to his daughter and smiled. Her eyes were closed, her little chest rising and falling beneath her thin nightgown with the peaceful breaths of sleep. He whispered a prayer over her before kissing her head once more. John stepped silently from the room, leaving the door cracked so they would hear her if she woke.

Neither of them had rested since the news arrived. After the shock of it had subsided, their little town had moved into a patriotic frenzy as they prepared to send their brave young men off to war. John had avoided the celebration because he knew what Beth wanted, but he couldn't avoid it any longer. He knew where he belonged in all of this; there was no point in denying it. He couldn't run away; he didn't want to run away. It filled him with pride to know that he could defend his family, that he had the strength to fight for this cause. Beth didn't understand how he could feel that way, and perhaps she never would. All he could do now was give her the love she deserved.

John could hear Beth in the kitchen, still washing the dinner dishes. They were already clean, but she kept scrubbing at nonexistent stains just so she wouldn't have to sit down and talk about it. The tension had been rising in the house the entire day. After he'd told her and left—disappearing into the fields to work and think—

he hadn't seen her again until she returned with her mother in tow. He knew she wouldn't want to talk; he knew she'd need the time to process. Beth understood what came next. John didn't need her permission, but he desired her support.

Perhaps she doesn't understand that it's my duty, but more than anyone she takes pride in her home, her family, and her country.

The thought of saying goodbye was killing Beth inside, but she would never admit it. She would blame it on the dispute over the Belgian border, she would blame it on their country, or she would blame John for thinking duty was more important than staying with his family and being here when their baby was born.

John could accept that, but he couldn't accept her coldness and growing distance between them.

"Beth." He stopped on the bottom step and reached up, pressing his hand to the ceiling for balance.

"What is it?" she asked without looking up.

"I think you've scrubbed that pan enough." John's boots thumped on the wood floor as he moved to her side. "We need to talk."

"I already told you." Beth dropped the pan and turned to him.

The strain she felt was evident in the dark circles under her eyes and the red splotches on her face. She always turned red when she was angry—or scared. John could always ease her mind, until today.

"I am not going to discuss this. There is nothing to talk about."

"Yes, there is." He sat down at the kitchen table, propping his elbows up and pressing his hands together. "I am going into town tomorrow, and you know what I have to do."

"You don't have to do anything." Beth hurried to the chair across from him, reaching out to grasp his hand. "Don't you see, love? You don't need to go. You are a husband and a father. You have given so much to this life, to this land. Why should you give your life for a cause we don't even understand?"

"It's not so simple, Elizabeth."

"But it can be … if you just let yourself believe it's possible." Beth dropped his hand and sat back.

"You know what I must do, sweetheart. I don't like it. The thought of leaving you and the children ..." His eyes moved to her belly, pressed against the edge of the table. "It kills me."

She bowed her head and moved her hands to her stomach.

"I know." Her whisper barely reached his ears.

"I don't ask you to come with me tomorrow when I sign up, but I would ask you to walk me down the lane. I would ask you to hold my hand and be my strength one more time, as you have been all these years."

When she looked up again, he saw her tears. How strong she was to keep from crying until this moment! He saw the acceptance in her eyes, the realization that he would be gone soon. John knew that wasn't easy for her to accept. Beth's struggle to let him go was real, and she fought it even now. Her shoulders trembled as she crumpled her apron in her fists. John wished he could ease the hurt, but his wife was strong.

She will survive this. John took her hand in his, squeezing tight. Then he bent over their twined fingers and whispered, "Dear Lord, You have brought us to a crossroads. Throughout our lives, You have challenged us, knocked us down and raised us up. We know Your will for us is perfect. Help us now as we face this new challenge. Protect my wife and ..." John choked and felt Beth weave her fingers into his hair. He continued, "... and protect my children. Watch them for me as I move forward toward this next challenge."

"Amen," Beth murmured.

John raised his head and saw tears shining in her eyes.

"Of course I will go with you." She used the corner of her apron to wipe her eyes. "I will always be your strength, John. No matter what comes."

John leaned across the table, pulling her forward for a kiss made salty by her tears.

Chapter Two

Canada
One Day Earlier

"What are we doing?" Emma giggled, her hands clasped around Jared's wrists.

"You'll see." Her husband kissed the back of her head, his big hands covering her eyes as he nudged her forward.

The heels of her shoes clicked against stone. Emma's brow wiggled as she tried to imagine where they could possibly be. It certainly wasn't town. There were no city noises, not even the distant rumble of an automobile engine. Wherever they were, it was far out of town, isolated. Her mind spun with a possibility, but she didn't want to get her hopes up. Since she'd met Jared she had discovered anything was possible. He had taught her so much about hope and faith. She didn't know what she would do if she were without him now.

Her nostrils flared as she inhaled, seeking out another hint to her whereabouts. She recognized one scent immediately, and her heart started racing.

"Daffodils?" She turned her head.

"No guessing." Jared was smiling. She could hear it in his voice.

Fresh soil mixed with a crisp breeze filled her nose when her toes bumped something wooden. Emma gasped, pressing her hands to her lips as though in prayer. Her shoulders rose and fell with another breath, knowing what was about to happen. Wet paint overwhelmed the scent of daffodils, confirming her hopes.

"Happy anniversary, Em," Jared whispered against her ear before his hands fell away.

Emma squealed and gazed up at the house. She had been watching her uncle build this house for months, waiting and hoping one day it would be hers. It was exactly the way she had imagined.

A white picket fence circled the two-story house, bordered by the fresh green yard. Emma looked down, rocking on her heels against the newly placed graystone walkway. Her dreams were coming to life right before her eyes, right down to the large porch with a swing and the gables framed by window boxes with small blooms peeking out.

She turned to Jared, who had stepped back, his arms crossed and one hip slack as he watched her. His once-irritating, ridiculous grin now made her heart skip a beat. Emma rushed him, throwing her arms around his neck. Jared chuckled, lifting her right off her feet.

"I can't believe you got it." She pressed her face against his neck. "Thank you."

Emma kissed him, her fingers slipping through his brown locks before he set her back on her feet. He took her hands, turning her around and leading her toward the house. She paused at the door.

"It's silly but … I'm nervous." She giggled again, taking a handful of his shirt to pull him against her and wrapping her arms around his waist.

"Don't be nervous. This is our home now." He kissed her nose. "I told you I'd make all your dreams come true, didn't I?"

She tilted her neck back, laughing.

"You did say that." She went up on tiptoe to kiss his cheek. "So far you haven't done a bad job of it."

"Well, thank you, my dear." He stepped back, bowing slightly at the waist before opening the front door.

Emma rushed inside. She passed the staircase, peeking down the hall toward the kitchen before stepping into the parlor adjoining the dining room.

The parlor was empty except for the alabaster rug her grandmother had given her when she turned eighteen. It was situated perfectly in the center of the room. Emma's grandmother, Judith Nickels, had told her this rug had been the first item to enter the very first home her grandfather had bought. Placing the rug first had become a tradition when Emma's father bought his first house for her mother. Then her father passed it on to her when she married Jared. Emma crouched, running her fingers over the soft material.

"You already started moving us in," she murmured, tears flooding her eyes. "I love you, Jared Cote."

His gaze sharpened on her when he reached down to pull her back to her feet, guiding her back out of the parlor and up the stairs. When they reached the top, he said softly, "Close your eyes."

Emma obeyed, wrapping his thick arm around her waist as he led her down the narrow hall and then stopped. She detected the flicker of candlelight and the faint scent of melting wax.

"Open."

Her eyes fluttered. Emma smiled, leaning back against her husband when she saw the lone mattress on the floor, surrounded by daffodil petals and new white candles. A breeze fluttered her favorite lace curtains in the windows, the ones she had boxed away for the whole year they'd been married, waiting to unpack them for an occasion such as this.

Jared pulled the pins from her hair, letting her blonde waves fall down her back before he bent to kiss her shoulder. She shivered and closed her eyes and turned her head when he pressed his lips to her cheek.

"Welcome home, Mrs. Cote."

Emma woke the next morning to the beating of her husband's heart. The candles had gone out long ago, the breeze from the open window pulling their aroma right from the room so all she could smell was her husband's scent. She breathed deeply, soaking in his pure fragrance. Three years ago, when she'd been eighteen and foolish, she'd turned up her nose at the poor young handyman who came to fix her mother's sink.

The first thing she noticed about him was his odor. She walked into the kitchen to find half a man sticking out from under the kitchen sink. She was overwhelmed by the mix of sweat and dirty water. When he stuck his head out from under the sink, he was covered in dirt. Emma immediately wondered if he'd taken a bath in a week.

Now she smiled when she thought about that meeting, how fixing one sink snared Jared into many family dinners at the Nickels' house and eventually an internship in her father's carpentry business. Every stick of furniture she now owned was built by Jared and her father.

When she was eighteen, Emma would never have imagined herself with him like this. She could feel the press of her wedding ring digging into her finger where his shoulder trapped her hand. Emma turned to the beat of his heart, and he stirred.

"You're awake." He moved his hand to her head, brushing aside her tangled hair.

"I am," she replied, reaching up to smooth her fingers along his cheek.

"What were you thinking about?" he asked.

"I was thinking about how we met. How one broken sink snared you into a hundred family dinners and parties."

"I loved every one," he whispered, "because you were there."

"I was remembering my early days as a nurse. Do you remember? I got that position at the hospital right before I met you. I had so many dreams and, at the time, I thought you'd get in the way. You were right when you called me high and mighty." She giggled softly. "I thought I was too good for you. How wrong I was."

"Hmm," Jared murmured and kissed her forehead. "How wrong we both were."

"You know I thank God for you every day. Every morning I wake up and think how blessed I am, how I wouldn't change a thing from the moment I met you."

His eyes burned with love as he leaned over to kiss her. "I think the same thing. Every day."

"We should get up." She yawned, sinking deeper against the curve of his body. "There's so much to do."

"Hmm." His eyes closed again.

Emma pushed up onto her elbow, the sheets tangling tighter around her body. She reached down to pinch one of the daffodil petals.

"You're right." He sat up, wrapping his arms around her. "Your mother and Sarah will be here soon."

"They're coming?" Emma jerked out of his embrace, clutching the sheets around her.

Her eyes widened when Jared lay back, clasping his fingers behind his head as he lounged against the pillows. His grin said it all, and she smacked him on the chest.

"You didn't think to tell me that last night?" she yelped, crawling off the mattress to quickly gather her clothes from the floor.

"If I had told you last night, you would have been awake before the crack of dawn to get the kitchen spruced up." He shrugged, his eyes never leaving her while she dressed.

"You're impossible." Emma crawled back onto the mattress to kiss him. "Will you go into town for the mail when you're able to drag yourself out of bed?"

Jared grabbed her waist and flipped her onto her back. Emma laughed, curling her arms around his neck, pulling him close so their foreheads touched. His eyes sparkled as his hand skimmed the side of her waist to her hip.

"You make getting out of bed very hard, Emma Cote." His lips were a feather touch against hers.

"You are wicked." Emma pushed him aside, her face flooding with heat as she composed herself once more and hurried to the door.

"I know." When she looked over her shoulder, he had resumed his position on his back, hands behind his head. "But you married me anyway. Best decision you ever made, admit it."

Her eyebrow curved into a perfect arc.

"My father would disagree." His face twisted sourly, and she grinned. "But if we give him ten years, I'm sure he will get used to you. To this day I don't know how you talked your way into that internship."

"I'm talented." Jared rolled his eyes.

"Hmm." Emma reached down to toss his trousers at his head. "Get dressed, Mr. Talented. Unless, of course, you want my mother to find you with your pants off."

A pillow came flying, just missing her as she ducked out of the room.

"Where's Jared, dear?" Grace Nickels set her basket down on Emma's new kitchen counter.

"He went into town with Simon to get the morning paper." Emma followed her inside, carrying the boxes of supplies Simon—Jared's childhood friend—had brought over from the room she and Jared were renting since they'd married.

"Grace, is there anything else that needs to come in?" Sarah, Emma's best friend, bustled in, tying her apron strings behind her back.

"No, just the baskets." Grace pulled back the cloth over the muffins she'd brought. "I still don't understand how Jared managed to purchase this house."

Emma eyed her, resting her hand on her hip. Her mother met her stare, tilting her head curiously as if she was about to ask what Emma was thinking. Grace Nickels was the most beautiful person Emma had ever seen. Her chestnut hair, streaked with silver, was twisted and wrapped in a bun at the back of her head, and her blue eyes still sparkled the way Emma always remembered. Her plain, gray dress was hidden beneath the full apron she wore for their day of cleaning and cooking. There was no one else in the world Emma would want to help more than her mother.

Yet somehow she manages to try my patience. A smirk tugged at the corner of her mouth, and she shook her head.

"He works harder than you think, Mother. We've been saving for a house since before we married. This is our dream."

"I know." Grace sniffled, turning her back.

"Mama." Emma hugged her from behind, resting her chin on her mother's shoulder. "It's been a year since I married him. Are you ever going to stop crying?"

"No." Grace laughed softly. "You were my baby and now … well, soon you'll have babies of your own."

Emma's cheeks turned rosy. She kissed her mother, snatched a muffin and moved to stand by the back door leading to an empty chicken coop. She grinned, staring out over green fields bordered by trees bent to the will of the wind. She could imagine her children running across them someday. She could see little versions of Jared, covered in mud and testing her patience.

Much like their father does now. Emma smiled, licking the last bits of muffin from her fingers.

"Now the cleaning begins!" Sarah announced, handing over a kerchief.

Emma smiled as she tied it across the top of her head to cover her braided hair.

"First eat, Sarah," Grace called as Sarah skipped from the room, cleaning supplies in hand.

"There is no stopping her once she gets started." Emma snatched up a broom, following her out. "I suppose you would like to start in the kitchen."

Grace just grinned.

Emma strolled out the front door and was immediately accosted by a cool breeze. Her kerchief fluttered against her hair, threatening to slip right off as she began sweeping sawdust and dirt from her new porch. She was halfway through when she heard an automobile rumbling down the dirt road. Emma looked up and smiled when she saw Jared behind the wheel. He stopped the car right in front of the gate.

"Mother's getting started in the kitchen." She turned, propping the broom up by the door. "She started crying again this morning. I think it's just all the excitement and—"

Emma stopped on the second step. Her husband stood at the gate, staring at her in silence, the morning paper clutched in his right hand. Something was wrong. Her heart filled with dread the moment she looked in his eyes. There was no devilish grin on his handsome face, no spark of light in his eyes. As he stepped toward her, he opened his mouth to speak, but she moved back, shaking her head. His fist tightened around the paper, making it crackle.

Emma's heart froze. The ten feet between them seemed like a hundred.

Chapter Three

East Hampton, New York
Evening of August 5th, 1914

A warm breeze wafted through her open window, throwing her curtains into the air like clouds of smoke. Christy Simmons turned over in bed, kicking her blankets off. With a sigh, she wiped a hand over the back of her neck to dry the drops of sweat gathering on her skin. Across the room, her sister was sleeping peacefully, unmoved by the news that reached America earlier that morning. Christy wished she could find such peace tonight. The world seemed to stand still for a few moments before it returned to as it had been. As much as the world was changing across the sea, her friends still believed it would not touch them. Christy's family—particularly her father—thought differently.

Turning again, Christy hugged her pillow as her eyes searched out the picture of her and Will on her bedside table. Having their picture taken together was Will's idea. On her fifteenth birthday, he surprised her with the photograph as her present. Her mother had viewed the picture of them smiling at one another as a symbol of commitment on Will's part. Her father had come close to forbidding her to keep it.

A pebble flew through her open window, clattering against the wood floors. Christy leaped out of bed, feet landing with a thud on the floor. Wincing, she glanced at her sister. Annie moaned, but simply turned over, her little leg falling off the edge of her mattress before she settled again.

Grinning, she tiptoed to her window and stuck her head out. Will waved his arm back and forth so she could spot him in the shadows. He must've moved after throwing the rock; he was now standing closer to the white fence that bordered their property. Christy waved back and then turned, snatching her robe from her bed and hurrying out of her room. Her toes sunk into the rug as she moved silently down the hall to the staircase. Looking over her shoulder, she climbed onto the banister.

Biting her lip so she wouldn't squeal, Christy slid down, sucking in a strained breath when the banister curved, taking her in a wide circle to the bottom. Landing with a slap on the cold floor, she wiggled her toes against the marble tiles. This old mansion had been in her family since her grandmother was a young bride, giving evidence to her family's prosperity. Each year something new was added, whether a piece of expensive furniture or a new room to the house.

Everything was always changing in the Simmons's home, almost always for the good ... until this morning's news. Christy shuddered, remembering the stern look in her father's eyes.

"It won't be long until the war reaches America," he'd said, carefully folding his newspaper beside his breakfast plate. "Then our own young men will be dragged into this nightmare."

No one had spoken. They simply let her father feed fear into their hearts and minds until he left for the day. Christy had never been more relieved to see her father go. The mere thought that war could reach them and possibly take Will from her was unbearable.

She slipped out the front door, pulling the ties of her robe tighter around her waist. Her bare feet sunk into the dewy grass as her body seemed to cut through the thick humidity in the air. Christy sighed, tucking a stray strand of her bright hair behind her ear. She sprinted across the yard, knowing exactly where Will would be waiting for her.

Looking over her shoulder, she stared up at the mansion she called home. The Simmons were descendants of British aristocracy, some said. Though Christy herself had never looked too deeply into her family history, she knew her father had inherited what was called old money. It was simply there. Her father didn't need to work—though he did, claiming he couldn't bear to be idle—and her mother had apparently been quite the heiress when she came to their marriage. Christy's face twisted in disgust.

They can keep their money. It's turned my father into a pretentious snob, and I won't let that happen to me. Christy nodded determinedly, then spun away.

She came to the lane, bending to squeeze between the rails on the fence. The roar of crashing waves reached her ears as she came closer to the beachside. Damp, salty air assaulted her, filling her with memories of the first time she secretly met Will down on the shore. Will had nearly broken her window with the rock he'd thrown. Christy was almost certain her mother had known exactly what was going on. But she'd let her go anyway.

Christy came to the incline and looked down. He was standing near the water, tossing rocks. Smiling, she followed the crooked stone pathway down the incline to the sand. Will turned as if he could sense her approach and dropped the rest of his pebbles. He held his arms open for her, and Christy flew right into them, burying her face in his shoulder.

"I thought you weren't coming," she whispered. "You were late."

Will answered her with a kiss. Christy sighed contentedly as she rested in his arms. She opened her eyes and looked up at him. She ran her thumbs over the contours of his face, memorizing the cleft in his chin, the slight droop at the corners of his eyes, and the thickness of his brow. She knew, deep in her heart, she would never grow tired of looking at his face, no matter how many years passed. Will tucked a strong arm around her waist and turned her toward the water.

They sat down on the sand, Christy leaning back against his chest as they watched the water in silence. She knew they were thinking the same thing. Will was never this quiet unless something was weighing on his mind.

"What was it like at the paper today?" Christy asked, leaning her head back against his shoulder.

"Busy." Will slid his arms around her waist. "Troubling."

"I read your father's article. It was very … informative." Christy said. "Did he agree to come to dinner tomorrow evening?"

"Do I have to answer that question?" He pressed his lips to her temple.

"I suppose not. He will never approve of us, will he?"

"For him, it's a matter of pride." Will tightened his grip. "You don't want to know his opinion of your father."

"I'm sure I can guess." Christy sat up, turning to face him. "He would say, 'Son, you will never be able to fulfill Christy Simmons's needs. That girl has money in her blood, and her father would never let her marry a poor reporter like you.'"

Christy cupped his face in her hands.

"There's just one problem with his assessment."

"What's that?"

"I happen to love you." Her forehead touched his as her eyes gently closed.

Will moaned deep in his throat and drew her tightly against him. Christy smiled, scooting onto his lap as her arms wrapped tight around his broad shoulders.

"Will?"

"Yes?"

"Do you think my father's right? Do you think the war is going to reach this far?"

The waves were moving closer to them, the gentle purr of water on sand the only sound Christy heard. Will remained silent, holding her firmly in his arms as if he was afraid she was going to disappear. Christy had her answer without his words. The way his muscles gripped with tension and his brow furrowed at the bridge of his nose was enough.

Finally, he spoke. "I want to marry you."

Christy opened her eyes, blinking rapidly to adjust once more to the moonlight illuminating Will's face.

"I want to marry you, too," she answered.

"I don't want to wait, Christy." His palm moved gently up and down her back. "Let's go right now. We'll run away, and our families will never come between us again."

"Will, we can't." Christy slipped off his lap, kneeling beside him. "We're too young."

"I don't care."

"I do." She combed her fingers through his hair. "I'm fifteen, Will. There's still so much I have to learn, still so much I have to know before I could be a good wife for you. I'm not ready."

She pulled him forward for a long, lingering kiss.

"I know that I want to spend the rest of my life with you. And I hope that we will both still feel the same way when I'm eighteen."

He exhaled when she paused for breath, his warm breath tickling her cheek.

"And if it's meant to be," Christy continued, "then our families won't come between us when the time is right. It's as simple as that."

She kissed him once more before she rushed away, hurrying back up the stone steps. When she reached the top, she saw Will standing by the water again, his hands in his pockets as the wind tossed his dark hair. Her heart nearly stopped when her mind raced back to that headline in the morning paper.

It won't reach us. It won't take him from me. Please God, don't let this war take him from me.

THE LOST GENERATION

Chapter Four

Canada

Two days had passed. Emma tugged on the edges of her kerchief, pulling it tighter on the base of her head. Taking a deep, determined breath, she pushed the couch, its legs groaning on the wood floor until it thumped to a stop at the wall. With hands on her hips, she surveyed the room.

With her father's help, they'd finished moving the rest of the furniture. Jared had been silent, disappearing for hours at a time to think. At least, that's what he said he was doing. Emma didn't wonder what he was thinking about. She didn't think about his time away from their new house at all. He could come and go as he pleased; Emma wouldn't question it.

If she questioned, she would have to look at the whole picture, and she was not going to do that. She was not going to ask what was in the paper this morning, nor would she ask why two of her new neighbors went into town waving flags, leaving their mothers dabbing tears from their cheeks as they sent them on their way.

Emma bent to smooth out the corner of her grandmother's rug. She paused for a moment, pressing her hand to her racing heart. She took a deep breath and squeezed her eyes to shut out the images of young men leaving her neighborhood or the look on her mother's face when she brought a meal this morning. Emma sent her away, insisting everything was fine, and there was no need for tears or charitable meals. She certainly didn't think the situation warranted sympathy.

Emma rose and, pulling the kerchief from her hair and removing her apron, headed for the door. After hanging them on the peg by the door, she smoothed the front of her dress, then snatched her reticule from the chair and stepped outside. Jared still hadn't returned with the morning mail. She wasn't going to wait any longer.

Emma lifted her face to the sun, bathing in its warmth as she made her way down the stone walk and out the gate. The neighborhood was quiet this morning, still waking up. She made the short walk to town where she would get a ride to the hospital with her fellow nurse, Rosie Trent. Jared was already at work when she headed out. Her father was strict about his interns coming in early.

Emma smiled and released the breath she'd been holding, her thoughts resolved.

This is the way it will be, always. Jared and I will work hard, as we always have. At the end of every day, we will meet back at our house to have dinner together. Nothing will change. Our lives don't have to fall apart because of a headline in the newspaper. Why should we have to sacrifice happiness because of something that has nothing to do with us?

Raising her head higher, she walked proudly into town. Everyone was bustling about, automobiles honking and swerving to avoid people crossing the street. Emma grinned and waved when she spotted Rosie stepping out of the shop across the street, but her hand froze in midair when she saw her friend's husband step out after her. Slowly she lowered her arm until her palm pressed to her skirt.

Emma turned away from the sight of the uniformed couple, tightly closing her eyes to remove the image. She took a deep breath and forced herself to put one foot in front of the other as she continued to the post office. Just as her hand hovered over the doorknob, she saw the figure standing at the counter. She froze.

She didn't have to see his face. She'd know him anywhere. His broad shoulders, squared and straight, exuded an air of pride. His dark hair curled slightly at the nape of his neck.

I need to give him a haircut. It's been too long since his last one.

When he turned, Emma spun away, her stomach twisting into a knot.

This isn't happening.

Emma's heels clicked rapidly against the sidewalk as she made her way back through town. The clicking heels and her beating heart were all she heard as she hurriedly took the shortcut to her house. She could feel his eyes on her the whole way as he followed slowly, keeping distance between them. He knew her well, and he couldn't approach her like that out in the open, not yet. She wasn't ready. She would never be ready.

This shouldn't be happening. This is wrong. This is all wrong. Emma's lungs constricted as she gasped for breath.

Rushing through the back door, Emma tossed her reticule onto the counter. Her trembling fingers reached for the apron on the hook. Emma tied the strings tight around her waist until it felt like a tightened corset beneath her ribs. She plunged her hands into the soapy water in the sink, fishing out the unwashed dishes. They clattered together, drowning out the sound of Jared's footsteps as he climbed the steps of the back porch.

The door squealed when he entered. He closed it with a thump behind him. Emma stared through the window behind the sink, her eyes unblinking as she concentrated on the meadow.

It is so peaceful. The slightest breeze makes the grass ripple like water. How can the world seem so quiet and peaceful when my heart is in such turmoil?

"Emma." The sound of her name on his lips had once brought such joy. "Emma, please look at me."

Her eyes squeezed shut, pushing tears from their corners. She shook her head, rolling her lips together.

"I can't." She choked, her ribs expanding with a deep breath. "This isn't happening. It's not real. This is a nightmare. We're both going to wake up and everything will be fine."

"Em, it's real. Just ... look at me."

Emma's fingers curled around the edge of the sink, her knuckles white. *If I look at him, then I'll have to give in. I will never have the choice to go back. I can never change it once I look at him.*

"Emma … we don't have much time." Jared's voice cracked. "*I* don't have much time. I need you now, more than ever. Please turn around."

Emma tilted her head back, causing the tears to flow down her temples and into her hair. Slowly she turned, forcing her eyes open. His hat was tucked beneath his arm; the crisp new uniform stretched across his chest. The dull gray-green color twisted her stomach into knots. He had never looked more handsome, his boots shiny and glinting in the sunlight, his hair combed back, and the golden buttons glittering above the harsh black belt at his waist.

It was overwhelming. It was too much. A sob wrenched from her throat, and Emma crumpled to the floor.

His wife was humming. Jared closed his eyes as Emma combed her trembling fingers through his hair. The snip of the scissors echoed in the kitchen as she cut away the locks at the nape of his neck. The tune to "Be Thou My Vision" slipped between her lips. It was her favorite hymn; the first one she'd ever sung. Jared had introduced her to their small village church the Sunday after they'd started courting. They'd both been so excited, and it had been important to Jared to share that part of his life with her, so she'd went. Jared had been overwhelmed when Jesus slipped His way into the heart of the woman he loved. He took a deep breath, his shoulders rising and falling.

"Hold still," Emma ordered, brushing at the back of his shoulders.

"It's almost time," he answered, turning his head slightly over his shoulder.

"I know." Emma pulled the comb through his hair.

A lock fell over his forehead, brushing against his eyes. Jared reached back, taking her wrist in his hand to bring her around to face him. Emma didn't meet his gaze as she trimmed the wave of hair that fell over his face. He let his gaze wander over her, taking in the way her dark golden hair was softly pulled back into a neatly braided bun at the crown of her head. A few loose strands gave the illusion of a halo. He admired her fair skin, flawless and glowing in the sunlight, and her full cheeks, defined by her curved cheekbones. Then there were her beautiful, blue eyes, piercing him with every emotion a man could possess. Jared felt her fear and her love as acutely as if it were his own.

"Emma." His fingers tightened on her hips.

"There." She smiled. "All done."

Emma gently pushed his hands away. Jared stood, pulling away the towel draped over his shoulders, dropping loose hair to the floor around his feet. He watched his wife as she returned with the broom to sweep up after him.

The silence between them was painful. Jared felt more helpless now than he ever had in his life. To see her pain was breaking him. He remembered a time when there was nothing but peace and faith in his heart. He remembered a time when Emma had helped him find that peace. But now ... now he saw nothing in her eyes, nothing in her that would help keep his soul alive.

Emma propped the broom against the kitchen wall and smoothed her hands down the front of her dress. Jared watched her, his eyes skimming down her trim figure to her delicate ankles. He ached to hold her, to draw her close, and tell her everything would be all right.

To tell her he wouldn't go.

"Are you ready?" Emma turned to him, clasping her hands.

He recognized her pasted on smile, the one she wore when she didn't want him to know what she was thinking, the one that covered the sadness in her eyes. He knew her too well. That's what his father used to say about him and Emma. He knew what she was thinking. He knew what she would say ... or when she wouldn't say anything at all. His father thought that wouldn't be good for them, but Jared was sure it would keep them together forever.

"I'm ready." He put his arm around her waist, guiding her out of the house.

"I'll drive," Emma announced. Snatching his hat from him, she offered, "Here."

She reached up on tiptoe to place his hat atop his head, brushing his bangs from his forehead and tucking them beneath the brim. Jared stroked his palms up and down her arms before she turned away, once again avoiding his gaze.

Jared followed her to the car, watching her every move, the way she shifted into gear, the way she bounced against the seat as the car rumbled past town. They were heading directly for the train station, not meeting up with any friends to say goodbye, avoiding their families in town. He didn't want to be with anyone but her at this moment. He wanted his last moments at home to be with the one person who meant everything, who had become his life. Jared focused on her, drinking in every little detail so she would be forever burned into his memory.

"You're staring at me," she commented.

"I am," he replied. His voice deepened, and his heart raced in his chest. "I just want to look at you for as long as I can."

He could hear the train from down the road. Emma didn't even glance his way. Her hands clenched the wheel as she pulled up in front of the station. Jared stepped down, tugging at the hem of his coat. His feet ached in the unfamiliar boots; the uniform scratched against his arms. He didn't know where he would go from here or what he would face, but at this moment, nothing seemed worse than leaving behind the girl he'd sworn never to turn his back on.

"Do you have everything you need?" Emma asked, hurrying to his side when he pulled his bag from the back of the car.

"Yes." Jared took her hand as they stepped up onto the platform.

He took in his surroundings. A sea of uniforms surrounded them both, accented by little flags flapping in the breeze. Mothers and wives dabbed moist cheeks, and men held their little children close. Jared turned to face his wife.

"Don't ever do anything foolish," Emma cautioned as she brushed her hands along his shoulders. "Take good care of yourself first. Don't be a hero, please. Don't make sacrifices. War is not the … it's not the right time for …"

Emma caught her breath and closed her eyes. Jared touched her face, lightly moving his fingertips from her temple to her chin. He smiled at her failed attempt to tell him to stay alive, to be careful. He gripped her chin gently between his thumb and forefinger. A tear formed on her lashes when he tilted her head back.

"Just be safe." Emma's fingers clamped his arms, pulling him close. "I'm proud of you, Jared Cote. I'm so proud."

He rested his chin against her shoulder, holding her. Emma exhaled, tickling his neck with her breath. Jared moved his hand along her spine, memorizing the feel of her warm body against his, the way the short, delicate strands of her hair curled at the back of her neck and the way she turned her body to lean against the curve of his waist, fitting them together like two pieces of a puzzle.

"This isn't forever, Em," he whispered. "I'll come back."

"That's a promise you had better keep." Emma lowered herself back onto her heels. Their foreheads pressed together lightly right before he tilted her head to the side and kissed her.

"It's not fair," Emma rasped. "I love you. We were supposed to have so much more time."

"I'm not gone yet, Em." Jared curved his hand along the top of her hair. "This war won't take anything from either of us. I promise you, I *will* come back. We will have forever."

"No more promises," Emma said, shaking her head. "Just … just be here with me. Just for a few more minutes."

Jared folded his arms around her waist. Their breath mingled as they waited for the last call. They waited for the train whistle, the final sound either of them would hear before he was forced to walk away. Her hand curled around the back of his neck, pressing his brow harder into hers. He took the pins from her bun, unfurling her braid. Emma didn't fuss this time as he ran his hand down her silky, smooth hair.

"It's time." Jared traced her spine with the tips of his fingers once more then pressed his palm against the small of her back.

Emma winced at the sound of the whistle.

"I love you, Emma Cote. I'll be home soon." He rubbed the tears from her cheeks with his thumbs.

"I know. God be with you, my love."

"He always is."

Emma looked up at him. Jared frowned, searching her gaze as concern pooled like acid in his stomach. "Remember that, Emma. He's always with us."

"He doesn't give us more than we can bear," Emma replied. "I'll remember."

"Pray for me, my love, as I'll be praying for you."

"Always."

Jared stroked her cheek, his worry easing. He bent close to her, and Emma closed her eyes. Their noses bumped, their lips nearly touching. Then he turned away. He felt cold without her, his movements sharp and stiff as he climbed onto the train, his bag slung over his shoulder. Jared turned, holding onto the rail.

Emma stood at the front of the crowd, red-rimmed eyes staring at him as her tears flowed. The train was moving now, the whistle announcing their departure. He leaned forward so he could see her for as long as possible. Emma rushed down the platform, following the train until she reached the edge.

Jared couldn't look away. Every fiber of his being wanted to leap from the train, to rush back to her side, and never leave her again. He yearned to take back all the hurt he'd caused when he put on this uniform.

But instead, he forced himself to look away. Instead, he turned his back and stepped inside the train.

Instead, he changed his life forever.

Chapter Five

England
The Same Day

Beth stared out the window, her hand moving in slow circles around her swollen belly. She inhaled a long, calming breath. The baby was moving, pressing a little foot against her stomach as he stretched. It was a boy. Beth knew it. John had argued with her on that point, but Beth had been insistent from the beginning. The difference between this child and Melody was like night and day. Beth couldn't explain it. She just knew.

A little hand touched her fingers, and Beth looked down, smiling as she reached to lift Melody from the floor. Her little leg curved across the top of Beth's stomach when she rested her head against her mother's shoulder. Beth closed her eyes, a gentle smile touching her lips.

"Mama sad," Melody whispered.

"Yes." Beth kissed her baby-soft head. "But we must be brave, my darling."

"It's time." John's voice rumbled behind her, causing her heart to flutter.

Beth set Melody back on her feet, resting her hand atop her head. For a moment, she didn't think she could do it. It had seemed so easy this morning. She'd woken and decided to pretend it was like any other day. John had already risen and was walking the fields. Beth prepared breakfast, washed and dressed Melody, and then waited for John to return. They'd spoken only briefly as they ate together, then he'd disappeared upstairs. Now it was time to face him again.

Now it's time to say goodbye. Beth turned, her chin trembling. His form blurred by the tears flooding her eyes. She stepped forward, smoothing her hands over his shoulders. Those big, broad shoulders she loved so much. Every time she looked at him, her stomach fluttered, and her heart raced out of control. This man who didn't think he was worthy of her love. This man who thought he was too ugly, too sinful to deserve her. This was the man she'd chosen to spend her life with because she saw something in him he didn't see in himself.

Unwavering faith. Unwavering love. He doesn't know it, but he's the strongest person, the most self-sacrificing person I know. When he let Jesus in, he held on tighter than anyone else I've ever met. He's perfect for me. Beth struggled to breathe.

"You look so handsome," she managed to say.

"Beth." His forehead touched hers. "I'm so ..."

"No." She framed his face in her hands. "Don't be sorry. You are a man of honor. This is your duty. It is *our* duty. I can accept that, John. I really can."

John's eyes softened. She knew he heard the lie, but he pulled her close and pressed his lips softly against hers. Beth groaned as his hand caught in her hair, bending her neck back. Melody giggled, pulling on Beth's skirt until they both looked down.

"Music, Mama!" Melody raced to the window, jumping up and down.

The music, faint in the distance, was sending off the soldiers. John was right. *It's time.*

"We need to go." Beth turned away, lifting her hat from the peg beside the door.

"Hey," John murmured and cupped her cheek, turning her face to look in his eyes. "Remember what I promised you?"

A tear escaped, trailing her cheek.

"Yes," she whispered. "You won't leave my side until you have to. You will always be with me, even when you're gone."

"Always." He touched her stomach.

"We have to go," Beth repeated, wiping the tears from her cheeks.

She slipped her arm through the crook of his elbow, then, with her other hand, took Melody's hand, pulling her close. Beth raised her head high as they stepped out of the house. The sun warmed her skin, sending rays glinting off Melody's fair hair. A wobbly smile tugged at the corners of her mouth when John looked down at her again.

Beth knew him well. His silence overwhelmed them both, covering the distance between their home and town. He wouldn't speak, not now, not as the road seemed longer, the walk less durable than any other day. Beth had been so sure when she married him, so certain she would never have to say goodbye to him again.

"Till death do us part." That's what we said. So why? Why is this happening now?

The music grew louder as they turned the corner. Soldiers were filing along the street, flags waving and horses prancing as they moved out. From here they would take the train, leaving behind their homes and families. Beth followed John through the crowds as their cheers drowned out the beating of her heart.

He turned to her suddenly, stopping on the sidewalk. Beth never felt further away from him as they stood there, a mere foot apart, just staring at each other. Melody was pulling on her hand, but Beth couldn't hear what her daughter was saying.

"I've made arrangements with Mr. Peters. He will tend to the fields and help with chores about the farm. You needn't worry about a thing, love," John assured her, even though he'd told her all of this before. Beth knew he was stalling.

Neither of us can bear goodbyes.

"Come home." She finally forced the words past her lips, holding back the tears, trying to muster the courage to see him go. "Promise me you'll come home to me. To us."

John pulled her close, clasping his arms tight around her waist. He lifted her up, kissing her right there on the street. Beth wrapped her arms around his neck, holding him tight. She smelled soap from his morning bath, the earthy scent of his skin and she stroked his face, smooth from his morning shave.

He took her wrists in his hands, pushing her arms away. Beth shook her head. John looked in her eyes and then bent, drawing Melody tightly into his arms. Their little girl wrapped her arms around his neck as he covered her in kisses.

"Tickles, Daddy!" Melody squealed, laughing. Beth sobbed.

John rose again, pulling her close.

"Close your eyes," he murmured. "I'll be home again soon. Close your eyes. The next time you see me, I will be walking home to you."

John ran his fingers lightly over her eyes. Beth closed them, memorizing the feel of his hands against her face. He kissed her cheek, her nose, her neck … her lips. Beth trembled, holding tightly to Melody as she wrapped her pudgy arms around Beth's legs.

"I love you." His lips brushed against her ear.

"I love you." She gripped his arms, clinging to him. "I love you so much."

He kissed her once more, his hands framing her neck. Then … nothing. Beth opened her eyes, spinning quickly. But he was gone, disappeared into the crowd. Beth bent forward, one hand gripping her stomach, the other holding tightly to her daughter.

Her sobs were drowned out by the sounds of joy in the town, her broken heart disregarded by the people. Her body was cold, and the void in her soul grew bigger. The people around her disappeared, just as her husband had. Melody looked up, her big blue eyes questioning. Surrounded by neighbors, by friends, Beth felt empty and alone. There was no comfort here, no one who could make this better.

Beth stood alone.

The church was rundown, white paint peeling from the walls and the hinges creaked, but Beth had grown up there. She had been raised in this church. The Porter family had sat in the third row from the front for the past fifty years. They had sung together, their voices rising high to fill the church with their worship. They had cried, prayed, and laughed together here.

I married John here. Beth closed her eyes as she knelt before the altar. She wasn't the first to come here today. Candles were lit, filling the church with a sweet aroma. Each candle represented one of the men she'd seen marching off to war today. But it was the third candle to the right in the fourth row Beth stared at. That candle—that little flickering flame—she had lit for her husband. The flame crackled and spat as a low breeze swept through the room from the open windows.

Beth braced a hand to her belly. The child danced inside of her, warm and safe. Beth smiled, wishing John was here to feel it. There was so much he would miss, so much he would have to catch up on when he returned.

Tilting her head back, Beth looked to the ceiling. Like everything else about the old church, it needed repairs. When it rained, the roof leaked and, if she looked closely, she could see sunlight streaming through a small hole in the far corner. But this was her home away from home. If it ever changed, Beth knew it would rip her heart out.

Closing her eyes, she released a low, raspy breath from between her lips.

"Lord," she whispered into the silence. "I have never asked why. I don't like to ask why because I know you are infinite. I know I must trust your will. But now I am absent a husband, and I have a child coming. I have a little one at home who doesn't understand. What am I to do? I need your guidance and love, more now than ever."

Beth paused, licking her lips lightly. Then she opened her eyes, looking down at the little candle. A tear rolled down her cheek.

"Bring him home to me, please. I have never loved—and will never love—anyone the way I love John Young. I was your instrument in his life. I brought him back to you. So please … bring him back to me. Keep him safe and whole, Lord. Guide his footsteps and make him steadfast. Do not withhold your light from him."

Beth pressed her hand beneath her belly and rose awkwardly back to her feet. Her knees trembled, and her hand shot out for her husband. But he wasn't there, so she steadied herself. Another tear escaped. She swiped it away. Her gaze drifted back to the ceiling, and she smiled and whispered words her father had taught her, "With everything I am, I will worship thee. With everything I have, I will honor thee. With my whole heart and soul, will I love thee. In the name of thy Son—who gave everything so I could live—Amen."

Chapter Six

East Hampton, New York

"Have you lost your mind?" Tommy leaned across the desk, glancing over his shoulder in search of Will's father.

Will grinned as he leaned back to prop his ankles up on the desk. He took another bite out of his apple, a bit of juice dribbling from the corner of his mouth. Tommy came with him to the paper every day after class. They were inseparable, and Will didn't mind. Having a best friend came in handy, especially since his family loved him like a second son.

"I've never been more serious. My parents are going to the Simmons's for dinner, and Christy and I are going to make our announcement." Will tilted his head back, tossing his apple core at the wastebasket in the corner.

"What announcement? That you'll be engaged for three years?" Tommy snorted. "You think a girl like Christy Simmons is going to stand by you for that long? All it's gonna take is one rich guy hand-picked by her father to turn her head."

"You don't know her!" Will snapped, his feet thumping back to the floor. "She wouldn't do that. As soon as she turns eighteen, we're getting married. There's nothing anyone can do about it."

"You know the war is overseas, right?" Tommy rolled his eyes. "Why would you want to start one in the Simmons's mansion?"

Will chuckled, turning back to his desk to lean over the morning paper. The headlines were always the same these days. He had a feeling they wouldn't be changing anytime soon.

"I know." Tommy leaned forward, his palms pressing flat against the desk. "Let's skip out now and meet up with Grayson on the shore. If you don't show up at home, your parents won't go to the Simmons's, and we avoid the biggest catastrophe of the year."

"No, thanks." Will interlocked his fingers behind his head, leaning back in his chair. "Our parents have to face the truth sometime. Christy and I are just meant to be."

"Now you sound like a girl." Tommy groaned as he perched on the edge of the desk. "What happened to my best friend? Why are you suddenly so willing to give up your freedom? You're only sixteen, Will!"

"I know how old I am." Will frowned. "I just ... I just have this feeling. Like every day brings us a little closer to this."

He lifted the paper, waving it in his best friend's face. Tommy glared, grabbing at the paper. Will pulled back, folding it over before tucking it beneath his arm.

"Your family just tells stories about the war, Will. We won't be fighting it," Tommy said, crossing his arms.

"Do you even understand what being allies means?" Will stood and turned to walk away.

"Don't talk to me like I'm stupid. Of course, I know what being an ally means." Tommy followed him. "But if we're not in this already, then what makes you think we will be soon? I'm telling you, this is not our problem."

"Maybe not yet." Will stopped in front of his father's office door. "But something like this only gets worse before it gets better. And we're fools if we think that the United States is going to come out of this unscathed."

"I'll see you later." Tommy waved his hand as he turned to leave.

"Where are you going?" Will frowned.

"Anywhere but in there. Whenever the Simmons are mentioned, your father turns red. I'm not going to be in the same room with him when he's facing an entire evening with them." Tommy saluted him. "Good luck, old friend."

Will waved him away and then took a deep breath. Tommy wasn't right about a lot of stuff, but he was right about this. His family wasn't poor. His father had nothing to be ashamed of, and he always denied that he was, but Will saw the truth in his eyes. They'd lived in the same small house since Will was little. The roof leaked and the porch creaked, but it was home, and Will loved it. As did his mother. Yet his father always griped about the lack of funds, the struggle of their little paper, and the worry that they wouldn't make it to the next year. Somehow, they always did. Will couldn't have been prouder of his family.

I only wish Father was as proud of our accomplishments. I only wish he could see what I see in Christy, a girl who doesn't care about money, who would gladly leave her rich lifestyle behind for me. He fisted his hand around the newspaper, crumpling it into a ball before he pushed the door open and stepped into his father's office.

Cigar smoke wafted up his nostrils the moment he entered. Joseph Garvin looked up and puffed again on the cigar tucked in the corner of his mouth. The moment his gray eyes fell on Will, he sat back in his chair, tucking his thumbs into the pockets of his vest. Will's father was still considered quite a handsome fellow, despite his receding hairline. He had a nice dusting of gray at the temples, a long, sharp nose, and a lean physique that turned many an eye. Will couldn't help but smile, remembering how his mother always talked about how lucky she was to have landed such a handsome husband.

"Son, if you're here to discuss that family, I'd rather not," Joseph grumbled.

"*That family* happens to be a well-respected family here in the Hamptons, Dad. And before you refer to her as *that girl*, my sweetheart's name is Christy," Will replied, taking a seat in the chair in front of his father's desk and crossing his ankle over his knee.

"Sweetheart," Joseph mumbled under his breath. "I've told you before, son, and I'll tell you again—"

"Please don't," Will interrupted sharply. "I love her, Dad."

That gave Joseph pause. He stood up, turning his back. "I'll go to the dinner tonight."

"Thank you," Will said, releasing a breath of relief.

"But she'll break your heart, son. Mark my words. Christy Simmons is not for you."

Will stared at his father's straight back, his broad shoulders hunched with tension, a stream of cigar smoke swirling above his head. Without a word Will stood and left the room, closing the door firmly behind him.

"It's going well. I think it's going well. Don't you think it's going well?" Christy turned sharply toward Will, her punch sloshing in the glass.

Will chuckled, taking the cup from her before she spilled it all over her white dress. He knew she would be nervous tonight, but he hadn't expected her to be so jumpy. They'd talked about it for weeks, planning carefully so they would pick the right moment. He knew Christy wouldn't back out. He knew they would be able to do this if they did it together. But he didn't know what her parents would do.

Glancing across the room, Will could practically see the tension radiating off both their parents, hers sitting on one side of the room and his on the other. Their silence was deafening. Will's mother attempted to talk with Mrs. Simmons, who seemed open enough to conversation, but Mr. Simmons's harsh scowl was holding her back.

Mr. Simmons hovered over his wife, watching her every move as if to be certain she wasn't forming any sort of attachment to Will's mother. He ran his finger and thumb along his prickly salt-and-pepper mustache before lifting his glass of brandy to his lips. The small pouch of his belly hiccupped when he snorted at something Will's mother said, then he turned, practically flapping the tails of his waistcoat at them as he went to stand at the hearth.

Will caught his mother's eye and she smiled, lifting her hand to wave at him. Will returned the gesture, wishing he could talk to her privately for a moment. He wanted to thank her, not just for her patience with their arrogant host but also for her open heart. She made such an effort in preparing herself for this evening. Her dark hair was pulled back in a full, twisted bun and she'd worn her best dress, blue silk and lace, the one she wore to every special occasion. Her neck was decorated with a string of pearls his grandmother had given her before she passed away. Her cheeks were dusted with light rouge.

Will frowned, wondering if his mother sensed what was going to happen tonight. She was smiling, but there was sadness in her eyes. He wondered if she knew tonight she might lose him forever if things didn't go well.

"Are you scared of the consequences?" Will turned back to Christy, rubbing the back of his finger down her cheek.

"He threatened to disown me." Christy bowed her head. "He threatened to send me away."

"We will face that if it happens," Will whispered. "I just can't imagine your mother agreeing to that."

"I'm not afraid of being thrown out of this house. I know that you'll take care of me." Christy smiled. "I just … I would so love their blessing."

"I know."

He kissed her forehead. Mr. Simmons cleared his throat loudly from across the room, and Will stepped back. Christy gulped down a long swig of her punch. Will grinned, pulling her arm through the crook of his elbow.

"Come on. Let's get this over with."

"Now?" Her eyes widened.

"Now's as good a time as any."

They set down their glasses, and Will guided her across the room. Christy was taking deep breaths, and her wide eyes were growing even wider. Their parents were sitting in stiff silence now. Christy's little sister looked back and forth between the two couples curiously. Will was sure Annie didn't understand anything that was going on nor why his parents and hers were so distant with each other.

"Mother, Father," Christy said, breaking the silence. "Will and I have something to tell you."

"What is it dear?" Mrs. Simmons smiled.

"Christy and I have been talking." Will took over, squeezing her hand beneath his. "We both know how all of you feel about us being together."

His father grunted, but Will pushed on.

"But I think you know very well how we feel about each other. We decided. We will admit all this news from Europe helped us finalize our decision." He took a deep breath.

"Go on, Will." Christy urged.

"I asked Christy to marry me," he said, looking down into her eyes. Her smile filled his heart with courage. "She said yes. We've agreed to wait until she turns eighteen, but we decided we wouldn't wait a day longer than that. We're going to get married on her birthday."

There was a moment of silence ... and then the room exploded.

STAGE 2:
ANGER

Chapter Seven

New York City, New York
June 1916

"I've got it!" Christy gasped as she burst into the office, her face flushed from running, and her hat tilted over her fair hair. She smiled and waved her notepad at Will's uncle. Charles Garvin grinned and reached out a hand to see her notes.

"I think they're good. I hope they're good." Christy bit her lip, her hand trembling as she handed over her idea for the piece. "I want to focus on the Pal's Battalions and what they will mean to the British Empire in the end. The war has not been going well, and all those working men are falling on the battlefield. I don't think anyone has even thought of the consequences of so much death."

"Hmm." Charles nodded without looking up from her notepad. Christy forced herself to wait patiently but allowed her mind to wander.

After that fateful dinner party at her parent's house, she had been given a choice. She could never see Will again and stay in her childhood home, or she could leave within the week and never see or hear from her father again. Christy had been terrified, but with the encouragement of the boy she loved and the promise of being allowed to visit her baby sister, she made her choice.

It had meant moving away from East Hampton altogether. Living with Will's family had been out of the question, and her father had ruined her in the eyes of their elite friends. Coming to live with Will's childless aunt and uncle in New York City had been the best option.

"If you go, you are no longer my daughter. I will never see you again," her father had threatened. It was a superficial response and completely expected. She knew he would say it; she knew he would be dramatic about it.

Christy remembered the tears on her mother's face and the shock in her father's eyes when she walked down the stairs at the end of the week, suitcase in hand. After the first year of living away from home, her mother finally received permission to come to the city with Annie for a visit. Her father even sent a note of greeting and concern. Still, he tried to make her come home, and she refused.

She thought she wasn't a child before, but after living with Charles and Louisa Garvin for two years, she realized she had been. But loving Will was not a mistake, and learning to love him even more over the past two years was what would keep them together for a lifetime. She was grown up now, and that was all that mattered.

"This looks wonderful, Christy." Charles skimmed through her notes. "You have a bright future here."

"Really?" Christy plopped down in the chair in front of his desk. "I never thought I was cut out to be a reporter, but writing these stories has been the most exhilarating experience of my life. Being right there at all the speeches and being the first to hear the news from overseas … it's just so fascinating and exciting!"

"Now you know why Will loves it so much," Charles said with a grin. "You two have more in common than you even knew."

"We discover new things about each other every day." Christy blushed as she pulled her hat from her head. "You know, I was so afraid we would grow apart. I was afraid my decision not to run away with him was a mistake, and if we waited three years, I would lose him. But now … now I know for certain that some things are just meant to be. Sometimes you just know, no matter how young you are."

"That's very true." Charles reached across the desk, and she took his hand. "Louisa and I once felt the same way about each other."

"Is he coming tonight?" Christy stood once more, bending over to take back her notebook. "I haven't heard from him since the letter last week."

"He said he'd be here, Christy, so he'll be here." Charles perched his spectacles on the edge of his nose, going through the papers on his desk. "Will has never broken a promise to you before."

"I know." She turned the ring on her left hand around in a circle. "I just miss him."

"It's not easy having such a distance between you and the person you love."

"No, it's not." Christy hurried back to the desk then, leaning over to kiss his cheek. "Thank you for being so good to me. I'll see you at home."

"Goodbye, my dear." He waved to her when she stepped out of the office.

Christy paused just outside the door, closing her eyes as she listened to the tap of typewriters. Strong scents assailed her—fresh ink and thin paper, sweat from hot bodies working over the presses. The newsroom had become one of her favorite places when she first moved here. It all started when Louisa sent her for the first time after Charles forgot his lunch. She had been swept away by the hustle and bustle and the excitement of stories coming to life on paper.

Christy also realized this was Will's life, the life he loved. From that moment, she decided to learn all she could. She never thought she would love it in the same way Will did.

Suddenly her feet slid to a halt. Her eyes widened when she took in the form coming through the front door. Everyone continued working as if the man in the fancy suit was a regular visitor to their place of business. But Christy knew he wasn't. Her thundering heart was all she could hear or feel. Her knees trembled, knocking together as she tried to step forward.

Christy's mouth went dry as beads of sweat formed on her forehead. She licked her lips, but it did little to help. Finally, she managed to force out a single word.

"Father?"

Christy gripped Will's hand, studying his expression. He just stared at her, blinking every now and again. She chewed on her bottom lip, wishing he would break the silence. Giving this news to Will, telling him her father's announcement had been more trying for her than seeing the parent she thought would never speak to her again.

"Please say something," Christy whispered. "I know seeing him at your aunt and uncle's dinner table was a shock. I understand. I felt the same way when he walked into the newspaper office. But after hearing him out, I had to bring him back here. You do understand, don't you?"

"Yes, of course. It's just so unexpected," Will replied, clearing his throat and flexing his fingers around her knuckles. "I was sure he was going to cut us off for the rest of our lives."

"He's my father, and somewhere in his hard heart, he does love me." Christy touched his face. "And because he loves me, he loves you too."

"I wouldn't go that far," Will said with a chuckle.

Christy sighed, tilting her head to his shoulder. They swayed back and forth on the porch swing, watching the twinkling stars in the night sky. Will's visits had been few lately. They were working hard to save enough money for a place in the city so he could begin working for Uncle Charles.

Leaving behind both their families and making a fresh start on their own seemed like a good idea two years ago. Now that they were less than a year away from marriage, it seemed like the best decision they could have made.

"Are you all right with this? With him wanting to be there?" Christy rested her hand on his chest, fiddling with the buttons on the front of his finely pressed white shirt. She slipped her hand beneath one of his suspenders, tugging on it.

"Are you?" His voice deepened, thick with sudden emotion.

Christy looked up into his dark eyes and saw the same thing she saw every time he was about to kiss her—his eyes growing heavy, his lips parting, his heart pounding against her palm. All evidence to the way she made him feel, all evidence to the fact that after all they'd been through to be together, he loved her more now than he had when she first snuck out of her house to meet him on the shore.

"My father came all this way to ask me if I still wanted him to walk me down the aisle at my wedding." She strained toward him, their lips almost touching in a light kiss. "Of course I'm all right with it."

"If you are, I am." Will kissed her, pressing his hand hard between her shoulder blades, bringing her closer.

Christy smiled as his hand tangled in her hair, tilting her head back at a sharp angle before he kissed her again. His lips moved along her jaw until he was nibbling on her earlobe. Christy giggled, curling her knees up toward her chest.

"Stop!" she cried, laughing as he nuzzled his face into her neck. His arm swept beneath her knees to draw her onto his lap.

"One more year," he murmured huskily, bending her back against the arm of the swing. Christy braced her arms around his neck, shaking her head as a hot flush filled her cheeks. "One more year and we'll have a place of our own."

"And we'll be alone," Christy whispered, turning her head around. "Completely alone."

The curtain fluttered behind her as his aunt ducked out of sight. Will ignored her, his hand clasping her neck to turn her back around so he could cover her mouth with his. Christy wrapped her arms tightly around his neck, his body warming her with its proximity. A cool breeze tickled her hair, tugging on the loose strands when he raised her up, his arms a solid support against her back to keep her suspended above the arm of the swing.

There was a sharp knock on the front door. Will jerked up, stroking his fingers through his hair. Christy tried to catch her breath, reaching over to smooth his hair from his face as she settled her feet back on the ground. A hot flush filled her face when he grinned sheepishly at her, taking her hand just as the front door opened.

Louisa stuck her head out. "Would you like something to drink?" she asked, winking at them.

"That sounds wonderful." Christy leaped to her feet. "I'll help you."

"Hurry back," Will called.

Christy looked over her shoulder at him, her heart still racing from his kiss.

"I love you."

"One more year," he answered and winked at her

Christy giggled as she turned to hurry after Louisa. She stopped at the door, pressing her hand to the wall for support. Her thoughts raced to the news she had collected from overseas earlier today. The thought that the war was getting closer to home was ever present in her mind.

One more year. We have one more year, and then we'll be together. This is meant to be, and nothing will get in the way of that. Nothing will ever come between us again, I just know it.

She took a deep breath, pasted a smile on her face, and stepped into the kitchen.

Will watched her go, his heart still racing from their kiss. Christy had grown more beautiful with each passing day. Her eyes seemed brighter, her hair softer, and there was a glow to her skin that he hadn't remembered before.

The glow of freedom. Will grinned. The shackles of her family had fallen away and left Christy to explore growing up in the real world. Will had discovered that he loved her all the more as they both matured.

Leaning his head back he thought of the many Sunday mornings he'd spent with her since she moved to the city. He tried to come out as often as he could on the weekends, and she always managed to convince him to attend church with her. Will closed his eyes, recalling their last conversation about it.

"Don't you attend on your own?" Christy had asked, worriedly.

Will smiled. "When the urge takes me, I go. It's not that I don't believe, of course, I do. I believe God exists."

"Then why don't you attend regularly?" Christy wondered.

"I don't know," Will said, shrugging. "Maybe it's just the way I've been raised. My mother attends every Sunday, but she's never forced me to go with her and my father ... well, he talks to God when he needs to. It's been a bit of a bone of contention between them over the years."

Christy's forehead had scrunched at that, and a contemplative gleam lit in her eyes. She'd squeezed his arms and smiled tightly. "I love you, Will. But if you don't attend church, then we may have some difficulties."

Will's brow rose. He'd covered her hand with his possessively and answered, "Sweetheart, if it's important to you, then, of course, I'll attend every day. I've told you, I believe in God."

Christy had still looked uncertain, but she hadn't brought it up again. He'd been sure to attend diligently every Sunday he was with her.

I hope she's satisfied with that.

"What are you frowning about?" Tommy's voice broke through his reverie.

Will looked up and found his friend standing on the top step, his shoulder leaning heavily against the rail and his thumbs hooked in his pants pockets. He grinned. Tommy always looked so relaxed at other people's homes, if not in his own.

"Nothing," Will replied. "What're you doing here?"

"Thought I'd stop by," Tommy said, looking down. He scuffed the toe of his shoe against the porch.

Will sobered. "Is it your father again?"

Tommy cleared his throat loudly and then nodded, without looking up. Will puffed out a long breath and leaned forward, elbows on knees. "You need to spend a night here?"

"No," Tommy declined. "Can't leave my mother alone with him, can I?"

"No, I suppose not," Will agreed.

The front door opened, and Christy stepped out, holding two glasses of lemonade. Her smile lit her entire face.

"Oh! Good evening, Tommy!" she greeted, handing one of the glasses to Will. "Would you like some lemonade?"

"No, thanks. Sorry, didn't know you two were visiting."

Christy sat with Will on the swing, snuggling close. "Don't be silly, Tommy. What brings you into the city?"

"My parents and I are here for a week because of Dad's work," Tommy replied. "Mom insisted on coming so she could visit her sister."

"I'm so glad you stopped by!" Christy said enthusiastically. Will draped his arm around her shoulders. "Are you hungry?"

"Well," Tommy hesitated, smiling sheepishly. "Just a little."

Christy shot out of the chair. "I'll get you something. Do you want anything, Will?"

"No thanks, Chris."

Christy bent over and bussed his cheek lightly before skipping back into the house. Then Tommy caught his eye.

"What are you looking at?" Will snapped.

Tommy's grin widened. "Nothing. She just … has a nice walk-away."

Will stood, fisting his hand in a fake threat and Tommy laughed. Will joined him, shoulders trembling as they stood side by side, looking out over the neighborhood dimly lit by the moonlight.

"So, you still plan to marry her, huh?" Tommy asked after a while.

"Yep," Will affirmed.

"Good."

Will looked at him, brows raised. Tommy ducked his head, avoiding his eyes.

"She's a nice girl, Will. We were all wrong about her, weren't we? Me, your dad ... all of us."

Will reached over and gripped his best friend's shoulder. "Yeah, she is a nice girl. She's the best person I've ever known."

"I wish——"

Christy came out before Tommy could finish and his friend was once again all smiles and jokes. Will watched him for a moment, curious as to what Tommy had been about to say. The boy was deeper than he liked to let on, but not many people saw that side of him.

Except me.

Will rejoined Christy on the swing and settled in, wrapping his arm around her as he listened to Tommy recount one of the parties he'd recently attended in the Hamptons. Christy's musical laughter filled the air, and all of Will's worries washed away as the sense that everything was going to be fine settled on his heart.

THE LOST GENERATION

Chapter Eight

Canada
The Same Day

"We need more morphine." Emma lifted the pile of sheets from the floor, hurrying through the ward. "Private Reynolds needs some relief."

"I'll let Dr. Kingston know." Rosie rubbed her forehead with the heel of her hand as she followed after her. "I've never seen this hospital so full."

"I know." Emma paused, looking over her shoulder.

The hospital had become a recovery home for so many soldiers needing constant care and therapy. Emma looked at the sea of men, some of them struggling on crutches with the help of nurses, others trying to sit up on their own in bed, still others moaning and crying. She turned away, her heart unable to bear the sight of men waking up not knowing where they were, screaming in the night, and reaching for invisible weapons to defend themselves.

"Has he let the doctor help him yet?" Rosie wondered.

"What?" Emma blinked, hurrying out of the ward.

"Private Reynolds. Has he let the doctor help him begin therapy yet?" Rosie took some of the sheets, lightening Emma's burden as they walked to the end of the hall.

"No." Emma shook her head. "We have to get him moving soon. It's not good for him."

"The man lost his leg, Emma," Rosie whispered as she dropped the sheets down the chute. "He needs time."

"He's had time," Emma answered, leaning back and pressing the base of her skull to the wall. "His leg was removed in England.

He was brought home for recovery, Rosie. Lying in bed and being pumped with morphine isn't recovering. I will relieve his pain, but I will only give him as much as he needs."

"You don't think—?" Rosie's eyes widened.

"That he depends on the medicine?" Emma's brow arched, her voice softening. "We've seen it before."

"I know."

Her friend kicked at the floor, stuffing her hands in her apron pockets. Emma took a deep breath. She knew exactly what her friend was thinking.

"He's on his way, Rosie." She rubbed her friend's arm.

"I know." Rosie cupped her hand over her mouth. "I just … I'm so scared."

"Of seeing Caleb again?" Emma put her arm around her shoulders.

"You know what I mean, Em." Rosie pulled away, hugging her arms around her waist. "You've seen it. These past two years we have nursed soldiers. There are no more children with broken bones or minor surgeries. We have assisted doctors with infection, disease, and amputations. We have helped treat every kind of wound there is."

Emma closed her eyes.

"Caleb is wounded, and they didn't tell me what to expect. I don't know if he's coming back to me whole or not. I don't know if he's …" Rosie stopped, trying to catch her breath. "I tell myself we are fortunate. He's alive, he's coming home, and he doesn't have to go back. But he'll be different."

Emma reached for her shoulders to pull her close.

"You will find a way to reach him again," she murmured. "Jared always used to say that God would show us the way when the world was at its darkest. That's what we're facing now. He'll help us both, Rosie."

Rosie placed her hand over Emma's, clasping her fingers until both their knuckles turned white. Emma closed her eyes and sent a silent prayer for her husband heavenward, just as she promised Jared she would. Every day.

Always.

"Have you heard from Jared?" she asked.

Emma stilled. With a gentle breath, she stepped back, smoothing the wrinkles from the front of her uniform. "No."

"He'll be fine, Emma. Jared's strong." Rosie didn't look her in the eye.

Emma opened her mouth to respond, but no words came out. She closed her lips with a click of her teeth and turned on her heels.

"Nurse Cote!" Dr. Kingston's voice rang out from the staircase.

With a sigh of relief, Emma rushed up the stairs. She didn't want to talk about Jared and the lack of letters. She didn't want to think about her pain. She wanted to be as numb as the morphine made Private Reynolds when overwhelmed by the pain of his lost limb.

She just wanted to work.

Private Reynolds's crutches trembled beneath the pressure of his hands. Emma held his arm, supporting him as they made slow progress down the hall. He had asked for complete privacy as he struggled to learn to walk again. He didn't want the other men to see him. He didn't want to be pitied. Sweat beaded on his brow; his lips pulled tight in a thin line as he took another step.

"You're doing very well, private." Emma encouraged, gently massaging his shoulder. "It will be second nature soon."

"Hmm," the private grunted. "It still hurts."

"I know," Emma comforted. "But the doctor said you need to cut back on the medicine."

Emma watched his reaction, noticing the drops of sweat trickling down his neck. It had to be from more than the struggle on his crutches. She had suspected for some time that Private Reynolds had found a way to get morphine without proper supervision. Keeping him under close watch had become a priority for her and Dr. Kingston. If they caught it in time, the withdrawal wouldn't be as difficult. If not …

"Have you heard from your husband?" Private Reynolds asked. He panted, his crutches thumping as he took another heavy step.

"Not yet." Emma pursed her lips.

"Maybe he's dead." Private Reynolds eyed her. "You have to be reading the news. All those casualties reported …"

"I am more aware than most," Emma snapped. "You don't need to be cruel just because you're angry with the doctor and me."

"Emma." Rosie's voice brought her around. "Go get some fresh air. I'll finish up here."

Emma nodded, waiting for Rosie to come support Private Reynolds' arm before she marched away. Tearing her cap from her head, she stepped out the door into a cool breeze. She curled her arm across her stomach as she tried to calm her racing heart. She stepped down and moved toward the yard where soldiers walked with the assistance of nurses.

Ever since they moved some of the patients from the hospital in town to the convalescent home, Emma felt less the nurse she used to be. Becoming a doctor had been her dream since she was a child, but becoming a nurse meant she worked with patients much sooner. But now … now she'd give anything to go back and pursue that education. She could do so much more good if she knew more.

Jared would say that she could still be a doctor if she earnestly wanted it. He would support her, he would love her, and he would go wherever she needed to be to get her education. But with him gone, Emma felt empty. She could never make such a big decision without him, and not hearing from him was killing her.

"Are you all right, nurse?" A voice stopped her, and she turned, the breeze pulling at the pins in her hair.

The soldier was tightly wrapped in a dull gray hospital robe, his feet tucked into warm brown slippers. A bandage covered his eyes.

"How did you know I was here?" she asked, tilting her head to the side and crossing her arms over her chest.

"I could smell your perfume." He licked his dry lips and shifted on the bench. "It's Nurse Cote, right? You changed my bandages yesterday. I'm learning," the private continued. "Dr. Kingston says I'm doing well."

"Private Jennings," Emma said quietly as she sat down on the bench beside him. "I remember."

"You're never outside," Private Jennings said. "You're always in the ward with Private Reynolds."

"He's struggling. I don't know how to help him anymore." Emma leaned back, sighing heavily.

"You can't." He shrugged his shoulders. "It's time for him to help himself. That's what I needed to learn. The doctor said I'll have to wear a patch for the rest of my life, but I should be able to see out of my left eye once the bandages come off. Being only half blind is better than not being able to see anything at all."

"That's a wonderful attitude," Emma said with a smile. "I should put you in the bed next to Private Reynolds."

"He will find his way. We all do." He licked his lips again and raised his hand in her direction.

Emma hesitated before slipping her hand into his.

"You know I still see everything. In this darkness, the images come so clearly. I can see the blood, and I can hear the screams." Private Jennings shuddered. "I just want the bandages off so I don't have to sit in this darkness, re-watching that last battle endlessly. I can still hear my best friend's last breath going out before I had to leave his body behind."

"I'm so sorry, private," Emma whispered, hot tears threatening.

"I just want the bandages off." His fingers tightened around hers. "Then I can forget for a few hours before I dream about it at night."

"Give it time." Emma sandwiched his hand between hers. "You don't have to go back. Now is the time for healing, in more ways than one."

"Emma!" Rosie called from the back door, waving her hand to get her attention. "It's time for rounds!"

Emma stood, but the private didn't let go of her hand. Emma looked down, bending slightly to massage his knuckles.

"I come out here every afternoon," he said. "I'd like to talk to you some more."

Emma hesitated. When the first wave of soldiers came in, she had promised herself never to connect. If she was indifferent, she wouldn't tie them to Jared. She wouldn't have to look at them and see her husband's face. But watching the way his head swayed back and forth, searching for her in his darkness, called to her heart.

"Of course," she rasped. "I'll see you tomorrow, private."

"It's Dan." He smiled.

"Emma."

Then she turned, slipped her hand from his, and rushed back inside.

Chapter Nine

Lancashire, England

"Melody!" Beth leaned her head out the kitchen window, waving at her daughter. Melody turned, her little face red with exertion. Her wide smile showed off rows of tiny white teeth. Beth's breath caught again, as it had for the past two years every time she looked at her children. They looked like their father, although the longer he was gone, the harder it was for her to conjure his image in her mind.

"Bring your brother inside now, darling!" Beth waved at her once more before closing the window. "They're always getting so dirty."

"They're children," her mother said, lifting her steaming cup of tea to her lips. "Of course they are going to play in the dirt. You did when you were four."

Beth folded her hands around her cup. Susan Porter smiled at her, the same smile Beth had come to expect since John enlisted. It brought that sympathetic sparkle to her dark eyes that stabbed Beth's heart. Susan had been coming over every week since John's last letter arrived. It had been months since she'd heard from him, and no one knew what to think. Every morning she waited for the news that he was gone. Every morning she waited for the telegram to come, telling her that her husband was one of many who wouldn't be returning home. Her mother's presence was the only thing that kept her sane.

The call to arms had come swiftly to their small town. By the time the campaign was finished, nearly every man she knew in Lancashire had enlisted and marched off to war. Beth had never seen anything like it: men of the same class going to fight alongside each other. It had been a brilliant idea, they said, a way to get the men to fight. They would be fighting alongside their friends, their colleagues. For two days, Beth had read the newspapers over and over, learning about what they'd aptly named the Pals Battalions. She continued to read them several times a day until her heart felt a little less troubled.

Perhaps it will work out. Perhaps fighting alongside friends and colleagues will help keep the men alive. Perhaps, in the end, it will all be worth it.

"Mr. Peters seems to be doing a fine job helping you keep up the place," Susan commented.

"Indeed," Beth agreed. "It's been difficult, though. Every morning I expect John to be there ready to do the morning chores, and I have to remind myself that it's my duty now. I must be up, dress the children and tend to the animals. It's so unusual, Mum. Even after all this time."

"You're holding up well, dear." Susan smoothed her gray hair back from her forehead and leaned back. "Better than I would."

"I have to for the children," Beth replied, slamming down her cup. "But I'm tired, Mum. I am so tired."

"Elizabeth ..." Susan warned, just as the children came inside.

"Mama!" Melody rushed in, dragging her little brother along behind her. "George ate dirt!"

Beth reached down and scooped up her son. George placed his hands on both her cheeks, giggling. Beth shook her head as she rubbed the ring of brown from around her son's mouth. Her heart swelled with love before the sadness started to overwhelm her again. Delivering him without John had been difficult, more than she'd expected.

"Let me, love." Susan snatched the baby from her arms. "Come upstairs, Melody. It's time for naps."

"Thank you, Mum," Beth murmured, wiping her hands on her apron. "Will you stay for dinner?"

"Of course!" Susan smiled over her shoulder before sashaying away with little George on her hip and Melody's hand in her own.

Beth cleared the table, taking the cups to the sink. She spent many hours in front of this window, cleaning up the kitchen and watching her daughter, and now her son, play in the yard. The rooster strutted ahead of the hens, leading them on an adventure around the house. So many times she had stood there, washing dishes and studying her husband as he worked. John did everything in his power to provide for her and their little family. Missing him was breaking her.

She closed her eyes and tried to remember the touch of his hands on her face, the way his kisses made her skin tingle. Two years she'd been without him, with only a letter every few months to remind her that he was still out there somewhere, thinking about her as much as she was thinking about him. He had never seen his son, and she didn't know if the picture she'd sent reached him. France never seemed as far away as it did now.

Beth slammed the tea cups down into the sink, and they shattered. Combing her trembling fingers through her hair, she tried to breathe through the pain of her memories. A tear escaped her lashes. She brushed it away quickly.

"Sweetheart." Susan was behind her suddenly. Gripping her daughter's arms, she rested her chin against Beth's shoulder.

"I'm fine." Beth raised her hands, turning away from her offer of comfort.

"Elizabeth." Susan's voice lowered to a foreboding whisper, the same tone she'd used whenever Beth had tried to lie to her mother and get away with it.

"You're right." Beth turned to her, bracing her hands behind her against the counter. "I'm not all right. But I'm not sad anymore. I'm not crying anymore. I'm not going through the sorrow I've been putting myself through anymore."

Beth took a deep breath, her chest expanding with the raspy breath.

"I'm just ... just ..."

"Angry?" Susan's eyes flooded.

"Yes!" Beth slapped her fist to the counter, her brow furrowing, and her lips tight. "I am so angry! I can't stand it. There's nothing fair about this. How can someone just demand my husband's service? How can the world be so cruel as to take him away from his family, maybe forever?"

Hot tears stung her cheeks.

"I have tried so hard to be strong, Mum, but it's too much. How can I be strong when the world is falling apart? We ... we're not doing well in this fight."

Susan bowed her head.

"New death notices line the streets of our town every day. John could be dead!" Beth gasped, clasping her hand over her mouth. "He could be dead, and I might not even know it."

"No." Susan took her face in her hands. "You would know." Placing her hand over Beth's heart, she whispered, "In here."

"I knew the day your father went to heaven. I knew it was time, even though I didn't want to admit it."

"This is different," Beth protested. "You were with him; you held his hand. Who will hold John's hand if it's time? Who will hold mine?"

Beth choked as she tried to catch her breath.

"You will find a way to be strong." Susan pulled her into a warm embrace. "You have me, and you have your children. You don't need to stand alone, my darling. Remember the words from Joshua. *'Be strong and courageous. Do not be afraid; do not be discouraged, for the Lord your God will be with you wherever you go.'*"

Beth sighed. For the first time in her life, she felt little comfort in the Scriptures.

"I know you think you understand, but you don't." Beth pulled away, turning her back. "I haven't seen his face in two years. I haven't held him or seen the joy in his eyes at the sight of his son. I don't even know if he knows he has a son."

Beth pressed her hand to her stomach.

"You think you understand, Mum. But you didn't lose Father this way."

"Perhaps you're right," Susan replied. "But if you think I don't share your pain, you're wrong. Seeing you hurt, hurts me more. Maybe one day, twenty years from now, you will understand that when you look into Melody's eyes."

Beth closed her eyes, rubbing her tears from her cheeks. She grabbed her mother, pulling her tight into her arms.

"I'm sorry, Mum."

Susan kissed her, stroking her hair lightly.

"It's all right, dear. It's all right to be angry," Susan soothed. "Just remember, you haven't lost him. You never will."

Beth turned her head, resting her cheek against her mother's shoulder the way she used to as a child. She heard her words and listened to her comfort, but she felt nothing. How could she believe these words? How could she trust? Every morning she woke to an empty space beside her in bed. Every morning she waited to hear his voice call to her from downstairs. Every morning she stared out the window, expecting him to come up the walkway from the fields in his coveralls and muddy boots. How could she believe that she hadn't lost him?

This is war. Nothing will ever be the same.

"I hear he came back scarred, he did. That's why he's holed himself up in that old house and won't come out," Mrs. Peters whispered confidentially over the rim of her teacup.

"Well, I hear that he's lost an eye and foot! Can't come out because his nurse won't let him and he frightens the children," Mrs. Toomey countered.

While slowly sipping her steaming cup of tea, Beth watched both women as they sat in Mrs. Peters' parlor. The windows were thrown open to allow a small breeze. Sunshine sprinkled the room in light, illuminating thick red rugs, a lovely stone fireplace, and floral printed settees, fading with age. Beth had accepted Mrs. Peters' invitation to tea reluctantly. She'd rather run around the yard with her children than spend an afternoon listening to gossip about Mr. Carter, the unfortunate soldier who was sent home absent a limb.

"Tosh!" Mrs. Peters exclaimed. "He's not lost an eye! That's just idle gossip!"

And what is this, I wonder? Beth thought, hiding her smile behind the rim of her cup.

"No, truly!" Mrs. Toomey insisted. "My poor little Lucy saw him, and she swears he had no eye! Just a hole where it used to be."

Beth shuddered at the thought.

"What about you, Elizabeth?" Mrs. Peters asked, attempting to draw Beth into the conversation. "Has Melody mentioned seeing him? Your farm is but a mile down the road."

"No, she's not. But I've heard the poor man was terribly damaged," Beth replied softly, setting her teacup down.

"Perhaps you should call on him, Elizabeth," Mrs. Toomey suggested. "After all, he may have been assigned to John's regiment."

Beth stiffened at the mention of her husband. She forced another smile and said, "Perhaps."

Mrs. Toomey and Mrs. Peters put their heads together once again, discussing the possibility that poor Mr. Carter had lost his entire leg, not just his foot. Beth listened to them as best she could before she let her mind drift. It was quite possible that Mr. Carter had been assigned with John; they'd left on the same day. But the more she thought about finding out, the more her heart ached. She still had received no word from her husband. If something happened to him and Mr. Carter knew …

No. I will never go to visit Mr. Carter. I couldn't bear it. Beth bit her lip.

When she looked up again, it was to discover the room had gone strangely silent. The two plump women before her had stuffed their round cheeks with tea cakes. Beth realized this was her opportunity. She stood quickly, nearly causing poor Mrs. Toomey to choke.

"Do excuse me, ladies," she requested, "but I must be getting back to my children."

Mrs. Peters stumbled to her feet, covering her mouth with her hand. Her pale eyes went wide as she tried to chew hastily. Finally, she spoke around her mouthful, "Of course. Tell Mr. Peters I expect him home for dinner *on time* this evening, please."

"Of course. Thank you for the tea, Mrs. Peters. It was lovely seeing you again Mrs. Toomey."

The other woman simply nodded. Beth turned before either of them could change their mind and protest, hurrying out of the parlor. She snatched her hat and coat from the pegs by the door and put them on as she stepped out. The wind tugged at the pins in her hair, but her hat kept her tresses firmly in place as she hurried down the lane toward home. Beth was thankful for the solitary walk when suddenly she heard a cart approaching up ahead. She stiffened when she saw young Penelope Gray walking up the lane toward her, leading the horse and cart along behind.

"Oh!" Penny exclaimed when she saw her. "Good afternoon, Mrs. Young."

"Hello Penny," Beth said softly. They stopped to face each other in the lane. Beth reached out, gently stroking the horse's nose. "How are you?"

"As well as can be expected, I suppose," Penny answered with a shrug. "Bobby left, don't you know."

"Yes, I heard."

"Couldn't wait to go, that one. Simply had to put on that uniform and march off. So handsome he was, missus. Couldn't take my eyes off him." Penny smiled affectionately as she spoke so easily of her brother.

It won't be so easy for her to speak of him in two years. Beth blinked, shaking the thought from her head.

"I'm sure he will make you proud," Beth said.

"Thank you, missus," Penny replied. "Well, I should be on my way. Mum is waiting for me."

"Of course," Beth said, stepping out of her way.

She watched the young girl hurry down the lane, clucking and whispering to the horse to make him move faster. Beth's heart ached for her, wondering if the girl fully comprehended the pain she would experience in the coming months, if she understood the loneliness she would feel as days turned into weeks. Beth and John had watched the brother and sister grow up. They were as close as any two siblings could be. Now Bobby was just like John—out there somewhere, fighting on distant soil.

A tear slipped down her cheek. She spun, running toward home. *Oh John, where are you?*

Chapter Ten

The Somme
July 1916

John's hand sank into the moist earth as he raised himself up, looking over the trench toward enemy lines. He could hear Bobby Gray breathing beside him, his mouth open, each breath a heavy wheeze. John slid back down the wall of the trench, his eyes closed against the shouts, against the screams. They were supposed to move forward, toward the village called Serre, but the field was already covered with the bodies of men from their battalion. John shuddered to think of how many young men were already gone.

"Let's go, Bobby." He grasped the young man's shoulder. "Don't think about it, son. Just shoot."

Bobby nodded and swallowed hard, making his Adam's apple bob.

"Yes, Sergeant." Bobby's fingers curled around the rifle.

"Stay close." John turned away, lifting himself up out of the trench.

He heard Bobby struggle up beside him before he took off across the field. Shots filled the air, surrounding him as he rushed across the field and attempted to rejoin the flank. His finger squeezed the trigger, firing blindly at the enemy as he searched for the rest of his men. The air was thick, making it harder to breathe as he moved further along the trench lines. A bullet breezed past his ear—too close.

John spun, his feet sliding out from under him as he fell into one of the trenches. He groaned at the pain through his back. His legs curled toward his chest in the narrow space; his heart raced as he pulled his helmet from his head and tried to get his bearings.

"Bobby, we've got to ..." He stopped, looking around at the empty trench. "Bobby?"

He was nowhere to be found.

"Bobby!"

John turned to the edge of the trench. A shot collided with the dirt, and he ducked, turning hard against the wall of the trench. Gasping for air, he reminded himself to breathe. He turned ever so slowly, stretching his neck until he could see over the edge. Gunfire exploded in the air all around him, and he ducked again. He hugged his rifle close, hearing only his heart thundering in his ears as he tried to regain his courage. Leaning back, he looked heavenward.

The light blue sky peeked in and out of fluffy clouds; the peaceful colors calmed him for a few moments. Suddenly something hit his shoulder. John jumped and turned sharply. A Canadian soldier slid down beside him. With a grin, he pushed his helmet up away from his eyes.

"Private Cote? Jared, right?" John asked as his fingers flexed around the barrel of his rifle.

"Yes, sir, Sergeant."

"Have you seen Private Gray?"

"The kid?" Jared shook his head, twisting his neck around. "We gotta get out of here, Sarge."

"Right." His rifle clicked.

"You ready?" Jared asked as he reloaded.

"Yes."

They both turned at the same time, leaping out of the trench. John landed, his foot sliding out from under him. He landed on his back, blood and mud splashing his skin. John rose up onto his elbows, just staring at the bodies piled across the field, blood painting the ground crimson.

"Sarge, let's go!" Jared grabbed his arm, pulling him back onto his feet.

John turned, aiming his rifle as they rejoined the flank. From left to right, men were falling; the cries of the wounded filled his ears as he and the young man ran into the fray. Jared's big shoulders were hunched, his knees bent toward the ground, moving as if he had the ground memorized. He did not trip over the bodies they passed; he did not step on one fallen soldier's hand. He moved with stealth and purpose, his gun rebounding over and over against his shoulder.

John suddenly fell to the ground, shielded by the dead. He propped his gun against his shoulder to fire.

"What do we do now, Sarge?" Jared gasped, falling onto his belly beside him.

"We need to fall back." John shook his head, searching.

"Should we find the colonel?"

John didn't answer. He was looking, listening … then he heard him.

"Bobby!" John leaped to his feet, racing back toward the trenches.

"Sergeant! Wait!"

John ignored Jared's call as the young man rushed to cover him.

"Sergeant Young! Help me please!" Bobby's scream filled his ears, filled the air.

John couldn't breathe, he couldn't think.

"Sarge, please!"

"Bobby, I'm here." John landed with a wet thud, dropping his rifle as he fell to his knees beside the boy.

"Sarge, we gotta get out of here!" Jared pleaded, looking over the top of the trench. "It's bad out there, Sergeant! Really bad!"

"Don't leave me," Bobby cried, reaching for John's hand as blood spurted from his mouth.

"I won't." John wrapped his arms around Bobby's chest, pulling him back against him. "I've got you."

"Sarge—"

"No!" John shouted, tears stinging his eyes. "Just … watch the perimeter."

He looked down, cupping his hand on the boy's bloodied face.

"I … I can't feel anything." Bobby's legs trembled, out of his control.

"I know," John whispered.

"Will you tell my family … I am so …" Bobby's eyes closed.

"I'll tell them," John promised.

"I didn't mean to fail you, Sarge."

"You didn't. You never could, son." John pulled him close, tucking the young boy's head beneath his chin.

"I'm tired," Bobby murmured. A dribble of blood from his mouth smeared John's uniform.

"Then go to sleep," John answered, allowing the tears to fall. "Go to sleep, son. It's all right."

Bobby was silent. John looked down, watching the boy's skin go pale, the life leaving his eyes right before they closed. He had come here willingly, joining up when his country called him to the Pals Battalion, coming to fight alongside his friends. He had been excited, invigorated … strong.

Now he knows only peace. John doubled his arms around Bobby, rocking him as he sobbed, his chest heaving. When he looked up, Jared was watching, his tears drawing stripes through the dirt on his face. His gun lay limp in his hands, and not a word passed his lips. They just sat there, staring at each other for what felt like hours.

Finally, John turned, resting Bobby onto his back in the trench. He stood and lifted his gun from the mud. Jared looked up at him, his eyes clouding with defeat.

John finally spoke. "Let's go, soldier."

Cigarette smoke swirled around his head in the dark trench. Jared took a long draw, the tip of the little white roll glowing in the night. He stared across the trench at his sergeant. They had decided to stay together until they could regroup with their divisions. The stench of sweat, filth and blood surrounded them as night finally fell, and they were granted a reprieve.

"Who was he?" Jared asked as he crushed the cigarette beneath his boot.

John lowered the photograph he'd been holding up to the starlight and looked up.

"The boy. Who was he to you?" Jared rested his elbows against his knees, shifting in the dirt.

With a sigh, John leaned his head back to stare at the sky. Jared interlocked his fingers, waiting quietly. John seemed to be thinking as if there were no simple answer to Jared's question. He supposed after seeing what they had seen today, there wasn't a simple answer.

"I watched him grow up," John said, breaking the silence. "He was a good man."

"He was a kid," Jared snapped. "They're all kids, Sergeant."

"I am aware, private." John crouched on the balls of his feet. "Stay put."

"Sergeant." Jared stopped John as he started to shuffle away.

"What is it, private?" John asked.

Jared hesitated before reaching inside of his coat. As he pulled out the photograph, he attempted to smooth out the crease where it had been folded before he handed it over.

"That's my wife," he murmured. "Her name's Emma."

John stared at the picture, angling it toward the moonlight before handing it back, along with the photo he'd been holding. Jared stared down at the picture. He swallowed at the sight of the little family staring back at him. The woman was lovely, her dark hair pinned loosely back in braids, her eyes shimmering with unshed tears, captured by the photographer.

"Your family?" Jared asked.

"Yes." John bowed his head.

"When was this taken?" Jared asked, running his finger over the image.

"Almost two years ago." John reached out, pointing. "That's my son. She named him George, for her father. It's what we discussed."

"She named him?" Jared frowned.

"Yes."

"When was he ... I mean, weren't you there?" He chuckled softly, but his smile quickly faded.

"He was born a month after I left them." John took back his photo, stuffing it inside his coat over his heart. "I've never seen my son."

The two soldiers stared at each other. The silence filled the space between them with thick tension. Jared finally broke away, looking down at Emma's picture once more. He traced his finger along her face, almost able to feel the soft texture of her skin, the silkiness of her hair, and the coolness of her lower lip against his thumb.

"I haven't seen her since I left. They won't let me go home. I know what she would say to me, right now. She'd tell me what I always told her when things got rough back home. To have faith, to hold onto the good things. To trust that God is watching us. I just don't know if I believe that anymore." Jared folded the photo, tucking it away next to his heart. "Sometimes I think I'll never see her again—like that kid will never see his family again."

"Bobby," John said.

Jared looked up again and caught the glimmer of a tear on John's lashes.

"His name was Bobby."

Then he turned his back again, disappearing around the corner of the trench into the darkness.

Jared winced as he stepped over the dead. His eyes watered as the fog settled all around him. Crouching, he took hold of one man's shoulder, turning him over slowly. Jared rubbed his hand down his face, shuddering as he looked down into the pale eyes of the youth. Beside him lay his twin, their faces mirroring each other exactly. Jared closed the boy's eyes before he straightened again. Flexing his fingers around the barrel of his rifle, he moved on, the stench of the carnage all around him, filling his senses, overwhelming him as he weaved around the bodies, avoiding stepping on any hands.

Gunfire popped in the distance, and he spun around. His heart thundered in his chest as he fell to one knee and raised his weapon. The fog rose higher, quicker than normal. Jared frowned, his eyes narrowing as he searched for the source of the bullets that peppered the ground near his feet. He slid down onto his belly, ignoring the stench of rotting bodies in the mud as he crawled back the way he came. Jared tried to breathe deeply, closing his eyes as mud smeared his uniform, splashing his face when he slid and rolled.

Looking up, he froze. Emma stood across the field, her wedding dress stained with blood and mud, her golden hair falling loosely down her back, rippling in the breeze. The smile he loved and missed so much tilted her full lips. Jared gasped in a breath, knowing this wasn't real. Yet there she stood, holding out a hand to him. He reached for her …

Jared jerked awake in the trench. Crouching beside him, Ralph Finnegan grinned and kicked his boot once more before he turned away. Jared pushed his helmet back, tilting his head to look at the sky still blanketed in stars, just as it was before he fell asleep.

How long have I been allowed to rest? One hour, two? He couldn't keep track of time here, and Ralph never offered the time when he woke him to stand guard.

"Come on, my turn." Ralph nudged him again, and Jared grumbled, pressing his hand into the soft earth wall before spinning himself around. He grunted when his chin connected with the trench wall. He pushed himself backward, landing hard against the other side. The narrow space was hardly enough for anyone to stretch out unless they were to lie horizontally. This place wasn't made for comfort, only for protection from the rain of bullets that would, no doubt, pound down on them in the next few hours.

"Sleepyhead's awake!" A youthful chuckle brought Jared's head around.

A knot filled his throat when he looked at the twins. They were huddled together, sitting shoulder to shoulder in the trench. He had met them the first day in the trenches, falling into the same small space after their failed charge across the field. They were two of many volunteers in the Accrington Pals Battalion—now two of the *few*.

They wanted to fight together, but no one ever mentioned that they would all die together. Jared shuddered, turning away from the boys' identical grins. After the dream he'd just had, the twins were the last people he wanted to see. Ralph was settling in. His long legs curled against his chest and his arms were wrapped around his rifle like a little boy hugging his teddy bear. Jared smirked at the sight. He knew every man here, if he had a brain, slept that way. But it was still strange to see a man as big as Ralph, who could snap another man's neck with his bare hands, huddled up against that dirt wall like a child.

"It was a long day, Jared," rasped one of the twins—Samuel he thought it was. His accent seemed thicker than usual. Jared didn't look, knowing the kid was about to cry. "An extremely long day."

"But we made it," Luke said, breaking in to comfort his brother. "That's what counts, isn't it?"

"Yeah," Jared nodded, peeking over the top of the trench. The air, thick with the scent of stale blood and raw flesh, sent quivers rushing over his skin. "We made it. We survived the day. That's what counts."

Surviving this war and getting back to Emma ... that's what counts.

Chapter Eleven

Paris, France

Jared leaned back against the wall, his arms tucked against his chest as he let the cigarette burn away between his fingers. He frowned as he watched the trucks making progress down the street and nurses bustling here and there with the wounded. Every time he saw a woman in uniform, he saw Emma.

He tossed the cigarette, crushing it beneath his foot and limped away. He'd been pulled off the line after twisting his ankle in a fall. It was stupid; frustrating. He'd stubbornly refused to let any of the doctors or nurses tend it. He knew John was responsible for pulling him off the line. Jared could have hidden it, allowing him to stay, but after losing half their division, John saw the defeat in him.

Jared moved among the people, stopping now and then to take a wounded soldier's hand. They didn't need to speak; their uniforms made them brothers, and there was no need for words between them. Just their presence and understanding were enough.

He leaned over one soldier, noting the blood seeping through the bandages wrapped tight around his neck and face. The dirt on his face led to infected wounds, turning his skin green. Jared swallowed, clasping his hand around the soldier's.

"Doctor?" the young man wheezed, shaking fingers curling around Jared's knuckles.

"No, just a friend," he answered. "Rest now. You've done well, soldier."

"Have you had enough?" Jared looked up.

Ralph cradled his rifle in both arms, one hip slack as he glared down at Jared. His lips tightened when he looked at the wounded man, then he turned his back on all of them. His shoulders tensed at the sound of their moans, at the soft voices of nurses comforting them as they were loaded onto trucks for the long journey home.

"I haven't been called back yet." Jared straightened, squaring his shoulders. "I am not going to sit around in a hospital. If you can get me back on the line, then yes, I've had enough. If not, then I am going to stay here and do whatever I can."

"You know she can't see you, right?" Ralph followed Jared when he turned away. "You think that being here brings you close to Emma."

"Don't!" Jared stepped close, their faces almost touching. "Don't say her name."

"She doesn't know that you're here. She doesn't know that you're helping them, so what's the point? She'll never know anything that you do over here," Ralph said with a shrug.

"You think I'm here because I miss my wife?" Jared hissed, his face twisting in disgust.

"If not for her, then you're doing this because of the twins," Ralph responded, voice thickening.

Jared's hands balled into fists at his sides. "I'm here because that boy over there could be me in a few days. I'm here because I fought beside them, and I didn't even know their names. I couldn't save them, and now they could die before ever making it back home."

Ralph averted his eyes.

"You can't know everyone's name, Jared. It's not your fault they're dying, and you're not," he said, softening his voice. "It's not your fault that the twins are gone."

"Maybe not. But I can at least try to make a difference before these men are shipped off without anyone to protect them." Jared stepped closer. "You remember those nights in the Somme? You said you had my back."

"I remember," Ralph answered, narrowing his eyes.

"I was supposed to have their backs too and I did. We gave each other courage, Ralph. Who's going to give that to them back home?" Jared spread his arms wide and backed away. "Look around you. You can feel the fear everywhere, and it's stronger than it ever was in those trenches."

Jared walked away, ignoring the pain flooding his ankle. He felt naked without his rifle, his constant companion of the past two years.

I can't take this anymore, the helplessness, the loneliness. I hate this country.

Suddenly he stopped. He immediately recognized the soldier by his posture, the way he held his shoulders straight and his rifle tightly in both hands.

Fueled by determination, Jared rushed forward, following the man down the street. He wasn't going to stay in this city a moment longer. He wanted to go back to the front. He needed to go back to the front.

"Sergeant Young!" Jared called out as he ran to catch up with him.

John turned, that constant frown creasing his brow once more.

"Private Cote," he said.

"Sir, I want to return to the front," Jared blurted as he caught his breath.

"You were pulled off the line because you could barely walk, soldier."

"And you just saw me run," Jared replied, desperately. "Sir, please ... I have to return to the front."

John hesitated, looking him over. Jared leaned into his bad ankle, ignoring the throb shooting through his foot. The sergeant pursed his lips but then nodded.

"I'll see what I can do," he said.

Jared released his breath as John turned on his heels and walked away.

Chapter Twelve

Canada
December 1916

"Emma?"

Emma looked up from her book, closing the cover over her finger to mark their place. She smiled as she reached to take Dan's hand.

"What is it?" she asked.

"You just ... you sound so sad." Dan's brow waggled in an effort to frown.

"So do you." The corner of Emma's mouth twitched into a half-smile.

"Dr. Kingston said that my bandages can come off next week." Dan sounded optimistic, but then he shuddered. "Now that we're so close, I'm frightened."

"You don't have to be frightened." Emma squeezed his fingers before pulling away to open her copy of *Oliver Twist* again. "You're going to be just fine, Dan. All the signs point to you seeing perfectly out of your left eye. You'll be heading home before you know it."

Dan raised his hand and reached out to her. Emma shifted uncomfortably when he ran his hand along her shoulder to her neck. He stroked her cheek with the back of his fingers. Emma looked down at him. His dark hair was still wet from his recent bath, and he smelled like lavender from Rosie's homemade soaps.

Emma took his hand from her face and cleared her throat.

"You shouldn't do that."

"Why not?" Dan asked, gripping her fingers before she could pull away.

"I'm married, Dan. It's inappropriate." Emma smoothed her hand over her hair.

"Your husband's not here."

"And that's an excuse?" Emma's brow lowered.

"No, of course not. I'm just saying … if he never … well, you know." Dan turned his head in her direction. "The doctor is confident I've improved. He seems ready to send me home. I can't wait to see your face when these bandages come off."

"That's enough, Dan." Emma stood up. "I know you're hurting, and you're lonely, but I do not want to hear this. Telling me that my husband may not …"

"I'm sorry." Dan reached out his hand. "Please sit down, Emma."

Slowly she lowered herself to the chair again.

"You will be there when the bandages come off, won't you?" Dan asked, biting his lip.

"I might." Emma opened her book once again. "Now stop talking, or I won't finish the book, and you'll never find out what happens to Oliver."

"Oh, and I just could not live without knowing the ending," Dan chuckled. "Proceed, madam."

Emma laughed softly. She ran her fingers over the cover. She was tempted to turn it back to the front, where her husband's handwriting graced the first page. He had given it to her the first Christmas after they met, her first present from him. He knew how she loved to read, and it was one book she hadn't read yet, making the gift even more meaningful.

Emma smiled. *He knew and picked it for that reason.*

Jared had showered her with literature, lining her bookshelves on Christmas and her birthday; sometimes, even when there was no occasion he'd bring home a book for her. Emma closed her eyes for a moment, squeezing the book in both hands. It smelled like Bay Rum; it smelled like Jared. More than once she'd fallen asleep beside him, holding this book, and when she woke, it was pressed between them. The pages held his scent as strongly as it held hers.

"Emma? Is everything all right?"

Dan's voice brought her back, and she smiled. "Of course. Now, where were we?"

"Emma," Rosie's voice interrupted. Emma glanced over her shoulder and then smiled at Dan.

"I suppose we'll have to finish later," she said, setting the book aside. "Besides, the doctor will be by soon. You do realize if all goes well, you might be discharged today?"

"Yes, I know," Dan hissed, his voice sharp with anticipation.

Emma patted his hand and then left him, hurrying to her friend. "What is it, Rosie?"

"The doctor has asked if you would go into town and fetch these supplies," Rosie said, handing her a small list. "Be sure to wrap up warm. I think it's going to snow."

"Thank you, Rosie." Emma tucked the list into her apron pocket and then paused, touching Rosie's hand. "How's Caleb today?"

Rosie's lip trembled, but she managed a smile. "We're living day by day, Emma. I think it's the only thing we can do."

Emma nodded slowly, hugged her friend and then hurried away. Would that be her and Jared someday soon? Living day by day? Dealing with the pain of what he'd gone through; what he'd seen?

Oh, Lord, we need Your love now more than ever. Please, don't let my husband suffer. Bring him home to me just as he was. Please. Emma put on her coat and rushed out of the nursing home, running away from her own thoughts.

Snow sprinkled around her as Emma hurried down the road back to the rest home a few hours later, holding the supplies close against her chest to keep her warm. Emma sniffled and rubbed her red nose as she climbed the steps to the door. Once inside, she leaned back against the door, sighing as she let the sudden warmth wash through her. Setting down the supplies, she pulled off her hat and scarf.

"You're back." Rosie came around the corner with a sigh of relief. "Private Reynolds insisted on walking outside all by himself. He said he didn't want any help unless it was from you."

"How far did he go?" Emma asked pinning on her cap as together they hurried toward the back door.

"Just to the bench. Then he sat, and he won't come inside. It's freezing out there, Em." Rosie stressed, rolling her eyes. "Honestly, the longer he's here, the more like a child he acts."

"He's been through a lot, Rosie. What happened to all that compassion you taught me to have for him?" Emma asked, touching her friend's arm.

"It's fading. Ever since ..." Rosie hesitated. "Ever since Caleb came home."

Emma's grip tightened around her friend's arm. Caleb had come home broken; his healing was slow. Now, a month after his return, Rosie spent more than one night at work. She explained they both needed some time, but Emma saw the fear in Rosie's eyes. Caleb's experience had changed him, and his mind needed as much healing as his disabling wounds.

"Will you cover my rounds for me?" Emma asked. "I will see if I can coax the private back inside."

"Of course," Rosie walked away, hiding her tears.

Emma watched her friend disappear up the back stairs before snatching a coat at the back door and bundling up once more to go back out into the cold. She saw him immediately, sitting on the bench, his crutches propped next to him. As Emma joined him, she saw the blank expression on his face. It broke her heart.

"You got a letter this morning," Emma said, breaking the silence. "It's waiting for you upstairs."

"It's from my fiancée," the private whispered.

"You should answer one of them, you know." Emma massaged his arm. "She loves you. She will always love you, no matter what."

"That's easy for you to say." He turned halfway toward her. "You can't understand this. As far as you know, your husband is still whole. How am I supposed to stand up with her at our wedding?

How can I do this to her? Look at me, nurse. I'm not a whole man anymore."

"Your heart is the same." Emma stood, lifting his crutches. "Come inside. You'll catch your death out here."

He hesitated before standing with her help. Tucking the crutches beneath his arms, he let her help him back into the home. Rosie, recovered from her tears, was waiting at the door to help him get back to his bed.

Stopping at the door, the private turned to look at Emma again. "You said my heart was the same," he said.

"Yes." Emma nodded, resting her hand on his shoulder.

"I'm just ... I'm not sure if you're right anymore." Then he stepped inside.

Emma's heart ached. A shiver from the freezing breeze rushed through her body. *Oh Lord, help him. I've tried, but I fear there's nothing else I can do!*

Trying to help him had been the hardest thing she'd ever done, but after his addiction had faded away, she'd come to learn who he was. Now a new monster was rearing its ugly head in Private Reynolds's heart.

Depression was a soldier's worst enemy. Worse than the infections, worse than the amputations, depression had claimed more than one soldier's life before he could leave the hospital to see his family again. Emma never realized coming home could do more harm than good for some of these men. She never realized that some of the men had dug themselves so deep into the lifestyle of the past two years that they didn't want to go home.

Emma grabbed the door and rushed inside. She gasped, and skidded to a halt, her eyes expanding as she saw the soldier standing a few feet from her. His hat was tucked beneath his arm; his medals glimmered on his shoulder. Emma's shock turned to a smile, and she shook her head.

"Dan?" she asked.

He grinned, reaching up to touch the patch over his right eye lightly before shrugging his shoulders.

"The doctor said I can go home," he announced. "I can finish healing and learning there."

"That's wonderful!" Emma's smile almost faded, her heart sinking.

Talking with Dan had made her feel so close to Jared. Now she was losing him too. She felt as if the whole world was working against her, taking every little bit of happiness that came her way and leaving her completely empty.

Dan reached out, taking both her hands. "Emma, come home with me."

"What?" Her lips parted in surprise.

"I want you to meet my family. I want them to meet the woman who saved my life."

"Dan, I can't do that," Emma protested, shaking her head. "I have to stay here. So many men need my help."

"Em ... I ..." He shook his head. "You were there for me. You have to know that I feel ..."

"Don't." She pressed her fingers to his lips. "I understand, Dan. But that's only because I helped you. You know that I'm married. I love my husband more than anything else in the world."

"You haven't heard from him in months. Please, Emma," Dan pleaded. "We may have a chance. He's not here. I am."

Emma closed her eyes.

"If you ever need me, you'll know where to find me," Emma whispered, her voice thick with tears. "You are a wonderful friend. When this is all over, you'll see that is all we were to each other. Good friends. Someone to talk to when we had no one else."

His hands slipped from hers, and she moved past him, not expecting anything else. But then his voice stopped her.

"I'll write," he said. "Then if you change your mind, you'll know where to find me. I'm ready to start over, Emma. I think by the time all of this ends, you will be too."

"You don't think Jared is coming home, do you?" Emma asked softly as she fisted her hand over her stomach.

"So long without hearing from him … all your letters to him coming back … it's not a good sign."

Dan turned to leave, his hand brushing against her shoulder as he went. Emma watched him disappear down the hall, her heart breaking again. If he meant to hurt her, he had done it. But then, she dried her tears and stiffened her jaw. She was done with being sad; she was done with crying about this. Two years of her life had been stolen from her and the man she loved.

It was enough, no longer a time for tears. Now the fury filled her, now the despair turned to determination. Her husband would come home, whole or not. She would not let this war take anything else from them.

Emma smoothed her dress, straightened her cap, and went back to work.

Chapter Thirteen

East Hampton, New York
April 1917

A breeze blew gently past the open windows, sending chills through the room. Christy didn't care. The church was quiet as Will slipped the ring onto her finger. She looked up at him, blinking back tears at the sight of him in his uniform. She never thought their future together would begin like this.

Her gown rippled in the breeze, white chiffon and lace rustling against her legs. She lifted her head as Will brushed aside the trim of her soft veil with his finger. A crown of pearls arched over her honey hair, shimmering in the lights of the church. Christy smiled, her chest rising and falling. She wasn't nervous. Nothing about committing herself to the man she loved made her nervous. But she had never felt further away from him than she did here, standing in her mother's wedding gown, looking at him in that green uniform she had come to despise.

Christy bowed her head to stare at the little golden band cooling her finger. She wanted this moment to last forever, but in truth, they would only have two days—two days before he would leave, two days before she would lose him. They had waited three years for this moment, to become man and wife, and with one headline in the newspaper, it was being snatched away. He told her, if it came down to it, he would go; he told her he would do his duty for his country. But having him as her husband for only forty-eight hours was an unbearable thought.

Shifting her flowers, Christy looked across the aisle at her father. He looked so stiff, his face only slightly red. It had taken eight months, one hundred dinners, and two engagement parties—one at her house and one at his—to bring her father around. Then as rumors of America joining the war circulated, she saw her father's eyes and heart open for the first time since she was a child.

"I now pronounce you man and wife," Father Keller pronounced, breaking the silence.

Christy lifted her head once more to look into Will's eyes. Smiling, Will cupped her face in his hands to place a gentle kiss on her lips. Her first tear fell when her eyes fluttered closed, the first tear she had shed since he told her he was enlisting. For three years she'd waited for him; for three years they had planned and hoped.

Now I have no time. Christy wrapped her arms around his neck, deepening the kiss. *Be strong, Christy. Don't let him see your fear.*

"I love you," Christy whispered.

He captured her lips again in a searing kiss, wrapping his arms tight around her waist as the church echoed with applause. Her breath completely left her. He wiped away her tears with his thumb when their kiss ended. Christy took his hand as they both turned, and he led her back down the aisle. The organ filled the little church with music, sending them on their way.

Christy glanced over her shoulder to watch the people, tossing rice high over their heads and shouting their congratulations as they rushed out of the church. They stopped in front of the car waiting to take them to her parent's house for refreshments. She caught Will's eyes, her husband's eyes, and she couldn't look away. He was happy, she could see it. His happiness mirrored hers.

Behind the smile, behind the twinkle in his eyes, she saw his sadness, his anger over having to leave her and his fear of not knowing what would come next or when he'd come back … if he'd come back.

Christy breathed deeply, telling herself everything would be fine. Then she climbed into the car.

"You must be so proud of him."

Christy stared unblinkingly at Mrs. Lane before turning slightly to look at Will across the yard. Once again a lump formed in her throat at the sight of him in that uniform.

Christy forced a smile, turning back to her neighbor. "I am, Mrs. Lane. More than I can say."

"He looked so handsome and strong standing in that church. He certainly is proud of you," Mrs. Lane gushed, sighing. "I think it's wonderful to see a young man is willing to sacrifice some of the happiest days of married life to defend his country."

"That's a common opinion," Christy muttered, fingering the present Mrs. Lane handed her.

"I'm sure this is hard for you, dear. But when he returns home triumphant, you will be so proud, and then your lives will begin." Mrs. Lane smiled. "He is making the world safe for your future children. Imagine if he did not go. Neither of you would truly be happy because you are both so honorable."

Mrs. Lane kissed both Christy's cheeks and then hurried to join her friends. Christy set the present down with the others, pressing her hand flat against her stomach. She wasn't hungry for the wedding treats. She wasn't excited about the many presents brought by friends and family.

Will's strong hand touched her waist, drawing her close against his side. Christy turned her head to look up at him. His warm smile greeted her, his hand stroking the side of her waist as he held her close.

"Ladies and gentlemen," her mother's voice rang out. "The bride and groom will now dance for the first time as husband and wife."

Will led Christy to the center of the tent, curling his arm around her waist. Their fingers twined together as her sister's violin began to sing. She smiled at Annie, so proud of how she'd grown up these past three years. She rested her cheek against Will's shoulder, her hand on the back of his neck. Her fingers fiddled with the delicate hairs at the nape of his neck.

"Please tell me we can make today last forever," Christy whispered. "I don't want it to end. I couldn't bear it to end."

"I know." He kissed her temple.

"Why is this happening to us?" Christy raised her head, looking into his eyes. "We waited so long and were willing to sacrifice so much ... why is this happening to us now?"

"It'll be over soon." Will pressed his hands to her face, rubbing his thumbs along the curves of her cheeks. "They're saying with us in the war, it'll be over in a month."

"They said that when it all began." Christy choked. His face blurred behind her flood of tears. "I don't think I can survive without you."

"We will find a way." Will held her flush against him. "Knowing you're here waiting for me, knowing you're mine, and you will be mine for the rest of my life ... that will keep me going. That will bring me back home to you."

"It'll keep us both alive," Christy answered, closing her eyes and pressing her hand against the beat of his heart. "Promise me you'll stay alive."

"Haven't I proved by now that I will never leave you?" He smiled. "I'm always with you, Christy."

"I know." Christy pulled him down for a kiss.

She melted against him, her hands tracing his shoulders. All around them, friends and family laughed and danced, but Christy felt completely alone. Alone with her husband, alone with the only man she had ever loved.

Will caught his breath after the kiss. "Let's get out of here."

Christy stood still as he took her hand and stepped back. She stared at him for a moment, taking the time to study him, to memorize his movements. The way his hair waved over the top of his head, the way his body moved in that stiff uniform. He led her through the crowd of people and rushed her into his car. No one seemed to notice as they disappeared.

Christy leaned her head against the window, watching the people dancing and wondering how long it would take all of them to realize that the bride and groom had left. She smiled and turned to him when he climbed behind the wheel. He grabbed her hand, squeezing until her knuckles turned white.

"Ready, Mrs. Garvin?" He leaned over until their noses touched.

"Ready," she replied, laughing softly. She pulled him toward her for another kiss.

The car sputtered as they drove away, leaving their wedding celebration behind. They wanted nothing more than to be alone, to be away from the people who kept reminding her how handsome her husband looked in his uniform and how proud they were of him for wanting to defend his country. It was too much. They had too little time.

I only have two more days. I won't share him for another minute of it. Christy brushed away her tears.

Will looked at her from the corner of his eye, and she smiled. He was her husband. They were promised, committed to each other, and for the next few hours, she could pretend she wasn't about to lose him.

THE LOST GENERATION

Chapter Fourteen

London, England

Beth's heel clicked rapidly against the floor. She twisted her hands around the strings of her reticule as she stared at the people in the office through her soft, dotted veil. The pins in her hat were digging into her skull, but she was too nervous to fix them. Beth wanted nothing more than to hold little George at this moment, but she had left the children behind with her mother to make this trip. Trying to find John was more difficult than she thought. Searching for a sergeant in a sea of sergeants in France was like looking for a needle in a haystack.

But she was still going to try. She had to find out if her letters had been lost in the Red Cross office. She had to see if they knew anything about his whereabouts. Surely all the inquiries they put in for her these past few days hadn't been for nothing! Surely by now they knew something about her husband. In the last letter she'd received six months ago, he had talked about being on leave in Paris, about a young man who begged to be sent back to the front.

She had read the despair in the tone of his letter. She had seen in the sharp curve of his handwriting, his concern for this young man named Jared, who had lost all his joy and his ability to look at the world and smile. Even now, in the middle of war, John thought only about the person beside him and not about himself. He gave no thought to how this war was changing him, but she could see it in his letters.

Oh, God, please let there be news! Something, anything to tell me that he's still alive and fighting to get back to me. Beth bowed her head, pressing her clenched knuckles to her lips.

The walk to the Red Cross office hadn't been easy. Death notices were all around her, down every street. The Pals Battalion had done its work at home when volunteers were needed, and now it was doing its work in France. How wonderful they had made it sound! She remembered the speeches so well, the notices in the paper, calling the men to fight. Now those men were dying, one by one, and the future was bleak. Beth knew no one thought of the world after the war, but she could think of nothing else. Already half the men of her village were gone, leaving widows and fatherless children to fill the space they left.

"Mrs. Young?" The officer behind the counter called her, breaking her free of her melancholy reverie.

Beth jumped to her feet, her heart pounding as she hurried to the counter.

"Yes. Do you have anything for me? Is there any news?" She asked anxiously, her fingers knotting in the strings of her reticule.

"I was able to find your husband's commanding officer." The officer licked his lips and cleared his throat loudly as he looked down at the telegram in his hands. "The last report on your husband's progress was a few months ago. He is on the front and finding him now … well, I'm sure you gathered that finding one particular man on the front lines is almost impossible."

"But he is alive," Beth whispered.

"He was." The officer nodded. "He received his orders and his commander sent him back to the front. I do have something for you."

He reached down behind the counter, pulling up a stack of letters. Beth gasped, covering her mouth with both hands. Tears stung the corners of her eyes as she accepted the letters, her hands trembling when she saw John's handwriting.

"They came over with a nurse. She was returning with the wounded and said that Sergeant Young asked her to send them along. He wrote them while on the front, but he was unable to send them himself."

"Thank you," Beth rasped, pressing the letters to her heart.

She turned on her heels and tore open the first letter. Her heart warmed at the sight of his handwriting but quickly turned cold at the subject. He had written again about Jared, the young man who had lost all hope. Beth moved a trembling finger along the page.

"'He has a wife named Emma,'" Beth read in a whisper, her brow curving into a deep frown. "'He believes he will never see her again. I am watching this young man lose his soul and little by little it is destroying us both.'"

Beth rolled her lips together, folding the letter back into the envelope. She started toward the door but then stopped. Turning around, she returned to the counter, catching the officer's eye.

"Pardon me, but if I could trouble you again?"

He smiled, his eyes softening. Beth winced, hating the pity she had chosen to ignore for so long. At least he seemed kind enough, unlike some who had been hardened by the harsh realities of the war.

"Of course," he said, nodding.

"I'd like to make another inquiry about a young private." Beth bit her lip as he pulled out a piece of paper and a pen.

"His name?" he asked.

Beth tugged her letter out again, skimming through it.

"Private Jared Cote. He was last seen in Paris, September 1916."

THE LOST GENERATION

STAGE 3:
BARGAINING

THE LOST GENERATION

Chapter Fifteen

Canada
June 1917

"Do you have everything you need?" Grace wrung her hands as Emma hurried her out the front door.

"Mother, you will only be gone for a few days." Emma smiled, drawing her mother close for a hug. "I have survived on my own for a long time now. Your absence for seventy-two hours will not bring my world to an end."

"It's just that, with another child coming, your sister needs so much help. Moving her here while Eddie is in France just seems like the right thing to do," Grace explained for what seemed like the thousandth time.

Emma sighed heavily. She didn't even want to think about what life would be like with her sister and nephews moving in with her. Laura hadn't been home in seven years, ever since she married Edward Hastings and moved to America. Emma had cared for disabled, grieving, and traumatized soldiers every day of her life for the past three years. The last thing she needed was her sister, depressed and pregnant, invading her home. She knew her mother would insist they be at Laura's beck and call from the moment she waddled over Emma's threshold.

Laura had begged Emma to let her stay at her house. She didn't want to stay with their mother. She didn't want to face her father's theories about how the war would end when she came down for breakfast every morning. Emma couldn't be selfish when her sister made that request. She couldn't subject her sister, still trying to accept that her husband was fighting for his life halfway around the world, to that.

"Mother, go. Help Laura get her things together and bring her home. Everything will be fine." Emma kissed her mother's cheeks.

"If you need anything at all—"

"I have Sarah and Rosie." Emma turned Grace around, guiding her down the porch steps toward the gate. "Stop worrying about me; focus on Laura. She's expecting and coming here with twin boys. She's the one we should be thinking about right now."

"Of course, you're right." Grace took a deep breath, then turned back again as she reached the gate. "I just ... I can't help worrying about you. No word from Jared, and that strange letter you received, about the inquiry?" Grace shuddered.

"I know." Emma's throat closed. She resisted reaching for her apron pocket, where the telegram rested.

She never sent in an inquiry about her husband's whereabouts, but she received a letter anyway, containing information that her husband was last seen in Paris in September of 1916 before he was sent back to the front. At that time, he had been well with no wounds reported. He had a short leave before his sergeant sent him back to the front per his request. Emma had read the notice repeatedly.

Why would Jared request to return to the front? Why had he neglected to send a letter while in Paris? Had he even tried? Had they been lost crossing over?

Emma would have given anything for a sign her husband was the same man she knew and loved, just one line that reminded her of the man he used to be.

But the few letters she had received only frightened her. They didn't even sound like Jared. Nothing about the tone of the letter, not even his handwriting, was like the man she had fallen in love with.

"We will be back soon. Contact us immediately if there is any word from Jared." Grace embraced her once more.

Emma smiled when she saw her father roll his eyes. She kissed her mother's temple, patting her back gently.

"We'll see her in a few days, Grace," he growled. "It's not as though we are going halfway across the world." He rolled his eyes again.

"If you receive any telegrams, any news ..." Grace stopped, sniffling as she rubbed away the tears from the corners of her eyes.

"She won't," Robert insisted. "There will be no telegrams."

Emma bent slightly, peeking into the vehicle at her father. Despite the harshness in his voice, she could see the spark of affection in his eyes. He always tried to act tough on his wife, but Emma knew his heart was much softer than he cared to let on.

"Even if it's a missing in action notice—"

"We all know that that's just the army's way of saying that they're dead somewhere, but they haven't found the body yet," Robert grumbled, tugging on his hat. "Jared is going to be just fine and so is Emma. Now get in the car, Grace."

"Just concentrate on Laura. She needs you more right now," Emma counseled. "You remember what it was like for me when Jared first went."

"Yes." Grace nodded, then climbed into the car. "God bless you, Emma."

"Be safe, Mama." Emma smiled, stepped back from the car, and waved as they drove away. Grace leaned out the window to watch her daughter until they turned the corner.

Feeling alone was no longer foreign. Ever since Dan left and Private Reynolds was finally sent home to complete his recovery, Emma had lost her purpose at work. She felt there was so much more she could do, but she didn't know what.

Emma pulled in a deep breath and hurried back into the house. Stepping through the door, she quickly tied her apron around her waist, then hurried to set a pot of tea on the stove. Steam blew up into her face as she poured herself a cup just as the telephone rang. Emma sighed, wishing for the hundredth time that she hadn't let Rosie convince her to install it. Setting down her tea, she lifted the receiver and said hello.

"Emma, it's Rosie. Are you coming to work today?"

Emma frowned as she answered, "I will be there this afternoon." Lifting her cup for a sip, she asked, "Is there a problem?"

"The ward is practically overflowing," Rosie replied. "A ship just came in with another wave of wounded."

"I have to start readying the house for my sister and her family." Emma stroked her hand through her hair. "I will be there as soon as I can."

Hanging up, she sat down heavily in her chair. She couldn't help pulling out the telegram. Her fingers trembled as she reread the words.

Mrs. Cote, in response to your inquiry, we regret to inform you that we do not know your husband's current whereabouts. As of September 1916, he was seen in Paris before receiving orders to return to the front. It was implied by our source that Private Cote put in a request with his sergeant to return immediately to the front.

Emma studied the letter again, frowning as she ran her hand over the script. It didn't seem like a normal, professional letter from the Red Cross. This seemed personal in some way. She couldn't explain why, but she was sure whoever had put in the inquiry on Jared had also been the one to send her this letter.

She put the letter away and got to her feet, pulling off her apron. If new patients were at the hospital, they needed all the hands they could get. Emma couldn't just sit here with that letter burning a hole in her pocket all day. As she climbed the stairs to change into her uniform, she reminded herself that the best thing she could do for Jared was to help the soldiers who came home.

It was what he would want, and it was what she needed.

Chapter Sixteen

New York City, New York
The Same Day

Christy sat with her hands suspended over the typewriter. The office was unusually quiet today, but it was better than being alone in her brownstone apartment with nothing to do. She dropped her hands to the edge of the table. Her hardest moments were having to report on the war while her husband was fighting.

Biting her lip, she looked around before reaching into her pocket. She had sent an inquiry to the Red Cross in London for reports on the progress of the war. She received a letter back, advising her that if she wished to receive an accurate report, she should come to London herself.

Christy pulled out the ticket she'd purchased. Her bags were packed, and she was ready to leave on the ship the next day. She just hadn't told anyone. Taking a deep breath, she stood and moved toward Charles's office. Her heart raced as she walked to the door and knocked briskly on the glass.

"Come in." His voice rang out.

Christy stepped inside, closing the door tightly behind her.

"Christy." He smiled, sitting back in his chair. "How are you, my dear?"

"I have something to tell you." Christy sat down in front of the desk.

He frowned as she reached across the desk to set the ticket in front of him. He stared at it, blinking slowly before turning his gaze back to Christy.

"I'm set to sail tomorrow," Christy said quietly. "I would have told you sooner, but I thought you would try to stop me. I just ... I must know what's happening. The closer I am to it, the more I will be able to find out. Especially now."

Nodding slowly, Charles said, "I thought this might happen. Christy, you do know this won't bring you closer to Will."

"Maybe not," she replied, "but at least I won't be sitting here at home, wondering about the details, trying to write about it without actually knowing what's happening."

"I don't suppose I can stop you."

"No, you can't."

Silence fell between them, filling up the space across the desk. Christy reached over to take back the ticket. Her heart raced as the finality of her decision settled over her. Rubbing her thumb over the ticket, she pulled in a deep breath, knowing that maybe she was foolish. But in her mind and her heart, there was no choice. She was going to London. She was leaving everything behind.

She was running into the mouth of war.

Chapter Seventeen

Paris, France
June, 1917

Will rubbed his palm across his chest. He swallowed hard and glanced over at Tommy. His friend just grinned and slapped his shoulder before they stepped inside. The near-empty bar was hot, smoke clouds fogging the room. This was Will's last night on leave before he would be transferred to the front. He hadn't seen much fighting in the past month, but he was being sent into the thick of it now.

His hand found the picture of Christy tucked over his heart. Pulling it out, he studied her face, determined to remember every detail before heading out the next day. He had mailed her a letter as soon as he reached Paris, praying she would receive it before her move to London. He hadn't argued with her, knowing she had to do something. He just hoped she would be safe and wouldn't attempt a trip to France. London was close enough.

Too close for comfort. Will shuddered, then tucked the photograph away.

"You've forgotten how to have fun since you put on that uniform," Tommy remarked. He rolled his eyes as he took a mug of beer from the counter. "Now isn't the time to be serious, my friend."

"You were never serious, Tom. I don't expect you to be now," Will replied with a chuckle.

"Come on." Tommy pointed at two Canadian soldiers. "Let's sit by them. Maybe you can get one of them talking and get some advice for us. You're good at that. Look at you, so serious. They look pretty mean if you ask me."

Will took a deep breath and settled at a table across from the two soldiers who slowly blinked at him and Tommy before returning to their drinks, mumbling to each other under their breath.

Tommy leaned in close to whisper to Will. "Loosen up, buddy," he said. "Flirt with the French girls and have a good time."

He winked and then walked away, approaching one of the women lounging at the bar. Will shifted uncomfortably in his chair as he fooled with his wedding ring. He watched the two men across from him, both sitting in silence, nursing their drinks. Will wondered how long they'd been fighting for the British Empire.

Have they been here the whole time? Will cleared his throat, but neither of the soldiers looked his way. He tried again, and this time one of them stood, muttering something under his breath before he joined the girls at the bar. The other looked at him, tilting his head slightly to the side. Will thought he didn't look old enough to be an experienced soldier, perhaps in his early twenties, with dark hair falling across his forehead and a fit physique.

But his eyes said everything about his experience. They were dark, clouded with things he had seen, things Will couldn't even imagine. Looking into his eyes, Will realized he was much older than he looked.

"Ignore Ralph," the soldier said. "He was grumpy before he came over, and he'll stay that way until we leave this damned country."

Will nodded, shifting again. The soldier eyed him before sliding a glass his way. Will chugged the beer, wiping his mouth with his sleeve.

"When do we head out?" Will asked. "I mean if you know."

"Anxious, are we?" The soldier turned his drink slowly in a full circle.

"No, I mean ..." Will coughed. "My name's Will Garvin."

"Well, Will Garvin. How long you been here?"

"Um ... a few weeks."

"You married?"

"Yes."

"Yeah, me too. You know how long I spent married to her be-fore this war?" He leaned across the table. "One year. I had her for one year. You know how long I've been fighting this war?"

He stopped. Will shook his head.

"Three years. That's three years they took from the girl I love and me. That's three years I've spent watching kids like you die. You want to know exactly when you'll be able to get yourself killed, go ask your commanding officer. You know that's why everyone ignores you. Because tomorrow you'll be dead anyway, and it's not worth it for any of us to grieve about it anymore."

"Hey, Jared, leave the kid alone!" Ralph called from across the room, his arm slung around the shoulders of a smiling girl.

Jared upended his glass, his Adam's apple bobbing as he gulped the last of the beer.

"See you on the other side, kid," the soldier growled, slamming the mug down. "And trust me, it won't be heaven."

He slammed the door on his way out.

Chapter Eighteen

Canada
August 1917

"Did the children get to school all right?"

Emma glared at her sister. She had spent the entire morning preparing her two young nephews for school. Baths, breakfast, and dressing them had all gone by in a blur as their mother sat in the kitchen with her feet suspended on a chair, eating half the fruit in the bowl on Emma's table. She understood Laura's need to rest, but she hadn't expected to be handed sole responsibility of her sister's children.

"If you had dressed when I told you to, you could have seen them off yourself," Emma grumbled, slapping her hat down on the table.

Laura was still in her nightgown, her feet propped in the same position as they were when Emma left. She balanced a bowl of porridge on her big belly, her spoon suspended halfway to her mouth.

"Em, I sense some hostility." Laura frowned, setting down her bowl. "You must have known what my coming here with the boys would entail."

"Yes, but I didn't think you would stop being the mother." Emma plunked her hands onto her hips. "Eddie left three months ago, and I've been taking care of your children ever since you came. It's not fair, Laura. They need their mother now more than ever. They're scared. They don't know why their father had to leave."

"I do not need you to tell me about my children," Laura said, pushing heavily to her feet. Pressing a hand to the small of her back, she waddled over to dump her bowl in the sink.

"Someone has to." Emma combed her fingers through her hair. "I don't have time right now. I need to go to work. Mother will be over by noon, and she will take you to pick up the boys from school." With that, Emma turned to leave.

"Emma?" Laura swung around, her chestnut braid thumping over her shoulder.

"What?" Emma asked sharply.

"When Jared left," Laura stopped short, pressing a hand to her stomach. "Did you ever think there was something you could have done to keep him here? That there was something you could have done to save him?"

Emma closed her eyes, dropping her head.

"Every day," she whispered. "And every day since I have thought the same thing of every patient I couldn't save." Laura hurried to her side, taking her hands.

"But you've saved so many. You're a wonderful nurse."

"It's not just their bodies I want to save, Laura. It's their spirit."

"I just want him to be home," Laura said, sniffling. "Eddie will never change. He never could. I just want him to make it through and come home to the boys and me."

"I said the same thing about Jared." Emma dropped her sister's hands and turned away. "In the end, there's nothing you can do. There's nothing that can be said to make any of this better."

"You'll never change, will you?" Laura snapped, turning her back. "This is where you're supposed to tell me that everything will be fine, that if I keep busy, it will all be over soon." ·

"How can I tell you that when it's not what you want to do?" Emma glared. "What you want is pity. You want everyone to hold you and take care of you and tell you that everything's going to be fine. But guess what? Nothing about war is fine. You are not the only wife whose husband could be killed any minute of any day."

Emma slammed her hand against the wall before storming from the kitchen. She wished, not for the first time, that Laura would move in with their parents. They got along better when they weren't under the same roof, and she knew her mother would love to let Laura sit around while she took care of her.

Emma snatched her nurse's apron from the peg beside the door, pulling her arms through the straps before tying it tight at her waist. She took several deep breaths, telling herself to be calm, reminding herself of what Jared would say if he was here. She recalled the last time Laura and Eddie had come to visit them, how well they got along because Jared was there to help even her temper with her idle sibling. In America, Laura had a maid and a cook, luxuries Emma would never have.

Jealousy wasn't part of Emma's vocabulary. She didn't want help around the house. She enjoyed making a home for her and Jared. But without her husband to hold her back, she couldn't handle her sister's selfish ways. Emma pressed a hand to her heart, her lips curving slightly in a smile.

"Every time she antagonizes you, answer with a smile. Show her love, Em, and maybe she'll improve." Jared's voice echoed in her ears.

Emma released the breath she'd been holding and started down the walk. Suddenly, her front door squealed open.

"Emma!" Laura called.

"Yes?" she answered.

"Just … be safe. And if there's anything I can do …" Laura bit her lip.

"I won't be back until late … if you could make dinner?" Emma waited for the excuse, wincing as she wondered what her sister would come up with. But when she looked again, Laura was smiling.

"Will chicken be all right?" she asked.

Emma nodded and turned again to leave.

"I love you, Em," Laura called.

Emma turned back and saw tears shining in her sister's eyes. She hurried back through the gate and leaped up the stairs to wrap her arms around her sister.

"Love you too, sis."

Emma held her gently. She knew she was right. There was nothing either of them could have done. But they could do this now.

They could hold each other, encourage each other, and forget about the past. It was time to look forward.

It's time to accept that nothing will ever be the same.

Emma rushed up the steps into the hospital. She had run most of the way from her house after going back to talk to her sister. Laura's sudden change of heart had taken Emma by surprise, and she wasn't quite ready to trust her. But talking to her had helped them both. Helping each other be strong during this time was the most important thing. They had more in common right now than they ever had as children.

As she pushed open the door, she had to sigh. She saw Rosie standing down the hall, whispering with Dr. Kingston.

"I'm sorry!" Emma gasped as she skidded to a halt in front of them. "I had to take my nephews to school, and my sister needed me."

"Emma." Dr. Kingston cleared his throat.

"It won't happen again, Doctor; I promise." Emma tried to calm her racing heart.

"Em," Rosie said, touching her arm. "We received news from Private Reynolds' fiancée."

"Oh, really?" Emma's face brightened with a smile. "How is he doing? Is he getting around better now?"

"Emma." Rosie shook her head. "The private ... he ..."

"What?" Emma's smile slowly faded, her heart sinking at their grim faces.

"Emma, the private has ... passed away." Dr. Kingston thrust his hands into his white coat pockets.

"He died last week," Rosie whispered, bracing her arm around Emma's shoulders.

"I ... I don't understand." Emma shook her head, her insides beginning to tremble. "He was fine when he left. He was better."

"No, Em, he wasn't." Rosie tightened her grip. "He was never going to be better again."

"Emma, Private Reynolds took his own life," Dr. Kingston said. "I'm sorry. I know how hard you worked to help him."

Emma gasped, clapping her hand over her mouth before she turned and ran from the hospital, slamming the door after her. Tears streamed down her cheeks as she sat on the top step and placed her head in her hands.

"Why, God?" Emma whispered. "Why is this happening? Is there something I could have done? Was there more?"

She tilted her head back. The sun glared on her face as her tears shifted their course, sliding down her temples into her hair. Silence answered her. Nothing about this was right.

He survived the war ... but coming home killed him. It's not right. It shouldn't be. I could've done something. I should've done more.

Emma folded her arms over her knees, pressed her face against them, and sobbed.

THE LOST GENERATION

Chapter Nineteen

London, England
August 1917

The building trembled.

Christy, startled awake, sat straight up in bed at the sound of someone pounding on her door. She threw back the covers and snatched her robe from the end of the bed before hurrying to the door. Cracking it open, she looked up at the landlord, his hair still dripping from his evening bath.

"It's time to come down into the basement, miss," he announced, pushing her door wide. "They're bombing the city again."

Clutching the collar of her robe, Christy slipped out of her room and headed toward the stairs with the other tenants. She spotted her landlady, Miss Porter. The sweet young lady smiled at her as she took her grandfather's arm. Christy stood close behind them, listening to the distant thundering that shook the building.

"Stay together, everyone!" Miss Porter called, stopping at the top of the stairs to rush everyone to the basement door.

Christy's legs shook as she squeezed between two other tenants, moving down the basement steps. They all gathered in a circle on the floor. The children looked up nervously at the ceiling as their parents hugged and rocked them back and forth. Dust hissed over their heads from another explosion. Christy brought her knees to her chest, whispering prayers as she tried to calm her racing heart.

Christy winced as another bomb rocked the building. The dark-haired woman beside her touched her arm lightly and asked, "How are you holding up?"

She looked to be in her early thirties, her blue eyes sharp but gentle, and her hair thickly braided over one shoulder. She didn't look as though she had been startled awake during the night by a bombing. Christy wondered how anyone managed to look so calm and put together in the middle of the night while explosions rattled the city.

"I know it's difficult," the woman continued. "Things must be so different in America."

"They are," Christy replied, rubbing her arms. "Everything is still just a headline in the newspaper, even though our men are over here now too. It's just ... waiting. Waiting for something to happen, helplessly reading about the battles and ... and the casualties."

She shuddered.

"I'm Beth." The woman took Christy's hand. "Beth Young. Ruth Porter is my sister."

"Oh." Christy smiled, squeezing her fingers. "I thought I saw a resemblance."

"Our grandfather says we have the same eyes." Beth smiled, tilting her head slightly to the side. "I just returned from the country. I have been making inquiries about my husband. He's on the front as we speak."

"Oh, I'm sorry." Christy rested her palm over her heart. "My husband is fighting too. I'm a reporter, and I came here for the story. It's like I'm helping him in some way. Making people aware of what he and so many others are going through helps me believe he will come back to me."

"That's a wonderful thought, Mrs. ?"

"Oh, Garvin. Christy Garvin. But please, call me Christy."

"Then you must call me Beth." Beth tapped her finger against her chin. "You know, if you need some work, I have connections with a local newspaper. They're not a very large edition, and they are relatives of mine ... but they have a decent number of subscribers. I'm sure I can get you a position."

"That would be wonderful!" Christy turned, tucking her legs beneath her to prop herself up. "I am very low on money since paying my rent in advance. If I want to stay here, I will need to make my own way."

"I'll take you there tomorrow, as soon as everything calms down again."

"What are you two whispering about?" Ruth scooted close to them, resting her temple against Beth's shoulder.

"I'm going to help Christy apply for a position with Uncle Matthew," Beth replied, putting her arm around Ruth.

"Your sister is very kind." Christy clasped her fingers tighter around Beth's hand. "My first friend here besides you."

"That's good." Ruth yawned behind her hand. "It's getting quiet out there."

"Maybe it's over," Christy said, looking at the ceiling.

"I'll check." Mr. Porter struggled to his feet. Ruth hurried over to help him.

"I'll go with you Granddad," Ruth offered.

"Be careful," Beth whispered hoarsely.

Ruth smiled as she walked with her grandfather back up the steps. Beth held onto Christy's hand as they both got to their feet.

"I pray these bombings end soon." Beth's voice trembled. "Every time I go home, it's harder to leave my sister and grandfather behind, knowing any day I could receive word that a bomb hit this place."

"In times like these, all we can do is pray," Christy answered. "I am tired, Beth. I'm so tired of it all and my country hasn't even been in this a full year. Ever since I came here ... I've felt so alone."

"Well, you don't have to feel alone anymore." Beth hugged her close. "Ruth and I will be your family now. It is the only thing to do during war times."

Christy's eyes flooded.

"Only God could have brought us together, Beth," she rasped. "I haven't felt this close to anyone, besides my husband, since I last saw my sister Annie. Thank you. Thank you so much."

Christy wrapped her arms around the woman, releasing a long breath as she held a prayer of thanks in her heart.

"Are you nervous?"

"Just a little." Christy bit her lip, her arm linked with Ruth's as they stood in the newsroom.

The space wasn't as large as Mr. Garvin's newsroom back home, but the atmosphere was the same. Desks lined the front room, and men bustled about, speaking quietly and smoking cigars, sending smoke rings to the ceiling. Butterflies fluttered in her stomach as Christy's excitement peaked. This was something familiar, something she loved. She smoothed out her sweater, wishing for a moment she had worn something else. But her cream dress and brown sweater seemed professional enough.

"This is what I love, so it shouldn't be hard to get the job, right?" Christy looked to Ruth for assurance. "Just because Beth has been talking in that room for twenty minutes with your uncle doesn't mean I'm not hired right? I mean—"

"Christy." Ruth giggled. "I think you're more than a little nervous."

"Maybe you're right." Christy sucked in a breath. "I'm just … this is what I came here to do. To find the stories and write about them."

"I have some connections with the Red Cross." Ruth offered, tilting her head so her temple rested on Christy's shoulder. "They can probably help you with your stories."

"Oh Ruth, that would be marvelous!"

Suddenly the office door opened, and Beth stepped out, grinning and winking at them before she hurried around the counters. She waved her hand back and forth as a puff of cigar smoke flew up from behind a desk.

"So?" Christy bounced from one foot to the other.

"He would like to talk to you." Beth took her hands. "Don't worry. Everything's going to be fine. He told me that on my recommendation, he believes he can find a place for you."

Christy nodded and stepped around her friend, holding her head up high as she marched toward the office door. She could feel the eyes of the men, watching her every move as she went. She stopped at the door, biting the scab that had formed on her lip. Turning, she caught Beth's eye.

Beth just nodded, her arm around her sister's shoulders as they watched her. Christy felt like a little girl, going to school for the first time while her mother watched. Her heart warmed at the thought as she knocked on the door.

"Come in, Mrs. Garvin," a deep voice rang out from the other side of the door.

Christy pressed a hand to her stomach to calm the butterflies before she pushed open the door.

THE LOST GENERATION

Chapter Twenty

Operation Michael
The Somme
March 1918

Jared crouched in the trenches, his breath wheezing in and out as he choked on the fog. Lifting onto the balls of his feet, he attempted to peek over the edge of the trench. His fingers were cold around the barrel of his rifle. He could see his breath, swirling in the mix of the white fog. As he crouched again, he caught sight of Ralph, slumped over against the wall of the trench.

He swallowed the lump in his throat; his jaw stiffening. Blood was still seeping from the fresh wound to Ralph's eye. His friend had gone silent, his chest no longer rising and falling. Jared had crawled on his belly along the trench, staying out of the Germans' sight, but he hadn't been able to get to Ralph in time to hold his hand at the end.

God, if You're still watching over me, then have mercy. Let this be as bad as it can get. He spared one last look over his shoulder at his dead friend before he put the man from his mind, just as he had done with all the rest.

Jared inched forward, pushing the rim of his helmet back to see clearly as he rounded the corner. There were men from left to right, most of them waiting to charge, waiting to make their move over the edge of the trenches. Jared looked for only one man in the crowd. Ralph was gone, leaving him with one friend, one other man he trusted entirely to watch his back.

"Where are you, Sarge?" Jared whispered, crouching by another soldier.

"Try around the corner." The soldier turned to him suddenly, his face covered in mud. "Sergeant Young went looking for the lieutenant."

"Thanks," Jared said, slapping him on the shoulder. "Stay alive."

"You do the same." The soldier grinned.

Jared moved on, weaving between the men as he went. Gunfire exploded in the trench behind him, and he tripped over his feet before rolling onto his back and firing into the air. German curses spewed through the air, and Jared struggled back up, running as fast as he could through the trench.

"Sergeant!" he shouted, firing over his shoulder. The Germans moved like ghosts through the fog, using the weather to their advantage.

Jared rushed around the corner and hit something solid. He fell back against the wall with a grunt, hitting his head hard. The world spun for a second before he shook it off, squinting to focus on what he'd run into. The two men held their rifles in midair. Their eyes expanded, pupils dilated as they gasped, sweat soaking their clothing.

His own eyes widened when he recognized them.

"What are *you* doing here?"

Will blinked, sharing a look with Tommy before turning back to address Jared. The Canadian was furious at the sight of them, his shoulders tensing and his gun death-gripped in both fists. Jared rolled his eyes and grabbed a fistful of Will's uniform by the shoulder.

"Never mind. Come on." He dragged Will a few feet before letting go, peeking over the top of the trench again.

Jared pushed back his helmet. His face was smeared with mud; his pants clung to his legs where the wet earth had soaked in. Will's nose wrinkled at the odors filling the trench. He wondered how long Jared had endured this place. He had done the best he could to deal

with this foreign land in the year he had been here, but Jared ....
Will hadn't understood what made him the way he was, but he was
starting to.

"We got separated from our officer," Tommy said, breathing
heavily, wiping the sweat from his forehead with his sleeve. "I think
we got a little turned around. We thought ..."

"Private Cote!"

Will spun at the harsh voice. The sergeant came boldly striding
toward them, his rifle slung across one arm, and his forehead creased
in a severe frown. He walked tall and straight through the trench,
not bothering to bend over to avoid enemy fire. He seemed not to
care. Even with the echo of bullets peppering the edge of the trench
a few feet away, he didn't flinch.

Will didn't know what it was about the man, but suddenly he
was relieved. He was thankful a commanding officer was in their
midst, and he wasn't left alone with Jared's harsh words and ways.

"Sarge!" Sighing with relief, Jared met the sergeant halfway.

They started whispering, their heads together as Jared gestured
back to Will and Tommy. Will leaned his palm against the trench
wall, his boots squishing in the mud. His feet ached from the running. It would be awhile before he could sit down again. They needed to get back to their unit. Will glanced at Tommy when he leaned
in to talk to him.

"What do you think they're talking about?" Tommy asked.

"A plan, hopefully," Will grumbled, shifting his rifle. "I just
hope they have the decency to share with us."

"Of all the men we had to run into, why did it have to be the one
who thinks we're useless?" Tommy rolled his eyes.

"He doesn't think we're useless." Will's tone gentled. "He just
... he's seen more. He knows more, and he doesn't want to deal
with it if we ..."

"Die?" Tommy shrugged. "Well that's not gonna happen, so
he's got nothing to worry about."

"All right." The sergeant approached them, chest heaving and his accent thickening. "Don't move, stay put, and use the fog to your advantage. I'm going to check the perimeter."

They nodded, following the sergeant to peek over the top of the trench. He glared over his shoulder at them when they moved close on his heels, stopping them dead in their tracks. But as soon as he looked away again, they took their chance to peer out into the fog.

Standing shoulder to shoulder, Will and Tommy slid back down the trench wall, turning to look at Jared who just grinned as he spoke softly with the sergeant. Sergeant Young rolled his eyes before approaching the edge of the trench. Bold as day, he lifted himself up, looking over the edge.

Bullets splattered the dirt, and the sergeant jumped down with a shrug.

"Only one way to go," he announced. "Watch each other's backs. I'll get you back to your platoon."

"We'll get you back." Jared's rifle clicked as he reloaded. "No way I'm letting you lead them out there alone, Sarge."

"It's too dangerous, Jared."

"Every part of this is dangerous, John. You should know by now you're all I've got left to keep me alive over here." Jared stood firm. "Where am I supposed to go anyway? Gotta rejoin the line, right?"

The sergeant nodded.

"On three," John said, bracing his palm on the trench.

Will positioned himself the same way, preparing to leap right out. His heart raced against his chest, a knot forming in his stomach at the prospect of running out into the open. He caught Tommy's eye. His friend smiled, slapping his shoulder.

"One."

"Keep your head down." Jared readjusted Will's helmet, slapping it twice. "Gun against your collar, shoulders hunched. You'll be fine."

Will nodded quickly, his mouth dry as dust. Jared moved on to Tommy.

"Two." John murmured.

"We'll see you across the field." Jared got between Tommy and John. "Got your back, Sarge."

"Three!"

Will held his breath and launched himself over the top of the trench.

Chapter Twenty-One

Operation Michael
The Somme

John spun, his feet flying out from under him as he fired into the thick of the fog. Heads flew back, bodies slammed to the ground as his bullets hit home. Landing on his back, he slid a few feet in the moist earth before flipping back onto his belly. Jared fell on his right side; one of the Americans was on his left. They stared at the tree line together as John tried to catch his bearings.

"Where's Tommy?" The American gasped, his stomach heaving.

"Do you know where we are, Sergeant?" Jared asked, ignoring the American. "Are we over the line?"

"What line?" the American asked. "What's he talking about?"

"I don't know." John shook his head, trying to concentrate. "I can't tell. Just … keep your heads down and be quiet."

"Did either of you see Tommy? He was right behind me!" The American started to rise up on his elbows.

John grabbed him, slamming him face first into the dirt.

"I said stay down and keep quiet, soldier!" he hissed. "We'll find your friend. Just stay down."

"He was right behind me," the boy whispered again.

"We'll find him, Will." Jared leaned over, looking past John. "He can't be far behind."

Will. That's his name. John committed it to memory.

"It's this bloody fog," John growled. "If it would just clear."

"I think we're over, Sarge." Jared reloaded. "We've got to be. They were behind us."

"I got turned around." John gasped in a few breaths. "This is my fault … I got turned around …"

"It's not your fault," Jared said, slapping his shoulder. "Come on, Sarge. We just have to turn around."

"Right." John nodded, stifling a cough on his sleeve. "Let's go."

He rose up on his haunches, preparing to spin around when a shadow fell over them. John raised his gun, preparing to fire when suddenly the form dropped, falling to his knees. John's brow curved downward when suddenly Will gasped.

"Tommy!" he shouted, dropping his gun to wrap his arms around his friend.

Jared cursed as he leaped to his feet, hovering over both boys, his gun at the ready.

"I've got them." John took the other side, down on one knee with his gun pressed hard into his shoulder. "We've got to get moving, boys."

"Tommy! God, please no!" Will cried, shaking his friend's limp body.

John looked down, frozen. He thought Jared said something to him, but he couldn't hear anything. Seeing the American holding his friend, Bobby's face immediately flashed before his eyes. This couldn't be happening all over again. He hadn't looked for a soldier he knew; he hadn't made a connection. The only one who he had allowed himself to bond with was Jared and that only because they would do anything to keep themselves and each other alive.

But watching this boy cradle his dead friend … it was too much. They had to get out of here.

"Let him go, son." John took hold of Will's shoulder. "He's gone."

"We can't just leave him," Will protested, sniffling.

"We have no choice, kid." Jared's voice softened. "We're over enemy lines. If we don't go now, we're all done."

"The best thing you can do for Tommy is keep fighting, keep going," John encouraged. "We've got to go now, Will."

"I … I can't …" Will shook his head.

"Get up, soldier." John lowered his voice, lifting Will's gun and holding it out to him. "Pick up your weapon and let's go. That's an order."

Will hesitated, his hand trembling as he reached out to grasp the barrel of his rifle. He gently laid Tommy down onto his back in the dirt. Turning away, John met Jared's gaze. They stared at each other for a moment, much the same way they had that day in the trench.

Will stood, rubbing his eyes with the back of his sleeve before he nodded. "I'm ready," he said.

John nodded as he positioned himself in front of Will. Jared understood as he also stepped halfway in front of the boy, creating a shoulder-to-shoulder wall to protect the young man. They looked at each other once more.

"You ready, soldier?"

"Yes, sir, Sergeant."

John aimed into the fog and together, the three men moved out.

Chapter Twenty-Two

England
April 1918

Beth sighed with relief as she stepped onto the boardwalk in her little town. Being home was such a wonderful feeling after spending so much time away. The crisp air reminded her why she didn't follow her sister to London. Everything about her home filled her heart with joy, even the chicken smell that wafted over her when she stepped onto her front yard. It was all hers ... and John's.

She pressed her hand to her heart, reminding herself he would come home. He had promised he would come home and it would only be a little while longer, she knew it. Soon he would be the one stepping off the train, soon he would hold out his arms and wait for her to rush right into them. That moment couldn't come soon enough. But Beth had faith.

It will happen.

"Mama! You're home!" Melody's voice rang out, and Beth looked up, her heart racing as she rushed forward.

"Oh, my darlings!" Beth's eyes flooded. She dropped her suitcase in the middle of the street and held her arms wide as both her children came running.

Melody squealed, leaping into the air to catapult herself into Beth's arms.

"I missed you!"

"I missed you, too." Beth wondered when her little girl had grown so big. She balanced her daughter on one arm just in time to catch up little George with the other. They both hugged her neck, little arms wrapped tight around her, their sweet, soft faces pressed against her neck.

"They were angels," Susan said and lifted Beth's suitcase from the ground. "I am almost sorry you came home so soon. How's your sister?"

"She's fine. She sends her love." Beth leaned over to kiss her mother's cheek. "Thank you for taking such good care of them."

"Come now." Susan took Melody from her. "We have to stop at the post office, and then we will go home. Your Mama can tell you all about her trip on the way."

"And how are you, son?" Beth asked, rubbing noses with her little boy.

"I missed Mama." George framed her face with his small hands.

Beth kissed his rosy cheek, hugging him tight as she followed her mother down the street toward the post office.

"It is so good to be home, Mum," she said, linking arms with the older woman.

"Then what's wrong?" Susan asked, arching a brow.

Beth shook her head. *She knows me too well.*

"I don't know. I have this … uneasy feeling. Leaving Ruth and Christy behind was difficult." Beth paused with a shudder. "I asked them both to come home with me, you know. But since Christy has settled into her new job, she wasn't willing to come away and Ruth … well, she'd never leave Grandfather or that boardinghouse."

"She knows how much it means to him," Susan agreed. "I'm sure you did everything you could, my darling."

Beth nodded. But she still wished she had pushed them to come to Lancashire. There was something in the air today, and her heart refused to settle. Beth cuddled her face against her son's warm neck and he squirmed.

"I am so happy to be home, George," she whispered as they stepped into the post office. "Mama won't be going again anytime soon."

"Oh! Mrs. Young!" Startled by their entrance, Margaret stood quickly.

"Hello, Margaret." Beth smiled as she set her son back on his feet.

"I didn't know you were back in town," the young woman exclaimed.

"I just stepped off the train," Beth answered.

"I have your mail." Margaret spun quickly, hesitating as she picked up the stack.

"Margaret has been a bit distracted," Susan whispered in Beth's ear. "She hasn't received news of her brother in months."

"None of us have received news, Mum." Beth bowed her head. "It is a feeling everyone understands."

"Mrs. Young." Margaret's soft voice brought her back around. "I … I'm sorry. I'm so sorry."

Beth froze. Her eyes focused on Margaret's shaking hand, her rapid breathing. She drew away from the touch of her mother's hand on her shoulder. Comfort was not what she needed now. She needed silence, she needed distance … she needed to be anywhere else but here.

Without a word she reached out and took the telegram from Margaret's hand.

Chapter Twenty-Three

London, England

Christy's fingers moved rapidly over the typewriter keys. She glanced down at her notes every now and again as she wrote. Her articles had quickly reached the front page of their little paper, and getting this latest story done before Beth's uncle kicked her out for the night was her priority. It was already getting dark out, and soon Ruth would arrive to drive her home. Leaning her elbows on the table, she stared down at her work.

"What are you thinking, miss?" a voice asked. Christy looked up and smiled at young Mr. Higgins.

"I am thinking there is nothing more frustrating than staring at a half-blank page and not knowing what to write next," she answered.

Higgins chuckled. "I concur, miss, I concur. Though I've not had many occasions to write, what?"

"No, I suppose not," Christy agreed. "But you will have your day, Higgins. I'm sure of it."

"I hope you're right, miss," he replied, rather loudly. "You know, they kept me out of the army on account of these ears of mine."

"Yes, I know," Christy said, long-suffering. She had heard this many times before from Higgins. "I don't pity you, you know."

"And why not? I can't serve my country. That hurts," Higgins pouted, pressing a hand to his heart.

"If you say so."

Higgins stared at her for a moment longer and then shrugged. "Well, goodnight then, miss."

"Goodbye, Higgins. Be safe." Christy waved as he marched across the room to the door.

She closed her notebook, tugged the piece of paper loose from the typewriter, and set it inside her portfolio. Christy pressed her hands flat on the desk and then rose. She decided to step out before Matthew had the chance to scold her again for staying late.

Gathering her things and slinging her coat over her arm, Christy slipped out of the office. Moments later, Ruth pulled up in front, waving her hand. Christy smiled and climbed quickly into the automobile. Without speaking, Ruth started back home.

"I'm almost finished with my article," Christy said, leaning her head back. "I wanted to finish tonight but ... I just came to a standstill. It's hard writing these stories without having any real experience. Sometimes I feel things would be different if I were in France."

"You don't want to do that. Things are bad enough here in London. You shouldn't even consider leaving." Ruth insisted.

"But isn't that the only way I'll find out what's going on? If I joined the Red Cross and went over there, I could tell the world what the soldiers are going through."

"You could get killed yourself," Ruth continued, shaking her head. "It's wrong. It's not a good idea."

"Ruth ... are you all right?" Christy reached over, touching Ruth's arm as they stopped in front of the apartment building.

"No, Christy." With a sigh, Ruth pulled off her hat. "My sister received a telegram."

"Oh no!" Christy gasped, covering her mouth. "Is he ...?"

"We don't know." Ruth reached into her pocket. "There's something else, Christy. I didn't want a stranger to give it to you."

Christy's heart stopped when Ruth began to pull her hand out of her pocket. The corner of a little envelope peeked out.

"I'm sorry, Christy. It came this afternoon."

Christy couldn't find her breath as she took the telegram in her hand, staring at her name typed in harsh black ink across the front. Her shoulders began to tremble as a single tear fell and splashed on the letter.

Chapter Twenty-Four

Canada
April 1918

Emma was out of breath. She had run all the way from the post office to her parent's house. Stopping at the porch, she leaned over, the paper in her hand burning her skin. She gasped back a sob, climbing the stairs. Pulling open the door, she stomped down the hall toward the kitchen. She knew that's where they would be so early in the morning, sitting calmly at the table, enjoying a quiet breakfast together, oblivious to the fact that her world had just ended.

They wouldn't understand her pain. She knew that as surely as she knew the telegram could only mean one thing. As much as she wanted to deny it, as much as she wanted to fight, bargaining was useless. Believing she could talk her way out of the truth was a waste of effort. But she would try. Despite how illogical it was, she would fight to believe there was hope, even now.

Her palm flattened on the swinging door, pushing it open. It rebounded against the wall, startling her parents out of their chairs.

"Emma, darling, what's wrong?" Grace asked, clasping a fistful of her robe at her neck.

Emma just stared at them, frozen in the moment. Her stomach twisted; her heart thundered so loud she could barely hear anything else. This was a moment she would never forget, a moment when the whole world seemed to stop. Through her blurred vision, she watched her parents share concerned looks. This was not supposed to be her life. This was not supposed to be the world that defined her.

"I … I just came from the post office." Emma finally spoke, the telegram trembling in her hand as she turned to her father. "Do you remember what you said that day when you and mother left to go get Laura?"

He was silent, his face blanching as she turned the telegram over again to read out loud.

"'We regret to inform you that your husband, Private Jared Cote, has been reported Missing in Action.'" Crumbling the telegram in both fists, she looked up at her father.

"Oh, Emma!" Grace cried, covering her mouth with her hand.

"What does that mean again, Daddy?" Emma didn't break eye contact with her father.

"Em …" He shook his head, taking a step toward her.

"No!" she shouted, holding up her hand as she backed away from him. "Tell me what that means! You said it so easily before when it wasn't about my husband!"

"Emma, love, please." He held out his arms to her.

"Tell me what it means!" she screamed, slamming her fists into his chest. "Is my husband dead? Is that what it means, Daddy? Tell me!"

"Emma, stop!" He grabbed her arms.

Emma stilled, bracing her hands on his biceps, her body trembling as she looked up at him. Tears flooded down her cheeks, soaking her neck as she looked in her father's eyes. The pity she saw there was too much, the understanding that this could be the end of her life as she knew it was overwhelming.

"Is my husband dead?" she whispered. "Is that what this telegram means?"

"I don't know, Em." He pulled her close, and she buried her face in his chest, her shoulders heaving. "I just don't know."

"No." Emma shook her head, pulling away. "No, he's alive. He has to be alive."

"Emma, don't go." Grace rushed after her daughter as she turned to leave.

"I'm sorry." Emma didn't turn back. "I just ... I have to be alone."

With the telegram still clutched in her fist, Emma left her parents' house. She would burn the telegram; she would get rid of it and pretend, for a while, that she'd never received it. Then, when the shock faded, when she released the breath she was holding, she knew exactly what she would do.

Her thoughts jumbled and her heart shattered, Emma somehow found her courage again as she marched home.

Chapter Twenty-Five

France
The Woods

They were surrounded.

Jared locked his fingers behind his head as the German soldier pushed him to his knees beside Will. The younger man looked at him, eyes wide with fear and jaw working as he gritted his teeth. It was a look Jared had come to recognize in soldiers when they were scared but trying hard to find their courage.

He closed his eyes. He'd promised himself he wouldn't be captured, that he would never be taken alive. But keeping John and Will alive was the only thing he thought of when he chose to lay down his weapon and raise his arms in surrender. Whether they would even make it to a prison camp, Jared couldn't be certain. The way the soldiers were eyeing them, the way one of them paced back and forth in front of them, his rifle at the ready—it wasn't a good sign.

Jared's bayonet made his ankle itch where it was hidden in his boot. He had a plan for every situation out here. He knew exactly what he would do. Glancing over at John, he knew the officer knew where he'd hidden the weapon. All they had to do was wait for the Germans to make the wrong move, to turn their backs. It would only take five seconds.

He would jump the big one first, putting down the strongest of their platoon. The rest would be easy. The rest were boys. Jared's insides knotted at the thought, but it had to be done. Nearly four years of his life had consisted of taking action that made him hate himself.

"Keep your head down, Will," Jared whispered from the corner of his mouth. "No matter what happens, when the time comes … run. Just get out. You got it, kid?"

"What are you going to do?" Will's eyes expanded.

"Just do it. Run and don't look back. Got it?"

Will nodded yes and shifted his arms.

"I'll take the big one." Jared turned to John then, keeping one eye on the enemy. "Can you handle the sergeant?"

John just nodded, his eyes narrowing. Jared could almost see him thinking it through, creating a strategy. Jared slowly began to lower his arms when the big one turned, the small group huddling together, discussing what to do with their prisoners. He licked his lips, wishing he understood what they were saying. Their sharp voices, their harsh language the only sounds to be heard in the middle of the woods.

"Now?" John asked.

"Now." Jared nodded.

The two rose up together. The world seemed to slow down as Jared lunged, grabbing the big German from behind. The others shouted and pointed their rifles as he pulled him back. Without thinking, he drew the bayonet across the man's throat, spraying blood into the air before the soldier dropped. John caught the German's rifle midair and aimed to fire at the startled troops.

"Now Will, go!" Jared yelled before tackling another to the ground.

He thrust the bayonet into the boy's belly again and again and again—his blood spurted up, splattering Jared's face. Suddenly, the boy grabbed his arm as he choked on his own blood. Jared stopped, his knife still lodged between the soldier's ribs. He stared down at the young man, his heartbeat drowning out the sound of John struggling with the last two Germans.

The soldier couldn't be older than Will, his face still smooth with youth, and his eyes filled with fear as his skin went pale. Jared gasped, yanking the knife loose from him as he stumbled back. The boy reached out to him; his tears mixed with the blood pouring from his mouth. As quickly as he drew away, Jared returned to his side, grabbing the boy's hand.

"I'm sorry," Jared whispered hoarsely, gasping for breath. "I'm so sorry."

The boy mumbled something in reply and then went still. His eyes glossed over as Jared rested his limp hand over his chest. Jared stood slowly, looking up just as John fired twice, dropping the last two enemy soldiers. Will was still there, leaning against a tree. The three men stood in silence; then Will turned and dropped to his knees, heaving behind the tree.

They waited for Will to finish, slowly rising back to his feet as he swiped his sleeve across his mouth.

"What do we do now?" Will asked.

"We try to catch our bearings," John answered, tossing Will a rifle and ammo. "Best thing we can do is get as far away from here as possible before the rest of their platoon comes back. There's no doubt now we're behind enemy lines."

"We don't get caught again." Jared recovered, snatching another bloodied rifle from one dead soldier's grasp. "If we're surrounded again, then we fight until we die. I don't know about you, but I'm not going to rot in a German prison camp."

"Do you think we can find our division?" Will wondered aloud as they loaded up. "We can backtrack, right? Get back to our guys?"

"I don't know," John replied, his voice low.

"But there's a chance, right? We can make it back and—"

"I don't know!" John shouted suddenly

"Sarge …" Jared shook his head, his eyes darting.

"We're behind enemy lines!" John slammed his fist into one of the trees, blood gathering on his knuckles. "We don't have a prayer! We're *behind enemy lines!*"

The words echoed all around them in the empty woods. Jared's heart turned cold as he looked down at the German boy he had killed. He crouched, resting his palm flat on the youth's still heart. After a few minutes, Jared said what they were all thinking.

"We don't have a chance." He looked up at them. "We're going to die."

A cold breeze rustled Will's hair as he hunkered down in the foxhole. Jared had dug it with his bayonet, covering all of them with leaves and branches until they blended into the woods like any other part of nature. Will had lost track of time, not knowing how long they'd been running and hiding, trying to find their way back. How far into the woods had the German platoon taken them? But more importantly, how much farther into the woods had they run when the rest of the men discovered the soldiers Jared and John killed and started to chase them?

John had tried to follow the direction of the sun, but when they were nearly caught again, they ran in the opposite direction. Twisting and turning in the woods, they completely lost their bearings once again, making it impossible for them to know if, at any moment, they would run into their own ... or another enemy division. They were desperate, alone, and completely void of hope. But running was their instinct, the only logical thing to do.

Will's stomach rumbled. Curling into himself, he pressed his palm against his stomach, trying to silence it. He felt Christy's picture crinkle, and he tugged it loose from its spot in his jacket. He couldn't see her face in the darkness, but he had her memorized. Everything about her he loved. Looking at her picture every day and knowing she was safe kept him going. It made him more determined to get back to her. He didn't care what Jared said. They'd made it this far, and they could keep going until they made it all the way home. They had to make some progress at some point, and the woods would look different when the sun came up.

Will closed his eyes, but sleep was far from coming. The moment he shuttered himself in darkness, Tommy appeared before him. Like a ghost, his friend knelt in front of him, his hand suspended in front of him and blood dribbling from the hole in his neck. He'd seen the wound and knew there was nothing he could have done, but he still hoped his friend had clung to life and not succumbed to his injury.

He gasped, jerking his body forward. The branches keeping them hidden stopped his progress, and he fell back, his head thudding against the hard dirt. He growled, slapping at the twigs in his face before turning his head and coming practically nose to nose with Jared. When he jumped back, Jared grinned. Rocking from side to side, the man turned onto his hip, his arm circled around his head like a pillow. He looked completely relaxed and comfortable in his spot in their hole as if the dirt was the softest bed in the world.

"So you've been out here a whole year now," Jared commented. "Fighting the front lines often?"

Will blinked at him, wondering where this conversation was going. After their first and only encounter before meeting in the trenches, Will decided Jared wasn't the type of person who was going to start a conversation without finishing it with something either nasty or insulting. He didn't strike Will as one who enjoyed small talk, especially not a casual conversation about the fighting.

"Some," Will replied, shifting again.

"Missing your wife?" Jared wondered.

"What do you want from me, Jared? Some kind of emotional response?" Will rolled his eyes and turned onto his back. "I've seen a lot of stuff now too. I understand why you are the way you are. Stop treating me like a stupid kid who needs a lesson."

"I don't want a reaction," Jared replied, his voice softening. "You know that boy I killed? He wasn't much older than you. I looked in his eyes as he died, and I wondered if there was something else I could've done, anything to spare his life."

"But there wasn't." Will looked at him again.

"Exactly." Jared nudged him. "Don't tear yourself apart over Tommy. It wasn't your fault, and there was nothing you could have done. Don't dwell on it because there was no moment when you could have done something differently, there was no split second when you could have changed anything."

"I-I don't think about …"

"You're not a good liar," Jared commented. "Everyone thinks about it when their first friend dies over here. I watched all mine die. That's why the sergeant is the only one I have left over here. We protect each other. Now you're running with us too."

"I'll try not to get you killed," Will said, grinning.

"Not the point," Jared growled. "If you let yourself, you'll dig yourself into a grave. You'll blame yourself until you don't think you deserve to live anymore."

Will's grin faded. He turned away from Jared's compelling gaze, fingering Christy's picture again.

"Your girl would tell you the same thing."

Will's smile almost returned as he wondered if anything got past Jared.

"You're right. She would. But she would also help me find a way to forgive myself. She'd know exactly what to do and say." Will folded his arms tight at his chest.

"So would my Emma," Jared said, and he stiffened. He started to turn over, but Will's next words stopped him.

"His father used to hit him."

Jared turned back slowly, eyes ablaze. "What?"

"Tommy's father. He used to beat him." Will shuddered, wondering why he was telling Jared this. "He was a drunk, and whenever things wouldn't go his way, he'd drink and come home to take his anger out on Tommy. Tommy always took it. He thought he was protecting his mother. When I could, I protected him. Now I've failed him when he needed me most."

"No," Jared answered. "You didn't fail him, Will. You did what you could, which is all anyone can do. What happened next … well, it wasn't in your hands."

Will looked at him again. "It should've been. He was right beside me. If I hadn't run ahead, if I'd stayed close—"

"Don't," Jared snapped. Will looked into his eyes and saw the truth.

Jared felt like this. Only a hundred times more than I have. Will's Adam's apple dipped when he swallowed.

"Like I said, there was nothing you could do. There was no moment when you could've changed it. It happened. It's done, and Tommy wouldn't want you to blame yourself."

Jared turned away sharply, bumping into John before he settled in. Will sank deeper into the earth, scratching where one of the branches had caused hives on his neck. When he closed his eyes this time, he saw Christy, her long blonde hair flowing in the wind, her wedding dress rustling as it had the night of their wedding when she stood in front of the windows.

He would find a way to get back to her. She would help him put Tommy's death behind him. She would help him find his joy again. Will knew Christy would tell him to turn to Jesus for his salvation. He knew she would say only the Almighty could help him, that her strength was small in comparison to the great magnitude of God's plan for Will's soul. But those words meant so little as he drifted off to sleep. Where was God now? Even Christy couldn't answer that question. Not if she was here. Not if she'd seen what he saw.

How can I rely on a God who abandons the ones He calls His children so easily? No, Christy *will save my life. Not some God I can't see or feel. She'll save me from myself. I just need to get back to her.*

Chapter Twenty-Six

London, England
May 1918

The door creaked as Christy stepped into the darkened hallway. She looked back and forth, listening for movement from any of the other rooms before she tiptoed to the hall. Her Red Cross hat scratched her forehead, reminding her that her life was changing forever. Christy clutched her notebook against the line of brass buttons down her front. The Red Cross symbol on her bag stood out in the darkness of the hall.

Clutching her shoes in her hand, she moved soundlessly down the steps. Pausing to sit on the last step, Christy pulled on her shoes before heading to the door. She looked back over her shoulder. They didn't know she was leaving, and she wanted to keep it that way. Christy had learned early in her life that she hated goodbyes. In times like these, goodbyes could mean forever. She didn't want to think she would never see Ruth or Beth again. She wanted to believe that the next time she saw them, she would be introducing Will.

All I have to do is find him. She closed her eyes. *Please, God, I must find him.*

The telegram was tucked away in her journal, a constant reminder of why she was doing this, of why she was putting herself in harm's way. They said he was missing, and they didn't know if he was captured or dead. Either way, she would find him. She would bring him home, no matter what.

"Christy?"

She froze with her hand on the doorknob. She closed her eyes and turned slowly, clutching the strap of her bag in both hands. Biting her lip, she faced Ruth.

"You're going." Ruth shook her head as she tightened the belt of her robe.

"I left a note. I hate sneaking out, but I knew you would try to stop me." Christy heaved a deep sigh. "This is just something I have to do, Ruth. Especially now."

"Do you think this is what Will would want?" Ruth hurried to her, grabbing her hands. "I don't. I think he would want you to be safe, Christy."

"Of course he would," Christy said, shaking her head. "But I want him to be safe too. He's missing, and the army can't find him."

"Exactly." Ruth dropped her hands. "If the army can't find him, what makes you think you will be able to?"

"Ruth, why are you acting like this?" Frowning, Christy stepped back. "Is there something you're not telling me?"

Ruth pulled her robe closer around her.

"Do you think you and Beth are the only ones who have received a telegram?" Ruth asked. "Mine came two years ago, and I still have it. We were engaged. He went missing, and I haven't heard anything since."

"Ruth, I'm so sorry," Christy rasped.

"You're not the first person who wanted to do more. I came so close to being where you are now. But you just have to open your eyes and realize that leaving home and doing what you're doing isn't going to help him." Ruth grasped Christy's hands once again. "You need to stay, Christy. You need to take care of yourself and return to your family when you're ready."

Christy stared at this woman, realizing how strong the war had made her. She couldn't imagine sitting back and letting go of whatever was happening over there. She'd already traveled across an ocean to be closer to him. Losing him now was not an option.

Letting him go has never been an option.

"I can't," Christy said, pulling away from Ruth. "He's my family. I can't just let him go like this. I can't live without knowing what happened to him."

She turned her back, pulling open the door.

"I'll write," she whispered over her shoulder. "Tell Beth I said goodbye, and I'll miss her."

"Christy, please!" Ruth begged. "Too many who go don't come back. That uniform will make you stand out to the enemy. They will target you! You've written about such things yourself. Please!"

Christy could hear the tears in Ruth's voice. "I'm sorry, Ruth. I have to."

Closing the door behind her, Christy released a long breath once she was out in the open air. Without looking back, she started down the street toward the Red Cross office. The sun was just beginning to peek over London, waking up the city.

When she arrived at the Red Cross office, Christy stopped and tilted her head to look up at the building. She was about to step into a whole new world, and she had no idea where that world would take her or what the result would be. But she had to go. That she knew as certainly as she knew this was not the end for her and Will. Their goodbye in New York was not their last. She knew that in her heart.

Leaving her doubts behind, Christy marched up the steps into the office. The air inside felt close, nearly stifling. She drew in a calming breath, telling herself it was just nerves. There was a small group of people standing nearby, all in the standard matching Red Cross uniform. Summoning a smile, Christy walked up to one of the girls. She was sitting by herself in the corner, a black leather book open on her lap. She looked up when Christy settled on the chair beside her.

"You're the American," she said without greeting. "The reporter, yes?"

Christy nodded and stuck out her hand. "Christy Garvin."

"Lucy Preston," the girl replied, squeezing Christy's fingers. "Is this your first assignment?"

"Yes." Christy nodded vigorously. "I requested an assignment to the front so I might be in the midst of the action. I think it would be the best place to receive an accurate report, don't you?"

Christy resisted biting her lip. The truth was, she'd requested an assignment to the front for a better chance at finding Will. But Lucy didn't need to know that.

"Well, you're getting your wish, miss," Lucy said, the corner of her mouth twitching but not quite smiling. "That's where we're headed."

A thrill shot through Christy so acute she thought her heart would burst open. She was headed for the front. Toward Will.

Lucy bent her head back to her book, running a gloved finger along the words as she read slowly. Christy leaned a little closer to her.

"What are you reading?" she asked.

Lucy did smile this time and tilted the book. Christy bent over, touching the fine, thin paper as she read, "*I will lift up mine eyes unto the hills, from whence cometh my help? My help cometh from the LORD which made heaven and earth.*" Christy raised her head again to look at Lucy. "I always loved the Psalms."

"Me too," Lucy agreed, carefully closing the book. "And I think, going to the front, we should be looking to the Lord for help as often as possible. Wouldn't you agree?"

Christy stared at this girl. A knot formed in the center of her chest. She hadn't attended church since she came to England. In fact, she'd relied on her own strength and merit alone to get to where she was today. Her Bible, even now, lay on the dressing table in her room at the boardinghouse. A sudden longing for its comfort twisted her stomach, and she thought about the verse and what Lucy had said.

I will lift my eyes to the Lord then. Christy thought resolutely. *He's the one who can help me—who can help Will—now.*

Christy covered Lucy's hand with her own. "Thank you, Lucy."

STAGE 4:
DEPRESSION

THE LOST GENERATION

Chapter Twenty-Seven

France
Field Hospital near The Marne
June 1918

Cries and moans echoed from behind the tent flap. Christy held her breath as she stepped inside, the smell of stale blood and raw flesh overwhelming her senses. She flexed her fingers around the strap of her Red Cross bag as she moved between the cots. Her shoes squished on the bloodstained ground, with puddles gathering here and there beneath beds. Christy stopped in front of two cots shuddering at the still forms of dead soldiers beneath the white sheets. They were packing up the dead and critically wounded, preparing to move the hospital.

The nurses and doctors would make one last sweep of the trenches, moving closer into the face of danger to see if there were any more wounded left behind. Christy licked her dry lips, pulling out her journal to take notes. She stopped in front of one soldier, noting his hands rested over his ribs and the bandage around his arm was half soaked with blood. He didn't seem to be in any pain; no painful moans came from between his cracked lips; no expression could be seen in his eyes.

A nurse came by, her hair pulled into a tightly braided bun, a stark white cap on her head. Kneeling by the cot, she slipped something beneath the soldier's tongue, then stood, slapping at her bloodstained apron. She turned sharply toward Christy, arching her brow irritably.

"Can I help you with something?" she snapped.

"I … I just wanted …" Christy fumbled with her journal, quickly putting it back in her bag.

"If you're just going to stand there staring at the suffering, then I suggest you leave. If you don't want to leave, then find one of the doctors and make yourself useful. There's no room for idle hands here."

She moved on to the next man before Christy could answer. Christy turned to leave.

"Miss?"

She stopped at the sound of the youthful voice and turned to the cot. His one eye moved back and forth unseeing; the wet, bloodied bandage over his other eye caused her stomach to twist. Christy knelt beside the cot. He lifted his hand, searching for her; she snatched it, sandwiching it between both of hers.

"What's your name?" he asked.

"Christy," she replied. Smoothing his hair with her hand, she asked, "And yours?"

"Michael." He gulped in air, his heavy breathing beginning to wheeze through his lungs. "Am … am I going … home?"

"Yes, Michael." Christy smiled, gently passing her knuckles down the side of his face.

He began to calm at her touch; sweat dripped down his temples as his breathing slowed.

"Yes, they're sending you home." Christy continued to caress his face. "You should try to sleep. They'll take you out soon."

"I … I feel strange." Michael shook his head. "I can't see anything."

"Maybe that will come back," Christy said, trying to reassure him. "Rest now, Michael. I will find someone to get you out of here."

"Thank you." He choked, tears gathering in his unbound eye.

Christy pushed to her feet and hurried out of the tent. She covered her mouth with her hand to mute the sobs wanting to erupt from her throat. Once outside, she gasped in a breath, cupping her hands at her waist. She watched as the wounded were quickly loaded into trucks, while doctors and nurses returned from the trenches with more men.

Blood surrounded her, everywhere she looked. Christy's stomach began to heave, but she swallowed it down. She knew she had to be strong, especially at this moment. At any time she could walk into one of these tents and find her husband. She needed to be prepared for anything.

"Hey!" A familiar voice called to her.

Christy turned and saw the blonde nurse who had scolded her earlier.

"Are you all right?" she asked, approaching her.

"Yes, I'm fine." Christy wiped the tears from her eyes.

"Is this your first time on the field?" the woman asked, tilting her head.

"It's the first time I've seen a wounded man," Christy whispered. "I'm a reporter."

"You're here for the story." The nurse nodded, understanding dawning in her eyes. "It's not so easy to write about when you're faced with them, is it? Now all you want to do is help."

"Yes, exactly." Christy turned to her eagerly. "All I want to do now is learn. Learn everything I can to help them before we send them home."

"That's a good thing." The nurse touched her hand lightly. "Thank you for talking to Michael. I think you helped him. It was a good start, and I will help you from now on."

"Really?" Christy bit her lip. "You'll teach me?"

"Everyone needs someone to follow. If you want me to, I'll teach you." The nurse smiled gently. "Just remember, it won't be easy. This is a different world, a harsh world."

"I'm ready." Christy lifted her chin.

"Good."

"Nurse!" a doctor beckoned.

"I have to make one last sweep. Be sure to get yourself into the same truck as Michael. I'll be close behind." She turned before Christy could reply, hurrying back toward the trenches.

Relief rushed through Christy and tears sprung to her eyes. Her hand automatically slipped into the bag over her shoulder, gripping Lucy's Bible. The train they'd taken to cross the French countryside had been hit, and Lucy had given it to her right before she died. Christy escaped with some others in her unit, but the result had been her here, alone, with no one to give her orders and no one who'd seemed to care who she was or where she went.

Until now.

"Nurse!" Christy called. "What's your name? I'm Christy Garvin!"

The woman turned and smiled.

"Emma," she replied. "Emma Cote."

Chapter Twenty-Eight

France
The Trenches

Emma kept her head down as she moved along the trench. The field was quiet, unusually so, but this wasn't the first time she'd stepped into one of the trenches. It was almost a silent agreement on both sides of the field that there would be a time for each side to gather their wounded without additional bloodshed. Emma couldn't make sense of it, but this was war, and she wasn't going to question the invisible rules.

Keeping close behind the doctor and soldier covering them, Emma turned her gaze away from the bloodstained mud. The trenches overwhelmed her with the stench of filth and death, though she was slowly becoming accustomed to it. Deciding to leave home had been easy. Knowing Jared was out here somewhere, needing her, pushed her forward and kept her going. Her nursing experience gave her an in; her talent and strength were priceless to the other nurses.

But Emma wasn't as fearless as everyone thought. At the end of every day, all she wanted was to run away. Now that she was here, she couldn't leave, especially not without the one she had come to find. But seeing so many men suffer was wearing her down. The number of wounded soldiers here tripled the numbers in her small hospital back home, a hundred times worse than she could have possibly imagined. Emma took a moment to remind herself this was what she'd asked for. She requested orders to the front because it was the only place she could truly feel close to Jared. It was difficult, going where they wanted her to and not questioning their orders. Emma took every opportunity she could to inquire after her husband, but the inquiries were becoming fewer the more she surrounded herself with the suffering soldiers that came into her care. It was time to focus on her work and hope, *pray*, she'd stumble upon Jared along the way.

"I don't think we're going to find more." The doctor, puffing for air, swiped his sleeve along his forehead. Looking up at the darkening sky, she could feel the fear radiating off of him. "We should head back before it's too late."

He was starting back when Emma stopped, holding up her hand.

"Wait … do you hear that?" She looked over her shoulder, listening for the source of the shouts.

Someone was crying, calling for help. She couldn't understand the words, but someone was in pain. She could sense it. Emma pressed her hands to the side of the trench, going up on tiptoe to look over.

"Be careful!" the doctor hissed.

"Do you hear it?" Her heart raced, the thought that it could be Jared filling her mind. "We have to find them!"

"It's too dangerous," the doctor said, shaking his head. "We need to go back. The trucks will be leaving soon."

"It could be a trap," the soldier added. "They may be trying to lure the doctors out into the open. The hospitals and Red Cross are some of their main targets."

"I'm aware of that, but what if it's one of our own?" Emma frowned. "What if it's someone who was separated and needs our help?"

"We can't take that chance," The soldier insisted, shaking his head.

"But we should. It's not right to walk away, no matter who it is."

"This isn't a game, nurse." The soldier grabbed her arm when she started to lift herself out of the trench, yanking her back away from the wall. "This is war, and we make sacrifices."

"Maybe you do," Emma said, pulling her arm from his grasp. "But I came here to heal people. If someone is hurt, no matter what uniform he wears, I'm going to find him."

"You're a fool."

"We all are." Emma lifted herself out of the trench.

The doctor said something indiscernible, but she kept going. She heard them shuffling after her as she followed the sounds toward the tree line, moving in the opposite direction of enemy lines. Whoever it was—even if it wasn't the enemy—they had wandered far from their division.

The screaming was closer now. Emma started running, not even sure if the doctor and the soldier were following her. She knew exactly what she was risking, but ignoring the suffering of any human being was something she could not do. She approached the tree line, stepping into the woods. As soon as she did, she saw them. Her heart nearly stopped at the sight of the rifle in the German soldier's hand, pointed right at her. The other soldier was lying across his lap, his middle ripped open and bleeding out.

Emma held up her hands and carefully stepped closer, her eyes fixed on the horrible wound.

"Can you understand me?" she asked quietly.

The soldier didn't answer, but the rifle lowered an inch. Emma stepped around the German helmet that had been tossed aside and crouched slowly beside the wounded man. Breathing deeply, she reached into her bag for bandages. The rifle clicked as he raised it again. Emma's heart raced as she ever so slowly pulled the bandage loose, pressing it into the man's torn side.

The soldier moaned again but didn't open his eyes. Emma slowly wrapped his side, slipping some morphine beneath his tongue. She knew it was too late, but she could ease his suffering. Looking over her shoulder, she found the doctor watching her cautiously, unwilling to get too close.

"He's going to die," he stated factually.

"I know. It doesn't mean we can't help." Emma turned back, pressing a vial of morphine into the other soldier's hand.

"We have to go," the British soldier said, stepping from the cover of the trees. The German jerked away, bringing his rifle up again.

"They're alone. We can't leave them," Emma said with a frown.

"We don't have a choice." The doctor grabbed her arm roughly, dragging her to her feet. "They're the enemy, and we don't have room in our trucks for prisoners."

The German said something sharply, his thick brow curving in a hideous scowl. Emma choked back her tears, turning her face away.

"Come on, let's go." The doctor pulled her out of the woods until the trees blocked her view of the two men.

Emma let go of the breath she'd been holding, allowing the doctor to guide her back to the departing trucks. They were almost halfway across the field when she realized they were alone.

"Wait!" Emma turned back. "Where's ...?"

Two gunshots echoed in her ears. Emma gasped, covering her mouth with her hands. One shot, then another. Then silence. Her chest swelled painfully; the doctor bowed his head as they both realized what happened.

The British soldier came out of the tree line, his rifle limp in one hand and his other fisted around something. He marched up to Emma, slinging the strap of his rifle over his shoulder before grabbing her wrist and slamming the vial of morphine in her palm.

"Don't ever waste my comrades' morphine on the enemy." He practically spit in her face; they were so close their noses touched.

"How could you do that?" Emma cried, rearing back from him. "That was ... that was murder!"

"We're all murderers." His face turned red with rage. "Murder is the only way here. The sooner you understand that, the better the chance you'll survive out here."

"They were only two men. You could have let them go."

He grabbed her wrist, clutching it so hard she thought the bone would split. She bit her tongue to keep from moaning in pain as she tried to step back to put space between them. But he leaned in closer, putting his mouth against her ear. "If you ever do something like that again, I will shoot you for a traitor."

He pushed her, marching past. Emma rubbed her wrist, glancing at the doctor before turning away. The trucks rumbled as the tents came down; the moans and cries of the wounded got louder as she approached the first truck. Without a word she climbed up into the seat next to the driver, holding her wrist close against her ribs. The truck roared to life as they followed the line back toward Paris, toward freedom for their soldiers, away from the danger.

Closing her eyes, Emma saw those men. Two more this war didn't allow her to save. She didn't see the uniform. She didn't hear the strange language. She saw only two souls, cruelly taken from the world. And her own hadn't let her save them, her own hadn't found the compassion to let two helpless men try to find their way home.

If our own won't let two soldiers like them go, then what will the enemy do to Jared if they have him? Emma shuddered and prayed for a miracle.

THE LOST GENERATION

Chapter Twenty-Nine

France
The Woods

"Jared, wake up." John shoved Jared's shoulder, tossing away the branches as his friend rose up on his haunches. John's shoulders arched forward as he scanned the woods.

Jared shook his head, blinking rapidly to rouse himself. From his sharpened gaze and tensed shoulders, John knew the moment Jared heard what had awakened him. They looked to each other, a flicker of hope shining in Jared's eyes as he shook Will.

"Get up, kid." Snatching his rifle from the ground, Jared climbed out of the foxhole.

"What is it?" Will pinched the bridge of his nose and rolled over onto all fours.

"Gunfire," John whispered, looking back and forth.

"Ours?" Will perked up, slinging the strap of his rifle across his chest.

"We don't know yet." Jared reached out a hand, and Will took it, letting him pull him carefully out of the hole.

"Which way?"

"West." John turned, grabbing hold of a tree for support as he rose.

"Stay close." Jared ruffled Will's hair. The boy pulled away, glaring at him.

They followed the sounds of the battle, John taking long strides, clenching his hands around his rifle. Jared and Will flanked him. Jared's strides were silent as if he knew the location of every twig, every leaf. Will wasn't so talented, cracking sticks and crumbling leaves beneath his boots.

John glanced over his shoulder at him, rolling his eyes before he turned back. The boy thought he was experienced, he thought he had learned so much, but he was wrong. John had listened to their conversation two nights earlier. Listening to Will say he'd seen things too and knew what they were going through angered him. But he also found pity in his heart for the boy. He hadn't seen anything. Who knew what this war had in store for them now?

Machine gunfire erupted ahead. John fell to his belly suddenly, crawling forward. Jared and Will mimicked him, following close on his heels. John's heart nearly stopped at the sight before him. He looked over his shoulder at Jared whose face had gone snow white, his knuckles clenching his weapon so tightly the blood left them completely.

A line of German soldiers bordered the woods, firing into the lines of what John recognized to be the Third Battalion, Fifth Marines. The Americans moved forward in straight lines, but none of them made any progress as the machine guns took them down one by one. The front lines were slaughtered like nothing he'd ever seen before.

"Those are my guys," Will gasped as he came alongside John. "We have to do something."

"We can't," John said, shaking his head. "We're behind the enemy. If they see us …"

"We can't just stay here!" Will shouted, his face reddening.

"Shut up!" John growled, sweat beading on his forehead. "Let me think!"

"If we move in, two things could happen," Jared murmured in John's ear. "The enemy will overpower us most certainly and kill us. Or we'll become victims of friendly fire. They won't see the different uniforms over enemy lines, Sergeant. You know that as well as I do."

"They're dying!" Will dug his hands into the dirt. "How can we just sit here?"

"We're three men." Jared didn't take his eyes off John. "Our dying now will serve no purpose. We should try to move around enemy lines and join up with them when the battle is over."

"That would make us cowards!" Will insisted. "We should move in now."

"Don't be so eager to die!" Jared snapped.

John felt like covering his ears, the way Melody used to do when she was being rebellious. When she didn't want to listen to her mother, she would curl up on the floor as though she were in the womb and press her palms against her ears. She would kick her legs and cry until Beth lost patience and sent her to sit in the corner. That was how John felt now as Will and Jared's arguments drowned out in the buzz of confusion.

"Sarge." Jared shook his shoulder.

John blinked, turning to him.

"It's your call, Sergeant," he said quietly.

John stared at his friend for a moment more before slowly drawing back and loading up.

"Let's go."

THE LOST GENERATION

Chapter Thirty

France
Field Hospital
Late-June, 1918

"Lift him up." Emma groaned, gripping the man's shoulder to pull him up into a sitting position. She searched for the exit wound, her hands slippery with blood.

"No exit?" Margie O'Brian, a fellow nurse, met her gaze.

"No." Emma shook her head, slowly lowering the unconscious man back to the cot.

"Can we take the bullet out ourselves?"

Emma looked over her shoulder at Christy. Her eyes were wide as she soaked in every move Emma and Margie made. The eagerness to learn spread across her face. Emma remembered when she used to have that same feeling, when learning and helping was all that mattered. Now, after all she'd seen, Emma yearned for those years of ignorance once again. Sometimes not understanding, not knowing, was easier.

"We could if we were desperate." Emma pressed thick bandages over the wound. "It's a shoulder wound and not too serious."

"There's a lot of blood," Christy said, frowning.

"There's always going to be a lot of blood. But it's not as bad as you think." Margie stood, slapping at her apron. "If the bullet was in his gut, we'd pull one of the doctors. But there are many men with more serious wounds. We'll clean it and wait."

When Margie walked away, Emma beckoned her, "Come here, Christy." The girl took Margie's place, kneeling beside the cot to place her palm against the soldier's forehead. "Help me raise him up. I'll wrap the wound tight."

"When will a doctor see him?" Christy asked as she braced her hands beneath the marine's shoulder, lifting him up and supporting him against her chest.

"They'll make their way through the tent and assess," Emma explained, rolling the bandages across the soldier's shoulder blades. "The ones who have a chance they'll tend first. The ones we got to first and are able to be moved out on the trucks, will receive attention first."

"You mean if the wounds are too serious …" Christy paled.

"We can only do so much. The doctors can't afford to spend hours on a man who they know won't make it no matter what they do." Emma tied off the bandage. "All right, slowly now."

Together they lowered the marine back to the cot. He moaned, his head lolling to the side as Emma strapped his arm up across his chest and haltered the bandage around his neck as a sling. She pulled a vial of morphine out of her pocket and handed it to Christy.

"Make the rounds, dear," she said.

Christy turned the vial over between her fingers. When she rubbed her sleeve along her forehead, a streak of blood was left behind. She searched the tent. Emma knew she was looking for the men she should give it to, the ones who wouldn't last much longer, the ones who wouldn't be going home.

Emma stood, moving away from the cot to approach a soldier who had just been dragged inside. She shuddered at the sound of gunfire in the distance. Explosions wracked the earth, sending waves of icy fear slicing through her. She rubbed her arms to warm herself before moving between the cots toward the tent flap.

The gunfire was louder when Emma stepped out in the open. Watching the doctors and nurses moving around, she slipped her hand into her apron pocket and pulled out a pack of cigarettes. Lighting one, she took a couple of puffs before removing it from her lips. Until she came here, she'd never smoked a cigarette in her life. Margie offered her one on that first day as she stood in front of a man who'd literally been torn apart. She had taken it without hesitation.

One of the nurses bumped into her, not bothering to even whisper an apology as she hurried to one of the trucks preparing to leave. They would have to move out quickly before the enemy confirmed their location and started bombing the area.

"Emma?"

She turned, tossing the cigarette on the ground and grinding it beneath her shoe.

"Yes?" She forced a smile when Christy approached.

"They're packing everything." The girl announced.

"Find Margie and see what you can do. I'll follow soon." Emma squeezed Christy's arm gently before turning her back once again.

She looked toward the forest, the source of this suffering. For just a moment, she wished she could see what was happening and know exactly what to expect next. Then she could know what she was leaving behind when she helped pack the supplies that could save the life of some of those American marines.

Tilting her head, she looked to the sky. "Where are You? My husband believed in You, I believed in You. He said You were always with us! So where are You now?"

Silence answered her. A breeze filled her nose with smoke and gunpowder. Emma shuddered, pulling in a deep breath before she turned her back on the forest and ducked back into the tent.

Christy lowered herself slowly to the ground next to one of the trucks. Her eyes flashed back and forth as she watched the soldiers carry the wounded on stretchers. Her gaze lingered on one man, his arms draped across the shoulders of two other soldiers. Blood-soaked bandages covered the stubs where his legs had been. Shuddering, she curled her knees up against her chest and leaned back against the truck tire. Even now she was sure she could hear explosions in the distance, the sounds of war echoing in her head.

She closed her eyes and reached for the pack of cigarettes Margie had passed to her as they left the field hospital. She turned the pack over in her hands, contemplating whether she truthfully wanted one. Emma always smoked one right before they left every hospital. She was calming herself as she prepared to leave behind the ones they couldn't save, the ones for whom they had no choice.

Christy shook her head and let her hand fall limp against her knees. Hugging her shins with her other arm, she pressed her chin into her knee. When she opened her eyes, she saw the hem of a nurse's dress, ankles covered in white stockings and stark black shoes.

Emma sat down next to her. For a moment, they just looked at each other. Christy's eyes flooded with cold tears, falling like ice crystals down her cheeks. Emma reached out to her; Christy grabbed her hand and held on for dear life.

"I knew what I was doing when I came here," Christy said softly. "The day I received that telegram telling me the world as I knew it might be over … it almost killed me."

"I know," Emma whispered.

"I couldn't imagine life without Will. I came here under false pretenses."

"I know." Emma dipped her head again.

A stretcher thumped as another soldier was loaded into the truck. Christy jumped. Her hands shook as she tugged one of the cigarettes loose. Emma lit it for her, shaking the match until the flame went out. Christy coughed as puffs of smoke slipped from her lips.

"I told them I had nursing experience. That was a lie. I came here to find my husband. That's the only reason. I didn't come for the story, or to help. I came only for him."

"I know." Emma's grip tightened.

"But now everything's changed." Christy wiped the tears from her cheeks. "I want to tell the story now. I want to help these men, to get them home the way I would want someone else to get Will home to me."

"Seeing their faces changes everything. Suddenly your man isn't the only one you see when you look at one of these uniforms anymore." Emma's forehead touched hers.

"I can't just walk away when this is over now." Christy gasped back a sob.

"None of us can."

"Everyone leaves. I can't be one of them." Christy crushed the cigarette between her fingers. "But it just feels like everyone leaves me."

"It will feel that way for a while," Emma said, stroking her hair. "It will go away."

"When did you come here, Emma?" Christy asked.

"In April." Emma's voice lowered.

"How long did it take for that feeling to go away?"

Emma hesitated, tracing Christy's cheek with the back of her finger.

"I don't know. Eventually, it just ... stopped. Everything just stopped."

Christy nodded, releasing another stream of tears when she closed her eyes.

"You won't leave me, will you, Em? When this is over ..." Christy choked.

"No." Emma pulled her close pressing her chin to the top of Christy's head. "I will never leave you. I promise."

Christy wrapped her arms around Emma, relaxing in the safety of her friend's embrace as she rocked her back and forth. Christy hadn't felt so safe since the last time she'd seen Will. Even as the trucks moved out, even as they were surrounded by the dying, Christy felt safe with Emma.

"Sometimes it's hard to walk," Christy said, hugging Emma's arm with both of hers. "I can't seem to move my legs. My feet feel heavy. Putting one foot in front of the other is a chore. I'm frozen."

"But you always find a way," Emma answered. "We always find a way, each of us in our own time. You have a good heart, Christy. And we will find our husbands."

"They're alive," Christy said, looking up at her. "They're both alive, Emma. I can feel it."

"Me too." Emma smiled though her eyes were murky with doubt.

"God will give us the strength we need," Christy said with a smile, assurance washing through her. "He is always here for us, isn't He?"

Emma didn't answer. She just smiled, tucking a loose strand of Christy's hair behind her ear.

"Ladies." Margie's voice drew their gaze. "It's time to go. We have twenty-four hours and then we head out again."

Emma rose up, taking Christy's hands to pull her to her feet. Margie was heading for the truck, beckoning them to follow.

"Come on." Emma interlocked their fingers, tucking her close. "Let's go get some sleep."

"Right," Christy whispered.

She looked down and smiled, finding her courage once again as she put one foot in front of the other. Christy didn't know what tomorrow was going to bring, but God had sent her another angel when she found Emma. Together they could do amazing things. Christy just knew it.

I know You're watching out for us. Thank You. Christy looked to the heavens and saw a stream of sunshine peeking through the thick clouds.

That one ray was a beacon of hope, all the answer she needed from above. She climbed into the truck.

Chapter Thirty-One

London, England

Beth turned her head toward the window as rays of sunshine showered her. She could feel Melody's heartbeat against her arm where her child nestled by her side. Little George was probably downstairs now, with Ruth feeding him his breakfast. Beth used to get out of bed at the crack of dawn. For the past four years, she'd awakened with the chickens. But ever since that telegram came, Beth couldn't find the energy to rise before the sun had reached the clouds.

Gently slipping her arm out of Melody's grasp, she slid off the side of the bed onto her feet. It had been her mother's idea for her to move into the city with the children, so she could be closer to the Red Cross without sacrificing time with her little ones. Susan would take care of the farm, and Beth would have the support of her sister during this difficult time.

Her sister. The one person Beth was close to who could relate to what she was going through. After Ruth's telegram had come, there had been no more word. They still didn't know if her fiancé was alive out there somewhere. But they had learned quickly that telegrams bearing the news of missing in action usually meant they would never see their loved ones again.

Beth froze at the window. Her fingers curled into her palm until she thought her hand would bleed. Turning, she snatched her robe from the end of the bed, tied it tight at her waist, and tiptoed out of the room. Melody would come down for breakfast when she was ready. She sensed her mother's fear; it kept her up at night.

Beth wished she could be stronger for her children, that she could hide the fear from them, but it was impossible to do so. Learning Christy had left London to search for her own husband hadn't helped. Beth had so longed to see her young friend, to share the support of another woman who was going through the same thing.

But Christy had done what Beth could only wish to do. Christy had been free to leave, to go in search of the man she loved, and help others along the way. More than anything, Beth wanted to do the same, but she could never leave her children.

She gripped the railing as she hurried down the stairs to the dining room. She could hear Ruth scolding George for sticking his hand in the honey. Beth smiled and stopped in the doorway. She leaned her head against the wall as she watched her sister care for her son.

Closing her eyes, she could picture John sitting with their son, feeding him. She longed for those days, knowing that it would come soon. A telegram was not going to determine their future. She wouldn't let it; she couldn't let it.

Ruth looked up, her face brightening with a smile. "Good morning, Beth."

"Good morning." Beth stepped into the room, leaning over to kiss the top of her son's head. "Thank you for getting his breakfast."

"Of course." Ruth grinned. "I only get my nephew for a little while. I'm going to spend as much time with him as possible."

"Still, it's kind of you to take charge for me during this time. I know you went through this too." Beth sat down and reached for a piece of toast.

"This feeling will pass, Beth." Ruth bowed her head. "You just need to give it time."

"I know," Beth said as she wiped George's mouth with her napkin.

A knock at the door brought Ruth around.

"That's Matthew," Ruth said, pulling off her apron. "He's my friend from the Red Cross. He said he was going to stop by this morning."

"Does he have news from my inquiry?" Beth asked, perking up.

"I don't know. He wouldn't tell me." Ruth frowned, then added, "But he did sound worried."

Ruth hurried away, rubbing her hands up and down along her skirt. Sighing, Beth pushed her plate away, suddenly not hungry. She folded her hands as if in prayer and leaned her elbows against the table. Deep down she wanted to pray, but praying had seemed to do so little these past few weeks. As wrong as that sounded in her head, she couldn't help feeling it.

"What did Matthew say?" Beth didn't look up when she heard her sister return to the dining room.

Silence answered her. Beth looked up, her brow creasing. Ruth stood in the doorway, her hands trembling as she stared down at the telegram. Her face was as white as the sheets on Beth's bed, her legs shook beneath her skirt. Beth pushed to her feet and hurried around the table.

"Ruth? What's wrong?" Beth braced her hands on her sister's shoulders.

"They ... they found Damian," Ruth rasped.

"What?" Beth gasped, her hand fluttering to her heart at the name of her sister's fiancé as she took a step back. "What does it say?"

"He's ... he's ..." Ruth shook her head, tears falling onto the telegram.

"Ruthie?" Beth's voice cracked. "What does it say, darling?"

"It says ..." Ruth shook her head. "We ... we regret ... to inform you that Private Damian Walters ... was k-killed—"

An animal-like sound erupted from Ruth's throat. Beth rushed forward, her knees slamming into the floor as they both fell to the ground. Beth braced her sister in her arms, her heart thundering out of control. She rocked her back and forth, her own tears falling into her sister's hair.

Beth never felt so helpless. She had always been able to fix things for her little sister, to give her hope again. But there was nothing she could do or say to make this better.

Beth tightened her arms around her sister. Ruth's cries filled the house.

Chapter Thirty-Two

France
The Woods
July 1918

Dear Beth,

After we saw the marines falling along the line on the border of the woods, we moved back. You know I'm not much of a writer, darling, but what I saw can't be described even in simple words. I would not burden you with such a memory, nor would I trouble you with the fear of knowing that I was afraid. How I long for the wonderful feel of your warm hands and the softness of your beautiful hair.

When we moved back, we tried to follow the line, but we were pushed back. We couldn't risk the enemy seeing us and shooting us down. Risking Jared and Will's lives is not an option, and I will not take any risks, even if Will hates me for it. I know what it's like to see your own dropping one after another and not being able to do anything about it. Will does not speak to me, and I cannot blame him.

Words cannot express what I feel for these young men, Beth. They are like my sons. How I long to hold ours. How I long to see your father's namesake, my firstborn son. I pray every night that God would give me this blessing, that He will get me through this so I may come home to you and hold our son.

The tip of his pencil broke where he pressed it into the paper. John looked up and saw Will lying on his belly, looking over the curve of the foxhole. All day he'd been watching a line that didn't exist, waiting for some sort of activity. Whether he was waiting for the enemy or their own men to show their faces, John wasn't sure.

"How are you doing, Sergeant?" Jared hunkered down beside him, rubbing his hands together.

"Fine." John closed the journal, tucking it away out of sight. "What do you think, Jared? What's our next move?"

"You're the officer," Jared answered, shrugging his shoulders. "You lead, and I'll follow."

"Is that how you run your home?" John asked with a grin.

"No. That's how Emma runs our home." Jared winked. "She makes me think I lead, but truthfully, I follow."

"Smart girl."

"She had the upper hand from the start," Jared continued, propping himself up on his elbows. "But in all honesty, Sarge, we're partners. A team. Neither one of us tries to rule over the other. It's just ..."

Jared stopped, his shoulders stiffening. He turned away suddenly and moved to crouch at Will's side. John hadn't heard much about Emma Cote in the time he knew Jared, but he understood the young man's reluctance to talk about the woman he loved when he might never get home to her.

John pressed his palm to the journal over his heart, and he closed his eyes. The longer he was lost, the more he felt he might never get back to Beth and his children. It had never been a question before. His love for them would drive him on, keeping him alive, and making him fight harder.

But here, he had found a new family. He had found something else, someone else, to fight for. John's eyes fell on the two young men who were now speaking softly, out of his hearing. He leaned forward, gripping his rifle.

They were his family here. They were what mattered, and he would take any means necessary to make sure they made it home.

Will turned to watch John, that sinking feeling returning to his stomach. They started running again after the sergeant had tried to move behind the line to regroup with the marines. But the German line had been too strong, and they had pushed deeper into the woods instead searching for cover.

Leaving behind those marines had been like leaving Tommy's body to rot behind enemy lines. He was almost sick at the thought. The marines' line had broken, and one after another, they'd fallen. Still, they kept coming. How many losses? How many of them fell never to rise again? Will wanted to believe he could have done something to help them. He had to believe it.

It hadn't been his choice. He knew John had done the only thing he could. If they wanted to live, they couldn't make foolish moves. But Will didn't have to like it.

When Will looked again, he saw John holding that little black journal. He'd been writing in it ever since they'd been lost together. Will didn't think the man had ever written anything in it until then. The journal was just where he kept the picture of his family, a safe place to shelter the faces of the ones he loved.

Being behind enemy lines had inspired him to use his last stub of a pencil to record what was happening to them. Will supposed it was something to tell his family when they got home, a story about how he went missing but survived with the memory of his family pushing him forward.

Will turned over onto his back, tired of watching the line. The forest was silent, and if they waited until nightfall, they could move out without being seen. Following shadows was a talent all three of them had learned well. He stared up, past the tall tree branches, toward the blue sky. How long had they been out here now? Time had no meaning out here; hours seemed like days, and days seemed like months.

"What are you thinking about, private?" John's voice broke the silence.

Will's head swung lazily in his direction, but he didn't answer. His lips tightened, eyes narrowing in anger. John frowned.

"What?" The sergeant bent his head, scribbling something else in the journal

"You sat there," Will whispered.

John looked up again, brow arched.

"You just sat there while those marines fell one after the other."

"What was I supposed to do, private?" John asked. "Run out there and get myself killed?"

"We should've done *something*. That's not ... it shouldn't—"

"Shouldn't have happened? No. It shouldn't." John leaned forward. "But you'll survive the pain, son."

"How do you know?"

"Because God never gives us more than we can bear."

Will rolled his eyes. "Yeah. Sure."

"Don't you believe in God, private?"

"After what we just saw? How can I? How can *you*?"

John's smile was sad as he sat back, tucking away his journal. "It's because of what I saw that I believe in Him with more ferocity than I ever have before. Because I have to believe those boys are at peace now. I have to believe that the Lord has taken them to His bosom, to live a painless life for all of eternity."

Will's lips tightened, and he turned away, staring at the empty forest. Jared nudged him.

"You listening, soldier?"

Will glared at him. "You don't believe all that too, do you?"

"I believe what I once told my wife when we were going through a rough patch. Once God has you, He doesn't let you go. There's nothing you can do about it." Jared's eyes flooded, and he sniffled, wiping his sleeve across them as he turned away. "No matter how much I doubt that, I always come back to it. I can't forget my own words. Even if I try."

"What, are you two on a mission to save my soul now?" Will growled. "Maybe you should mind your own business. I'm done talking, and I'm definitely done praying."

He rolled away from them, crawling on his elbows to the tree trunk. He felt their stares, heard their soft murmurs, but he ignored them.

He heard a heavy sigh slip from Jared and then John appeared at his side again. He was all soldier again, not the soft-hearted, God-preaching man of moments before.

"We have to keep moving." Sweat poured down John's face.

"Do you think we should move out into the open while the sun is still up?" Jared asked, rubbing the back of his neck.

Jared always rubbed the back of his neck when he wasn't sure about their next move. John would sweat until they could see the stains on his back. Will wondered if he could know the two men on either side of him any better than he knew them now. Tommy had been his best friend, but the closeness he felt to these two men was so different in comparison.

"I'm not sure we have a choice. I don't like this," John grumbled.

"Don't like what?" Will frowned. "Nothing's happening."

"Exactly." John's Adam's apple bobbed. "No distant gunfire. No shouting. Nothing. It's too quiet."

Will rolled back onto his belly, watching the woods.

"I think we're being watched." Jared scratched at the stubble on his face.

"But shouldn't we stay put then? Wait for them to make the first move?" Will asked.

"Maybe, maybe not," John answered, pulling off his helmet. "I don't know."

He ruffled his hair, brushing to the side the damp strands sticking to his forehead.

"We're all tired." Jared hunkered down. "Maybe we should give it another hour and see what happens."

"No." John shook his head, strapping his helmet back on. "We keep putting it off. We keep holding back. The only way we're going to find our men again is if we push through. It's time to start running toward the enemy, not away."

"All right then." Jared nodded.

"Ready?" John nudged Will's arm.

"Yes," Will said. He raised his rifle.

Together the three men rose up, their weapons raised as they strode between the trees, always keeping each other in sight. Will stayed close to Jared's side. Until their little exchange, he hadn't spoken to John since the decision had been made to turn their backs on the marines.

Deep down he knew there hadn't been any other choice. Jumping out at the enemy would have been a foolish move ending with the three of them dead. That would have served no purpose, but it hadn't made it any easier for him to walk away from his own.

Jared said there was a difference between self-preservation and being a coward. Will was still trying to understand exactly what the difference was. He was sure he would understand someday. Maybe the day he saw Christy again and was happy to be alive once more, maybe then he'd understand the difference.

They stopped in unison. Each fell to one knee, aiming at possible hiding places.

"Anything?" Jared broke the silence.

"Nothing." John shook his head.

"Clear." Will lowered his rifle an inch.

"Follow me."

John stood again, sidestepping ahead of them. They jogged forward. Will leaned slightly to the side to see around John's tall form. Was that the border of the woods he saw? Had they been this close the whole time without knowing it?

Excited, Will surged forward, not watching where he was going. He took another step and suddenly the ground dipped. With a shout, Will went down as the ground sank beneath his boots. Something below his feet growled as Will fell hard onto his side.

He spun onto his back, propped on his elbows and came face to face with a German rifle.

Chapter Thirty-Three

France
Field Hospital

Explosions rocked the ground as Christy pressed her hands onto the shoulders of a wounded soldier. He struggled against her hold, clawing for his leg. Reaching behind her, she snatched some more bandages to press into his mangled knee. Leaning far to the right she looked around Margie's shoulder where Emma was making her way down the line. One soldier at a time she assessed and did what she could before moving on.

"Don't we have more morphine?" Christy asked, smoothing her hair out of her eyes.

"We can't spare it right now," Margie said, shaking her head as she braced her arm across the soldier's chest, pressing him down on the table. "Until the doctor gets to him and says he can have more, he's had his share."

"That sounds so harsh."

"I thought by now you'd realize that everything about this place is harsh." Margie rolled her eyes.

"Emma told me the ones with more serious wounds can have a larger dose," Christy argued.

"Well, Emma has her own way of doing things. It's not my way." Margie turned to look over her shoulder.

"She is in charge, Margie."

"That's what the doctor said." Margie's jaw stiffened.

"It's not a competition. You said yourself this place is harsh. It's war. You shouldn't be competing for a position, and you shouldn't be jealous just because Emma has been doing this longer than you have."

The soldier moaned and tried to turn away from them. Christy clamped her hand on his thigh, wishing she could soothe him.

"You have to keep still." Margie lowered her voice, turning her attention to their patient. "You'll only make the wound worse."

"How are we doing?" Emma finally reached their table.

"I think it needs to come off," Margie answered.

Christy turned away as Emma peeled back the bandages. Her finger brushed against the bone sticking out of his skin. The flesh around his knee was torn like paper, shredded pieces of skin folding over to reveal raw flesh beneath.

Emma didn't even flinch as she used her fingers to push aside bits of skin to find the cause of the wound. With a wet hiss, she yanked a piece of shrapnel from inside his knee. The soldier screamed, causing Margie to nearly lose her hold on him. Suddenly he sat up, his arms flailing to push Emma away.

Christy's stomach swirled, but she swallowed it back. She regained her composure as she turned back to thrust her hand inside the wound, halting the stream of blood.

"I can't repair this," Emma said, shaking her head. "You're right, it has to come off."

Another explosion shook the hospital, nearly deafening them with its proximity.

"But not here," Emma announced. "We need to pack the wound and strap him tight so he doesn't move it too much. He needs to be moved on the first truck out."

Emma began to do just that when a sergeant entered the tent. She turned, whispered something to Margie, and then hurried away. Margie took over, packing the wound tight and strapping the leg before she beckoned two soldiers to carry him out.

Christy wiped her bloodstained hands on her apron and moved slowly toward the front, keeping one eye on Emma as she pretended to work. When she got close enough to hear them, she knelt beside one of the unconscious privates, taking his hand gently in hers.

"We need to move out," the sergeant was saying, his hand on Emma's shoulder. "The doctor was … wounded."

"Is he dead?" Emma clenched her hands on her hips.

"Close to it." The sergeant ran his hand down his face. "He had just left the tent when it went up. They've pinpointed our location. We need to move now."

"What are you saying?"

"I'm saying take the ones you can save."

Christy's heart stopped.

"You're asking me to make the choice to leave men behind?" Emma shook her head.

"You've done it before, nurse. Tell me which ones you can save, and I will load them in the trucks. But we need to go now." He marched out before she could say anything more.

Emma turned, and their eyes met. Christy rose slowly, her vision blurred by tears she wouldn't let fall. Lifting her chin, Emma resolutely strode the length of the tent to pull Margie aside. Christy shook her head.

I can't watch this.

She rushed from the tent, past the trucks being backed toward the flap. Suddenly, she stopped gasping for air. A breeze lifted the stray strands of her hair. She nearly choked on the smoke as she stared at the demolished tent and twisted, broken bodies strewn across the ground. A nurse bumped into her, nearly knocking her off her feet as she rushed away from the bomb site.

"Christy?" Emma's hand touched her shoulder. "It's time to go, dear."

"I couldn't … I couldn't bear to watch you suffer through that." Christy spun to hug her. "How could you make that decision and be so calm?"

"I'm anything but calm," Emma whispered. "I'm anything but at peace right now."

"You're the only friend I have out here and seeing you hurt so …"

"I know. But it's over now." Emma gripped Christy's shoulders, pushing her back to look in her eyes. "I'm not leaving anyone behind, and that sergeant can gripe all he wants. But we have to go now."

Just as Emma started to pull Christy toward the trucks, they heard it. Christy slowed, looking over her shoulder. It started as a whistle in the air, growing louder as it came closer. Frantically, Christy's eyes searched for the source.

The wind picked up, pulling the pins from her hair. Christy's eyes widened; she turned to Emma.

"Christy, get down!" Emma shouted, lunging at her.

Christy hit the ground just as flames erupted behind them. Metal debris flew into the air as the truck was torn to pieces; shouts echoed all around them. Christy's eyes rolled to the back of her head, red dots invading her vision. Her head throbbed where her skull hit the hard ground; scrapes stung her back and shoulders.

"Emma?" Christy whispered.

She took hold of her friend's shoulders, turning her over. Emma flopped to the side, and Christy jerked up, her trembling hands hovering over Emma's body.

"Em? Oh, God, no, no! Please don't take her!" Christy lifted her in her arms, holding her close. "Emma, please. You said you wouldn't leave, you promised!"

Tears cut off her air. Her chest tightened with panic as she looked around wildly, screaming for help. She couldn't bring herself to check, not yet, not alone. Christy closed her eyes.

What would Emma do if I were hurt? Christy calmed at the thought. Bowing her head, she forced herself to look.

Blood streamed from the gash along Emma's hairline, flowing down her cheek and along her neck. Christy pressed her fingers into the side of Emma's neck. Relief flooded her when she felt the faint pulse against the pads of her fingers.

"Sergeant!" Christy screamed when she saw the man rush from the tent, Margie close on his heels. "Help, please!"

"What happened?" Margie fell to her knees.

"We were right beside the bomb. She saved me."

"Get her on the truck!" Margie looked up at the sergeant. "We need to move now. Get your men moving faster; take the ones she labeled first!"

"Right." The sergeant pulled Emma out of Christy's arms and rushed her back to the trucks.

Christy rose to follow when Margie grabbed her arm, her grip so tight it would leave a bruise.

"Next time, don't wander like that," Margie hissed. "Don't ever put her in the position where she has to run after you because she feels obligated to look after you, to keep you safe. Emma looks at us all like her sisters, some of us she thinks of as her kids. She feels older than she is and that's this war's fault. Don't make her feel like she's responsible for you if you choose to run off and put yourself in harm's way." With that, Margie shoved her and walked away.

Christy watched her go, the gnawing in her stomach growing.

"Nurse!" The sergeant rolled the truck to a stop beside her. "I have Nurse Cote in the back."

Nodding, Christy circled the truck to climb in next to the sergeant.

"Are you all right?" he asked. The truck rumbled as they followed the line.

"No." Christy touched her fingers to her lips. "But I will be. We all will be."

"Hope you're right, nurse." He reached into his pocket, slipping a cigarette between his lips to light it.

He puffed and then held it out to her.

"I know I'm right." Christy took the cigarette, her hand trembling so hard the ashes tumbled from the end before she took a long draw. "It won't be long now. I have this feeling."

"You sound so sure." The sergeant took back the cigarette. "I wish I had your confidence."

Christy turned halfway to the side, hugging her arms against her ribs to warm the icy feeling in the pit of her stomach. It would all end soon. This war was coming to an end. It had to.

It will end, and I will find my husband. I know it. I believe it. Please God ... please make it so.

Knives were stabbing her temples. Emma moaned, turning over on the lumpy cot. She pressed the heels of her hands hard into the sides of her head. Feeling the thick bandage around the top of her head shift, she tugged on it until it fell to the ground beside the cot.

Without opening her eyes, she searched for her wound and found it. The stiff stitches along her hairline had been crudely sewn, but her hair would cover it nicely. It wasn't a large wound, but since it was a head wound, she knew there must've been a lot of blood.

Finally, she sat up, blinking rapidly to adjust her eyes to the dim lighting. She noticed she was surrounded by the wounded and realized they must've just put up the tent. Everything inside was still fresh; there were hardly any blood stains on the ground. Emma sighed, wondering how Margie had handled packing everyone up after she'd been hurt.

Pushing aside the thin blanket, Emma swung her legs over the side and stretched her neck from side to side before attempting to stand. The pain in her temples was nothing; she could ignore it just as she'd ignored every little ache and pain that meant nothing compared to the pain of the soldiers she treated.

"Emma." Christy's voice drew her, and she turned to look.

Christy sat up, her eyes glassy. She'd been sleeping in the cot next to hers, taking a moment to get some rest before the next wave came in. Emma sat back down on the edge of her cot, reaching out to her. Christy went right into her embrace, falling on her knees to wrap her arms around Emma's waist.

"Were you hurt?" Emma whispered.

"No," Christy assured her. "I was never so happy to feel someone's heartbeat than I was to feel yours. When I saw all that blood, I thought ..." She shuddered.

"I'm fine. That's the important part. We're both fine."

"Margie said you think of us as your children." Christy sat back to look up at her. "You love us all so much."

"I do." Emma smoothed her hand along Christy's hair.

"Promise me you won't put yourself in harm's way for me ever again. I couldn't live if something happened to you because of me. I don't want to be your child, Emma. I want to be your best friend. We need to protect each other. It can't be your responsibility to protect all of us."

Emma didn't answer. Instead, she stood, turning to look around. She was surrounded by soldiers, doctors, and nurses, yet she felt all alone. Christy was wrong. It was her responsibility to protect all of them. It was her responsibility to find her husband. It was her responsibility, more than anything else, to make sure she didn't lose one more person to this war.

If she never saw her husband again, then she wouldn't be able to bear knowing that one of these courageous people died on her watch. No, she would gladly do anything to protect these nurses.

Christy may never understand, and perhaps I don't understand it either. But it is my duty. It is the reason I found her. Emma closed her eyes.

"I have to believe …" She hesitated, licking her parched lips. "I have to believe that I'm here for a reason other than healing, because after spending over a month here, healing is something that comes only once a day. I can't heal all of them. So I have to believe I'm here to save the lives of the people fighting beside me."

Emma looked down at Christy where she still knelt, her big eyes innocent and frightened. Emma leaned over to kiss the top of her head.

"We're fighting a different war inside these tents, Christy." She pulled in a deep breath, turning to look at the line of cots, all of them full. "Look at them. They're not soldiers. They're bakers and bankers and farmers. It's not fair that they're here, but they came willingly, and I can't change it. All I can do is move forward. I don't know what's going to happen next, but the only way I can go on is if I protect you."

She turned and started to walk away.

"But who will protect you?" Christy's words stopped her.

Emma closed her eyes.

"Let's get back to work," she whispered.

Emma crossed the tent in search of one of the doctors. She needed to keep her hands busy. Her fingers searched for the stitches again, following the pattern. It was tender, the bruise creeping toward her eye. She never thought she would be grateful for pain, but she was. The pain would drive her forward.

May it remind me why I'm here. May it give me the strength to do whatever is necessary. Emma clasped her hand to her throat. *May I never fail these soldiers.*

Chapter Thirty-Four

France
Field Hospital

"How are you feeling?" the doctor asked, pressing back her hair with his thumb, examining the stitches.

"I'm fine, Dr. Evans." Emma rubbed her arms.

The doctor eyed her fondly. "I think after all this time you can call me Walter, Emma."

Emma smiled wanly. "No headaches or dizziness. It was just a concussion."

"It's been quiet out there," Walter commented as he probed the sensitive skin around her scar. "This is healing nicely, Emma. In a few weeks, you won't even notice the scar."

"Thank you." Emma's arms felt heavy as she placed her cap back on her head and pinned it in place before she stood again.

She forced a smile when Walter stepped in her way, blocking her from hurrying away. Emma clasped her hands together, the desire for a cigarette overwhelming. She'd been more anxious than usual since the explosion, and she knew she depended too much on the calming effects of those little white rollups.

"Are you sure you want to stay?" Walter braced his hands on her shoulders. "It's still not too late to take my offer. I could have you on a boat headed for home tomorrow."

"I can't go home." Emma shook her head. The letter she'd received from her sister was burning a hole in her apron pocket. "Ever since Paris ... well you know."

Walter nodded.

He'd been there when she'd received her sister's letter through the Red Cross, the letter that said her sister was a widow. Emma couldn't face her; she couldn't go home and look into her sister's eyes, knowing that Laura could never have done what Emma was able to do. Emma was able to help; Emma was able to seek out answers for herself instead of waiting helplessly at home.

Emma could handle many things, but not her sister's grief. She knew it was selfish, but she couldn't go home to face an entirely different kind of suffering than what she faced in these tents.

"I need help!" a soldier shouted suddenly, bursting into the tent.

Emma and Walter moved together to the soldier's side. The man lifted his friend onto one of the tables. Blood streamed steadily from the wounded man's mutilated arm.

"There was no warning ..." The young soldier stepped back.

Emma recognized the look. These men were brothers, perhaps not by blood, but they had fought together for a long time. They would risk anything for each other. The soldier who stood before her couldn't save his friend. The panic in his eyes even now told Emma that he knew.

"It's not your fault," Emma said. She reached back to squeeze his arm. "There never is any warning for this. Don't blame yourself."

"Emma." Walter's voice brought her back. "I can't save this arm. The flesh is practically torn away and the bone ..." Walter shook his head.

Emma bent over the wound, mopping the blood with her own apron to get a closer look. The flesh of his arm was torn in bits like paper with white bone sticking up from the foot-long gash, splintered in his shoulder. Emma reached her hand carefully into the wound, searching for any bits of shrapnel.

"I don't feel anything foreign." She turned her face away, using only her fingers to examine what remained of his arm. "Christy!" she called.

The girl's head came up where she knelt by one of the cots. Setting aside the cup of water she'd been serving to one of the wounded, she hurried to her side.

"I need you to hold down his legs."

"Please." The first word from the soldier passed his blood-crusted lips.

"What is it, soldier?" She leaned in, turning her ear to his mouth.

"Please don't take my arm," he rasped.

Emma's eyes fluttered. She had heard this plea so many times.

Please don't take my arm ... please don't take my leg ... please save me ... please ... please ...

Emma shook it off, knowing none of them had a choice.

"Bite down on this." Walter put the stick in the man's mouth. "Bite down hard. It'll be over soon."

"Nurse." The soldier who brought the wounded man in grabbed her arm, stopping her. "Please, he's my best friend."

"We'll do everything we can." Emma forced the words past her lips, patting his hand lightly before turning away. They were all best friends, all from the same place, all neighbors or family. Emma rubbed her swirling stomach.

She administered the morphine, humming softly to soothe the man. His chest swelled and his eyes closed as her song slowed his heart rate. Emma nodded to Walter, seeing that the morphine had already taken effect. She glanced Christy's way. The girl had never assisted in an amputation before. Emma had made sure of that. But there was no one else to help now.

"Hold his shoulders, Emma." Walter gently nudged her out of the way.

She did as she was told, averting her gaze when Walter lifted the saw. Emma licked her lips, squeezing her eyes tight. Assisting in over a hundred amputations didn't make them easier to handle, especially under these circumstances. Needing to take limbs under these conditions could make the wound worse. More than once after taking a limb, they had to cut even more because of infection. Too many of the men had to be operated on immediately and then moved, sometimes within minutes.

"Ready?" Walter asked, tightening the tourniquet an inch or two above the wound.

"Ready," Christy answered.

Emma's eyes found hers. Christy dipped her head, holding her gaze. Emma's body rippled with tremors as Walter lowered the saw. The grate of it against human bone echoed in her ears, the sound so familiar it sickened her.

The agonized cry broke through the soldier's clenched teeth, his shoulders shaking in the struggle against her hands.

"Hold him!" Walter shouted.

Emma flattened her palms against his chest, her elbows digging into his shoulders. Blood sprayed the side of her face as Walter proceeded, not even slowing at the sound of the man's screams. She lifted her eyes once more, her gaze colliding with Christy's.

They held there, each of them drawing strength from the other. Soon the cries faded away as the soldier's eyes grew heavy. He passed out from the pain, the stick in his mouth falling with a thump onto the table. The blood that sprinkled Emma's face slid down her cheek, creating lines all the way down her neck to stain the collar of her dress.

"Done." Walter wrapped the stub, all that remained of the man's arm. Blood immediately soaked the bandages as Walter doubled them, tying them off as tightly as he could. "You've done enough, Emma. Go find Margie to finish up."

Emma nodded, taking the escape he offered. The heaviness inside of her grew, forcing her to drag her feet out of the tent. Emma stumbled, nearly falling in the dirt when she stepped outside. A breeze tried to dislodge her cap, tugging on every loose strand of hair that had fallen from her bun.

Without much thought she reached into her pocket, flipping the package of cigarettes repeatedly in a nervous gesture. She wanted one more than anything, but at this moment, just fooling with them helped. Knowing she could calm herself without smoking made her feel better. It was becoming a talent, one she used to hope she would never have because it meant she was going numb. It meant that with each passing day, amputations and death were normal. An everyday occurrence that didn't bother her anymore.

"Emma? Are you—?" Margie appeared at her side.

"I'm fine. Walter needs you." Emma cut her off and gestured behind her.

"It's almost too quiet out here." Margie hugged her ribs and Emma sensed the avoidance. Margie didn't want to go into that tent any more than Emma did.

"I know what you mean," Emma answered. "It's like the quiet before the storm. Those few minutes when everything is still and quiet outside before the thunder fills the sky."

"Do you think this war will ever end?" Margie wondered. "It's become a way of life."

"Please don't say it." Emma massaged her temples. "Please don't ask me how we will ever go back to normal life. Everyone asks me the same thing. I can't take it anymore."

"I'm sorry." Margie's jaw creaked, her lips pursing. "I thought we were friends who encouraged each other."

"That's fine, Margie." Emma hissed, glaring at her. "But I'm not your mother. It's my turn to ask if we will be all right. It's my turn to seek comfort instead of giving it. I am exhausted, Margie, and I don't have the energy to hold and comfort another human being right now."

Emma stuffed the cigarettes back into her pocket.

"I need to take care of myself now."

"Whatever you say." Margie turned on her heels, her braid swinging against her back as she ducked into the tent.

Emma leaned her head back to look up at the sky. Her neck arched at an almost painful angle, she breathed in through her nostrils. Her nose burned with the smell of stale blood, the stink of infection and melting flesh from gas burns.

It was a scent she would never forget, one she smelled in her dreams. She would smell it for the rest of her life. In her first years as a nurse, she had learned that there were always some patients she would never forget, some hurts and deaths that would stay with her forever.

When she had chosen this career, she never imagined it would bring her here. She never thought it would bring her to a place where such horror would break her soul.

Emma started to turn when she caught sight of it. She blinked slowly, squinting as she looked closer at the uniform. He was wearing a pin on the front of his jacket, one she recognized. She had seen it before. Her heart thundered in her ears as she hurried across the field, passing by the other tents, moving nurses and doctors gently out of her way.

"Excuse me!" She reached out, grabbing the soldier's arm.

He turned, dirt smudged all over his face and oily red hair sticking to his forehead.

"What?" he snapped.

"I'm sorry. I just ..." She shook her head. "You don't remember me, but I think we're neighbors. I recognized your family's pin. Your father said it was a good luck charm."

The soldier covered the small, unnoticeable pin with his palm. He nodded, asking, "You're Canadian?"

"Yes." Emma smiled.

"I remember. You're Jared's wife."

The sound of her husband's name stabbed her chest. She pressed a hand to her heart, swallowing the lump at the base of her throat.

"Have you seen him?" Emma grabbed his arms. "He went missing. I've been searching for weeks."

"I'm sorry, ma'am, I haven't." He clasped her wrists, removing her grip from his arms. "I wish I could help, but I'm sure you understand that finding someone in this place ..."

"Yes, I know but ... but you did see him?"

"A long time ago." He nodded. "Time means nothing here so I can't tell you when. Don't lose hope. More often than not soldiers go missing and dig themselves in, hoping to be found. Then they wander into a field hospital somewhere."

"Really?" Emma's heart lifted.

"You're right where you need to be if you're trying to find him." The soldier stepped back. "Either way ... he'll end up here."

"Either way ..." Emma's hand slid up to curl around her throat. "Oh ..."

He bowed his head, kicking the toe of his boot against the dirt.

"I'm sure you thought of the possibility."

"That he would come to me dead?" Emma tensed. "It's all I think about."

She turned, hugging herself as she marched back to the tent. When she looked over her shoulder, he was still staring at her. For a moment Emma thought of going back to him. She thought of talking to him again, offering some comfort. But just as she was about to return to him, thunder broke overhead. The soldier looked directly into her eyes before the explosion lifted him off his feet.

Emma stood frozen, unable to move as she watched him fall, shrapnel flying all around. She turned, her arms coming up to shield her face as she crouched to the ground, pelted by debris and dust. The heat from the burning tent reddened her face. When she lifted her head again, half of their hospital tents were gone.

"Emma!" Margie took hold of her, lifting her up. "Come on. You were right. It was the calm before the storm."

Emma gripped her hand, letting Margie lead her back toward the trucks. They were always moving, always running. It was the way of life out here.

"Nurse!" She recognized the soldier, the one who had brought his friend.

"Good." Emma recovered, tugging her hand out of Margie's. "We need your help."

"What can I do?" He followed her into the tent.

"Start loading up the wounded. Help the doctor."

"Em!" Christy's sigh of relief brought her around in time to wrap her arms around her. "I heard the explosion ... I was afraid to look outside."

"It's getting worse," Emma murmured. "They're getting closer."

"Let's move, ladies." Walter passed by, shuffling along with one of the wounded. "There's no time to waste."

"Stay close," Christy whispered as they both bent to lift one of the cots.

Emma nodded, reaching across to run her finger down Christy's temple. She forced a smile, even as her heart sunk into her stomach.

"Always."

Chapter Thirty-Five

France
The Woods

Will's breath stopped; the whole world went still in that moment. He wasn't staring at the rifle. He didn't see his life flash before his eyes. Instead, all he could see was a mirror. He was just a boy, and Will knew they saw the same thing in each other's eyes—the same youth, the same inexperience. He opened his mouth to speak when suddenly a boot flew out, kicking the rifle out of the German's hands.

"Get up!" John growled, grabbing Will's coat to drag him to his feet. "Run!"

The German's face twisted suddenly as he opened his mouth to shout. Another figure rose up out of the foxhole, rifle ready.

Will turned, stumbling as he ran with Jared in front and John behind him.

"We need to find some cover," John gasped as they ran for their lives. "We need to go deeper."

"Deeper in?" They stopped, their backs pressed against a tree.

They could hear the Germans pursuing, shooting at anything in the woods that moved. Will closed his eyes, slamming his head back against the tree over and over again. How could he have been so foolish? How could he have missed the cover of the foxhole?

He had spent this whole time believing he was now experienced in war. He had begun to believe that he knew all the tricks of these woods. He had been running and hiding for so long, how could he not know every trick to staying alive? But now the enemy was here, on their tails.

And it was all his fault.

"Those are the first enemy troops we've seen in a while," John commented. "They must be extras, maybe as lost as we are. I was sure after this amount of time the marines must've cleared the woods."

"They're getting closer." Jared gritted his teeth.

"All right," John agreed. "We run, don't look back. We don't know how many are back there so we just run, no matter what happens."

Will nodded, loading his rifle.

"Now!" Jared ordered.

They strode forward, long legs leaping across the ground toward the thick of the woods, searching for cover. Sweat poured down the back of Will's neck when he heard shouting behind them, bark flying around his head where bullets hit the trees.

"Keep moving!" Jared shouted.

Suddenly Will stumbled, rolling on the ground. John fell to his knees beside him, wrapping his arm around his waist.

"Come on, son." He started to pull him to his feet.

It happened so suddenly, Will wasn't sure it was real. A rifle popped in the distance. John shouted, falling into the dirt. Jared said something, his voice echoing words Will couldn't understand. He turned, his eyes expanding as he watched John lift his hand, bright red glittering in the sunlight off his fingers.

"John!" Jared grabbed his friend by his shoulders.

"Oh my God!" Will tangled his hands in his hair.

"Come on!" Jared snapped, slinging John's arm around his shoulders to drag him along.

With Will supporting his other side, they started running, turning west where the trees were closer together. Jared's eyes never stopped searching, not until he found the fallen log. The three of them fell; John's back propped up against the fallen tree. Will knelt there on all fours, his hands pressing into the dirt as he watched Jared pull John's hand from the wound in his side.

"You're fine," Jared assured John with a smile while rubbing the drops of sweat from his eyelashes.

"Jared." John shook his head as Jared pressed his hand against the hole in his side.

"It's fine. You'll make it," Jared insisted.

"No."

Bullets suddenly exploded all around them. Jared turned with a shout, firing rapidly into the woods until silence surrounded them. Will bowed his head, his shoulders trembling as he fought emotion.

"Jared." John grabbed the front of the man's coat with both fists.

Will looked up, watching the two men look into each other's eyes like brothers. He could see the bond between them, the invisible cord that had bound them together and kept them going, a fraying cord, about to break before his eyes.

"You and Will have a chance now." John struggled, turning away briefly to spit blood from his mouth. "I can hold them off long enough for you two to disappear."

"I am *not* leaving you behind," Jared growled.

"You have to. You and I both know that I can't go on."

John reached into his pocket, pulling out his journal. Turning, he grabbed Will's wrist, yanking his hand up to slam the book down into his palm.

"You write this story, Private Garvin," John ordered, his face beginning to pale. "You write it. Do you understand me, soldier?"

"Yes, sir, Sergeant," Will whispered as he tucked the book safely into the front of his coat.

John smiled gently and turned back to face Jared. He grasped the back of his friend's neck, bringing him forward.

"Don't let them forget, Jared Cote," he whispered. "You make the world remember us. You make those people know what we gave for them. You tell the world. Do you understand?"

"Yes." Jared nodded.

"Good man." John released a satisfied breath and leaned his head back. "Give me my rifle."

Will snatched the weapon where John had dropped it. He placed it in his hands, sparing some of his own ammo for the sergeant.

"Now go!" he said. "Run and live. You get home, boys. That's an order."

Will stood and turned, his rifle aimed behind them to cover them both.

"Let's go, Jared."

But Jared didn't move. He just stared at John, his head swaying back and forth.

"You are like my son," John choked. "This is what I need you to do. I need you to live."

Tears forced their way onto Jared's face as Will watched his struggle. The man stood, his hand coming up sharply to salute.

"I'll see you soon, Sarge," he murmured.

Will backed away as Jared set his rifle down beside John. The weapon was fully loaded, ready so John could quickly switch to it without having to reload. Jared pulled his handgun from the back of his belt.

Without a word he moved past Will and started running. Will hesitated, looking down at his commanding officer once more. John smiled again before raising the rifle, aiming into the quiet forest behind Will.

"I'll never forget," Will promised.

He ran after Jared and didn't look back.

Chapter Thirty-Six

France
The Woods

John's blood formed a puddle on the ground. His arms trembled as he held the rifle. He could hear them coming, their low murmurs echoing in the empty woods, louder than they thought. John struggled to breathe, the bullet in his side pressing hard against his ribs.

"God, please." He tilted his head back, looking through the canopy of tree branches to the sky. "Please help me hold on. For Jared and Will."

Suddenly something moved to his side. He turned sharply, his stomach dropping. For a moment he thought it was Jared, coming back to drag him along. But they were out of sight, on their way to safety. The sight he saw before him ... couldn't be possible.

John lowered the rifle slowly as he stared at the man, standing there as if he'd never left. He knew him so well. His salt-and-pepper hair glistened in the sunlight, a bristly mustache covered his upper lip, and compassionate gray eyes smiled at him. The man John had missed for years knelt by his side, surrounded by an unearthly glow.

"Hello, John," George Porter said.

"This isn't real." Shaking his head, John stared up into the eyes of his wife's father. "It can't be you."

"I thought my daughter taught you to believe that anything was possible," George said with a chuckle. "It's real, son. I'm here with you."

John closed his eyes.

"I'm close then." He shook his head. "I have to hold on."

"Jared and Will are safe. You can come home now." George held out his hand to him.

"I missed you."

"I missed you too." George smiled. "Come home, son. It's time."

John was tempted, the rifle lowering another inch. But then he turned away, shaking his head.

"Not yet," he whispered. "I'm not done yet. There's one more thing I need to do. For Jared."

He raised the rifle as the first German came around the corner.

"Do what you must, son. I'll be here." George's voice echoed in his ears.

John pulled the trigger.

Chapter Thirty-Seven

The Woods
July 1918

Jared's chest was throbbing as he bent over, his arm curved across his middle, gasping in as much air as he could. He flexed his fingers around his pistol before straightening and arching his back to look up at the sky. He glanced over his shoulder, but the woods were quiet, the moon illuminating the trees with bright white rays between the branches.

Jared unbuttoned his jacket to let the night breeze cool him. Will stumbled to a stop beside him, wheezing as he fell to the ground. They'd been running for hours, even after the sound of gunfire faded behind them. They had run until their legs burned, their hearts were about to explode, and sweat soaked their hair—running for their lives.

Running like cowards, Jared thought. He dropped his pistol and pressed both palms against the tree trunk.

"Were we wrong?" Will panted.

"About what?" Jared frowned at his companion.

"To leave John behind; were we wrong? Should we have tried harder?" Will gulped loudly.

"No." Jared shook his head. "No, we weren't wrong. We might be cowards, but we weren't wrong. John wanted it."

"But ..."

"He was dying!" Jared spun on him, shoulders heaving. "We couldn't have carried him. We couldn't have stayed behind and fought if we were to live. He didn't do everything he did for us so we could die there when we had a chance."

"But you're not all right, Jared. You're trying to make me think you are, but you're not." Will turned onto his back. "Well, neither am I. I think the best thing to do is talk about it."

"Talk!" Jared snorted. "Yeah, sure, let's talk. Let's talk about how I left my best friend behind to die. Let's talk about how I didn't protect him when I should've. Let's talk about how it's your fault, with your clumsy feet, that he's dead!"

Jared spun, slamming his fist into the tree.

"Let's talk about how he saved my life repeatedly in the trenches." He hit the tree again causing blood to ooze from his knuckles. "Let's talk about how he sent me back to the front with a busted ankle because he knew I'd die if I couldn't go back! Let's talk about how he showed me the picture of his family! The picture of the son he *never met*!"

Jared had bloodied the tree; his own blood splattered his chin. He fell against the tree, his forehead scraping against the bark. His hand trembled at his side; blood dripped between his fingers onto the leaves. Tears burned beneath his lids when he closed his eyes.

The image of John sitting against that tree, his face twisted in pain and his eyes full of sorrow caused Jared's insides to turn cold, his blood suddenly hot on his skin. Jared would carry the knowledge that he couldn't save his best friend for the rest of his life.

"Let's talk about how I walked away from him when he needed me most. How I saved myself when I shouldn't have listened and stayed to save him instead," Jared continued as a tear slipped down his nose.

"He saved us both, Jared." Will stood up again. "We didn't have a choice. You were right. We didn't do anything wrong. He was dying, and there was nothing we could've done."

Jared shook his head, rubbing his hand down his face. "Let's dig in," he said, turning away.

Walking a few feet from Will, Jared searched for softer ground close to the trees. He could hear Will following him, could feel the young man's eyes on him, watching his every move. Jared knelt, reaching behind him to pull his bayonet loose. He broke the ground, overturning dirt in a space large enough for both. He thrust the bayonet into the ground and started using his hands.

Will suddenly appeared in front of him. Jared tilted his head back, looking up at the young man shadowed by darkness. Will knelt, burying his hands in the dirt to help dig.

"It wasn't your fault," Will murmured. "And it wasn't for nothing."

Jared closed his eyes. It was as if Will could read his mind.

"We go on now." Will held out his dirt crusted hand. "Together. Deal?"

Jared exhaled, the corner of his mouth tilting up. He grasped the boy's hand, squeezing hard.

"Deal."

Will muttered under his breath as he tried to turn over, the small space barely enough room for him and Jared. The branches scraped against his face, but he welcomed the sting. He deserved so much worse for getting John killed.

"What are you doing?" Jared mumbled, spinning around onto his side to face him. "And what are you muttering? Praying or something?"

"No," Will snapped, barely able to make out Jared's face in the dark. "I'm done praying."

Jared grunted, turning over onto his back. "That's interesting, my friend. I thought the same thing awhile back."

"Don't do that," Will's voice lowered. "Don't try to sound like him."

"Who says I was?" Jared squeezed his arms past Will, clasping his hands behind his head as he tried to get comfortable. "Maybe I sound just like me. Before this cursed place changed everything I thought I was."

Will rubbed a hand over his stomach when it roiled. "Yeah."

"You said you were done praying," Jared murmured, staring up into the tree branches covering them. "I was wondering what Christy would say about that."

Will tensed and squeezed his eyes shut.

"I know what my Emma would say. Well, first she'd slap me silly. Then she'd tell me that praying was second nature to me now; I couldn't stop if I wanted to. Then she'd throw everything I ever said to her back in my face." Jared's voice broke. "She'd tell me prayer was my lifeline. If I broke that cord, I'd die inside. I'd forget who I was because Jesus embodies my heart and soul. Even in sin, He's there to pull me out of trouble because He never leaves. She'd tell me I was the one who taught *her* how to pray, so she doesn't believe for one second I would give it up."

"My father once told me," Will licked his lips, "that he and God weren't on speaking terms. I didn't understand that because I was little and had never heard God's voice. I thought God wasn't speaking to him because he did something bad." Jared chuckled, and Will joined him, raking a hand through his hair. Then his voice quieted.

"I understand now what he meant. He meant he was angry, and *he* wasn't speaking to *God*. Well, that's how I feel right now. I don't *want* to talk to Him Jared. Especially now. Especially because of John."

Jared held his breath for a moment. "And it's because of John ... that we should."

Will turned his head and watched as a single, glittering tear rolled down Jared's temple. "It's what he'd want."

Will exhaled, his chest deflating. He knew his friend was right.

It's what John would do for us.

"Let's start with something easy, huh?" Jared closed his eyes. "Just a simple prayer."

Will swallowed the lump in his throat and nodded his agreement.

"Good." Jared nodded.

Then together, they whispered into the silence, "Our Father, who art in heaven, hallowed be thy name ..."

Chapter Thirty-Eight

London, England

Beth pressed her cheek against her son's, holding him tightly in her lap. George wiggled, a little sigh slipping out. Beth turned her lips against his cheek, kissing him softly before looking up at the priest once more. The service was almost over; family and friends gathered around to speak, expressing their goodbyes to the man who would've been Beth's brother-in-law.

Ruth sat tall and strong between their grandfather and mother. Restraining her tears, she gripped Susan's hand when Damian's father stood up to speak. There was no body to bury, nothing but the tags that had been returned and the word of another soldier who had witnessed Damian's demise.

The service hardly seemed like closure to Beth, but having a ceremony to say goodbye and having a stone made for him seemed the best way to let him go and be at peace. But Beth knew it would take more than a goodbye ceremony to heal her sister's heart. Beth reached past her mother to touch her sister's hand. Ruth smiled gently, a solitary tear dripping from her lashes to her cheek.

Melody shifted on her other side, leaning her head against Beth's shoulder. Ruth watched her with unmoving eyes, unable to look at Damian's father. Ruth's face was beginning to pale, her eyes widening as her breathing raced. Susan looked back and forth helplessly between her daughters, but Beth simply smiled and passed George to his grandmother.

"Do you need some air?" Beth whispered.

Ruth's head bobbed rapidly. Beth gripped her hand as they stood and moved silently out of the pew and toward the large church doors. Once outside, Ruth gasped, leaning entirely against Beth as she sucked in the cool summer breeze. Beth held her, pressing her hand to the back of Ruth's head.

Slowly Beth lowered her sister to the church steps, holding her the way she held Melody when the little girl had nightmares. Ruth interlocked her fingers at Beth's waist, curling her legs up against her chest as she cuddled against her sister's heartbeat. Beth didn't mind. More than anything she knew her sister needed to be held.

"Have you heard from John?" Ruth broke the silence. She sniffled, rubbing her tears away with her thumb.

"No." Beth rested her chin on her sister's head.

"I don't understand this. They won't tell me any of the details. They won't tell me why it took so long for this soldier to come forward about Damian's death."

"Some things cannot be explained," Beth said, stroking Ruth's hair. "We just need to believe there is a plan."

"A plan?" Ruth shook her head. "I just can't ... I thought I was done grieving for him. I thought I'd accepted that he was dead, that he was never coming back. But seeing it on paper ... it just ... it changed *everything*."

"I know."

"It was so final on paper. It was horrible."

"I know."

Ruth looked up at her through eyes blurred by her tears.

"We're all praying for John, Beth. He'll come back; I'm sure of it." Ruth squeezed her hand. "I feel it in my heart. It will be the one bit of happiness out of this nightmare."

Beth pulled her sister close. She had no words. She couldn't speak of the man she loved when her sister had just lost hers. Beth cleared her throat, pressing her hands to Ruth's shoulders to look her over.

"Now, let's wipe away those tears." She tugged her handkerchief from her sleeve and dabbed her sister's eyes.

"I don't want to go back in there," Ruth protested, shuddering.

"I know, but you have to. Moments like these were never meant to be easy." Beth pulled Ruth back to her feet. "I'm right here with you."

Ruth nodded and, turning on her heels, marched back up the steps and into the church. Beth watched her for a moment, her own heart racing. She reached for her locket with John's picture nestled safely inside. Having his likeness against her heart at all times eased her pain. Feeling he was close made things seem easier. But she couldn't help this overwhelming feeling that something was terribly wrong.

It had started right after the news about Damian arrived. Her mother said it was just the fear talking, the fear of receiving word in the same horrible way that was giving her that feeling. But Beth knew the feeling well. This was completely different from the way she felt when her telegram arrived.

It was the feeling she had every time George fell and scraped his knee when she wasn't looking. It was the feeling she had when Melody fell into the creek while she ran to the house for their picnic lunch. It was the feeling she'd had when George had smallpox a year ago, and her mother insisted it was just a child's cold.

It was the instinct of a mother, the instinct of a wife, that told her someone she loved was in trouble. It was a feeling all women knew well, and she couldn't shake it. Someone she loved was in trouble. Someone she loved was in pain, and there was nothing she could do about it.

Beth was helpless, and she hated it.

"Mama?" Melody fisted her small hands around her blanket, pulling it up to her chin.

"What is it, darling?" Beth asked as she settled herself on the edge of her daughter's mattress.

"When are we going home?" Melody turned slightly, reaching to pull her sleeping brother against her side. "George and I miss home."

"I miss home too, sweetheart."

Beth twirled one of Melody's darkening curls around her finger. Melody had her father's hair. It had been fair when she was born, and they both thought she had inherited his mother's blonde hair, but then it darkened to John's chestnut locks.

"But your Aunt Ruth needs us right now."

"Because Uncle Damian is gone, right?" Melody tilted her head. "I remember Uncle Damian."

"I know you do." Beth smiled.

"Grandmamma said Aunt Ruth loved him very much, but now he's gone to heaven."

"That's right, love."

"But why, Mama? Why would he go to heaven if Aunt Ruth loved him so much?"

Beth blinked, her mind racing as she searched for an answer. Melody had become so curious lately, watching and listening to everything so attentively. Sometimes Beth didn't know what she would do with her when her daughter truly started to understand what this war meant for their family. It was a harsh time for a child growing up, and it was never what Beth wanted for her children.

"I don't know, Melody. I think your Uncle Damian didn't want to leave, but he didn't have a choice. God wanted him to come home, love." Beth leaned in to kiss the top of her head. "Now get some sleep. I love you, darling."

"I love you too, Mama." Melody wrapped her arms around Beth's neck, pulling her down.

"All right now." Beth laughed softly as she tucked the blankets around Melody's little form. "Sleep, little one. Next time you open your eyes, it will be morning."

Beth turned out the light, stepping silently out of the room. She looked back once. Melody was already asleep, little breaths puffing from between her pink lips. Beth closed the door to a crack before hurrying down the hall. She stopped at the top of the stairs.

She could hear the muted conversation coming from the dining room. Beth tightened the ties of her apron. She didn't want to go down there. She didn't want to know what they were talking about. News of Damian just brought up the fact she hadn't heard from John in over a year.

Beth turned away from the stairs, hurrying toward her sister's room. She knew she couldn't avoid her mother and grandfather forever, but she also knew her sister needed her. Beth had to check on her to make sure Ruth was sleeping, not lying in bed crying.

Her hand curled around the glass doorknob, turning it silently until she could peek in. Her sister's hair was disheveled, sticking to her feather pillow as she slept peacefully. But she wasn't fooling Beth. She could see the rash on her sister's cheeks where she had scrubbed away her grief. She could see the pocket puffs forming beneath Ruth's eyes.

Beth closed the door before the light from the hall woke Ruth. At least she was sleeping, and Beth would let her get as much rest as she could before the nightmares woke her. It took weeks before Beth could sleep without nightmares after she received the news that John was missing. She couldn't even imagine the kind of dreams Ruth would have tonight.

Her heart stuttered as she stepped down toward the dining room. Her mother's voice reached her ears when she was halfway down the steps. Beth scooted to the side, pressing herself to the wall so she could listen. Her mouth watered. Drinking a glass of milk before bed had become a habit when she was a little girl, one that continued into her adulthood. John teased her about it, but she didn't care. She couldn't sleep until she'd had some.

She prayed they would get up to go to sleep soon so she wouldn't be stopped and forced to face them. Beth was exhausted. She just wanted some peace and quiet. She didn't want to worry anymore.

She pressed her ear against the wall, licking her lips as she listened.

"... so strong, Papa," Susan was saying. "So much stronger than I could have been. Stronger than I was."

"We have both seen death, sweetheart," Malcolm Porter replied in his scratchy voice. "I know your pain and mine were the same when Georgie passed."

"I thought I would die." Susan gasped, and Beth knew that her mother was about to cry. "But seeing Ruth and Elizabeth like this ..."

"You know my dear," Malcolm stopped her. "I thought there could be no greater pain than when I lost my son. I thought there was no greater tragedy than for a man to die of a heart attack so young. But seeing my granddaughters in pain, seeing his children suffering ... it is an equal hurt."

Beth covered her mouth, her fingers trembling against her lips as she lowered herself to the stairs.

"I worry so about Elizabeth," Susan whispered. "She doesn't talk about John anymore. She has everything bottled up inside because she wants to help her sister. Being here in London has separated her from her memories, and I know it can't be good for her."

"Perhaps you should take her home," Malcolm suggested.

"I have thought of it. But I don't think she'll go. Not until this tragedy with Ruth has passed. She thinks only of her sister."

"You raised them well."

"But I'm scared, Papa." Susan's voice broke. "I don't know what to do."

Silence filled the house. Beth turned and quietly tiptoed back up the stairs. She stopped at the top, sitting beside the rail with her knees curled up against her chest. She felt just like a child, hiding where she wasn't supposed to be.

Beth hated that her mother felt helpless. She hated that her mother felt forced to share her pain. It wasn't what she wanted, and she knew it wasn't what Ruth would want either. She knew her mother would never go home unless she thought they were all right.

Beth buried her face in her knees; her shoulders trembled as she fought tears. Maybe her mother was right. Maybe she wasn't thinking of herself enough. But there was one thing her mother couldn't understand.

Beth couldn't think of herself. She couldn't think of John. Thinking of her sister, helping her sister, was the only thing that kept her sane for the past week. It was the only thing that made her get out of bed in the morning. When she looked at her children, she saw John; when she looked in the mirror he was standing behind her; but when she was comforting Ruth, her self-pity disappeared.

God help us both. How will I ever be able to return home?

Chapter Thirty-Nine

France
Field Hospital

"How are we doing?" Emma scrubbed her hands, the rag red from blood that also stained her skin. She dunked her hands into the bowl again, continuing to rub her hands raw. She looked over her shoulder at the wounded lined up inside the tent, tickets pinned to their coats. Their painful moans vibrated through the air.

She bit her lip. In just a few short hours, half of these men would be heading home; the other half would be dead. In moments like these, Emma knew for sure knowledge was a curse. Knowing with certainty that half of these men would soon be dead was breaking her.

"Margie and I have done everything in our power to ease their pain." Christy joined her at the bowl, dipping her hands into the pink water. "Until the trucks come to take them to the ships, there's nothing else we can do."

"It won't come out." Emma dropped the cloth into the bowl, causing water to splash over the rim. "After a while, blood stops coming off."

She dried her hands on her apron, smearing it with dried brown blood. Her hands were splotched with blood stains, seemingly permanent after so long without being able to wash them properly. With a sigh, Emma leaned back against the table.

"Maybe we should take Walter's offer," Christy murmured, sidestepping around the table to stand beside her. "We could be on one of those ships home today."

"Do you want to leave?" Emma frowned. "Because you don't have to stay here because of me. That's your choice."

"I couldn't leave you behind," Christy protested, kicking at the ground. "You almost died out there for me. I can't walk away from you after that. But we could go home together."

"Don't you want to find Will?"

"Of course I do. But after seeing all of these men ..." Christy shuddered, rubbing her arms. "Sometimes I think it would be better to get the telegram than to find him in one of these hospitals."

"Have you given up hope that he's alive out there somewhere?"

"Honestly?" Christy looked directly into her eyes. "I don't know. I don't want to give up on him, but I also know I couldn't bear to see him torn apart like some of these soldiers. Outside the Belleau ... well, you saw the same things I did."

"But Will wasn't there," Emma said.

"We don't know that for sure, Em." Christy bowed her head. "How many men die and are never found? How many of our dead get left behind?"

She walked away before Emma could answer.

"Emma, it's Connor!" Christy called.

Emma turned over on her cot, darkness shrouding the inside of the tent. Blinking the sleep from her eyes, she tried to adjust to the dim lighting. She swung her legs over the side of the cot and weaved her way between the cots toward Christy's voice. Connor O'Hare was tossing on his bed, his face red with fever.

Emma grabbed at the bandages from his double amputation, then reared back at the smell. His legs, green with infection, were swelling with bleeding beneath his skin. Emma closed her eyes. They'd already cut further above the knee because of infection, but his body wouldn't fight. He was too susceptible to the poison of gangrene to fight it back.

"It's all right, Connor." Emma lifted his shoulders, positioning herself behind him.

Heat radiated from his body; beads of sweat formed on her forehead as he leaned back into her. His head lolled to the side, eyes rolling back.

"Shh." She combed her fingers through his hair. "I've got you now. You're fine."

"What do we do?" Christy knelt beside the cot. "He … he was going home in the morning. He's just a kid."

"I know." Emma kissed the boy's temple.

"What's going to happen to me?" Connor rasped, his stiff fingers reached for her arm.

"Nothing. You're fine, Connor. You just need to sleep," she cooed as his fever rose.

"Emma?" Connor kneaded her arm.

"Yes?"

"Do you believe in heaven?" His body convulsed in her arms as he struggled against tears. "Do you believe there is a place for us when we die?"

"Of course I do, love," Emma whispered, pressing her cheek against the top of his head. "It is wonderful there, a place where God heals you of all the pain of this world. Heaven is a promise, Connor. A promise of eternal rest, and God would not break a promise."

He nodded, his grip loosening on her arm. Emma's eyes met Christy's and held for a moment. She could almost hear the girl's heart pounding in rhythm with her own. Neither of them wanted to be here. Neither of them was prepared for what was going to happen next.

Emma pressed her hand to Connor's chest, turning her lips against his ear.

"Is Jesus here, Connor? Is He in your heart?"

Connor nodded, his body trembling beneath her palm.

"Then don't be afraid." Tears streamed her cheeks as Jared's words flowed from her tongue. "Don't ever doubt, Connor. Because once Jesus has you, He doesn't let go. That's it, sweetheart.

You're His, and there is no power great enough to take you away from Him. God's promise of heaven was made for *you*. As long as you love Him, you have nothing to fear."

"Will you sing?" Connor whispered, his Irish lilt thickening. "The one I taught you?"

Emma closed her eyes, remembering how he had told the story. The song was new, but his mother had an ear for music. She had taken to singing it to Connor's little brother mere weeks before he left home for the war. But he remembered the song, the sound of her voice, better than he remembered anything else from back home.

Lord, give me strength, she prayed.

"Of course, darling."

Christy rested her head on Connor's chest, hugging him tight. Emma placed one hand atop Connor's head, the other on Christy's. She took a deep breath, closing her eyes as she began to rock him ever so slightly. Opening her mouth, Emma's throat vibrated with song. Her eyes fluttered, her chest swelled. She had almost forgotten what music sounded like, what her own voice sounded like in rhythm with song.

As her voice filled the tent, Connor's entire body relaxed. His arms fell limp at his sides, his ragged breaths hissed between his pale lips. Emma kissed his forehead, closing her eyes again as she murmured the song into his ear. Christy's fingers twined with her own over his chest.

"Emma," Christy whispered.

She looked up and stilled. A sea of eyes were staring at her, men propping themselves on their cots, boys weeping softly at the sound of her voice. Emma's heart thumped louder against her ribcage when her eyes met the soldier sitting directly beside Connor's cot. Fresh blood seeped from the bandages around his temples, a sheen of tears glittering in his empty gaze as he rasped the words along with her, his accent thick and his hands clenched in his lap.

Emma turned away, unable to bear the look in his eyes. Looking down she rolled her hand through Connor's wavy hair before she kissed the top of his head, humming the tune ever so softly. Christy's tears were dripping onto his shirt, her hand moving back and forth against his chest to soothe him.

At that moment Connor's chest stilled. Emma's face twisted with the pain, her eyes squeezed shut to keep the tears at bay when Christy began to sob. She slowly lowered the boy to his cot. Christy sat back as Emma crossed his arms over his chest. She reached up to close his eyelids over his half opened, glazed stare. Emma bent over him, forehead pressed to his shoulder.

"May you find peace in heaven, love," Emma whispered. "I'll meet you there soon."

THE LOST GENERATION

Chapter Forty

The Woods

Will's mouth was parched. Finding water was the only thing on his mind as he tossed around on the ground trying to get comfortable. His stomach caved toward his spine, growling at him loudly. He and Jared had scrounged around in the woods for food, catching a rabbit or squirrel every day or so. But it had been days since they'd had a meal. Their last one had been before John died.

He froze, his hand pressing against his heart. Dwelling on what happened didn't do him or Jared any good. They could grieve later, once they were out of here. Once they were back home safe. Now they had to concentrate. They were getting close; he could sense it. There was something familiar about this part of the forest, about the way they'd been circling in search of the border.

If they could find the river, he knew they would be just a few miles from the army. They had to be getting close now. The marines had to have cleared the woods. Will didn't even know how long it had been since they went missing. He wasn't counting days anymore; he didn't want to.

He felt like a coward, running and hiding for so long. How many men had died fighting during the time he'd been dug into the ground with Jared and John? How many lives had been lost? How many sleepless nights had Christy spent wondering if he was alive or dead?

"What's wrong, Will?" Jared nudged him in the side. "Can't sleep?"

"Can you?" Will grumbled. "I'm hungry and exhausted, but most of all I'd die for just one sip of cold water. I have never been so thirsty in my life."

"I know what you mean." Jared pushed back the branches over them, peeking out. "We should get moving anyway. Sun's about to come up."

"Right," Will agreed but didn't move.

"Yeah, you're right." Jared fell onto his back again with a heavy sigh. "What's the point?"

"Hmm." Will nodded. "You read my mind."

"Is it just me, or do you think we know each other a little too well?" Jared grinned, closing his eyes again.

"I guess this is what it's like to have a brother." Will turned to look at him. "Do you have any siblings?"

"No. You?"

"I had a brother, but he died when I was five."

"I'm sorry."

"I'm not." Will furrowed his brow.

"What do you mean?" Jared finally looked at him.

"He went peacefully back then. If he hadn't passed away when he did, then he'd be here with me, or he'd be dead on a field somewhere on foreign soil." Will crossed his arms, trying to curl into himself. "I wouldn't wish that on him just so I could have had a few more years with a brother I have trouble remembering."

"I understand," Jared said. "You shouldn't feel guilty about it."

"Wouldn't you?" Will turned, propping himself up on his elbow. "You feel guilty about John."

"It's different. I left him behind. You didn't have a choice when it came to your brother. But feeling guilty because you're glad he passed on and didn't have to go through this misery … you just … you shouldn't feel that kind of guilt."

"Maybe so, but—"

The branches started to cave. Will's eyes expanded when a boot slammed into his gut. He grunted, and Jared burst into action. His hand wrapped around the ankle, pulling it off of Will's chest.

"*Argh!*" The growl echoed in their ears.

Will spun, his rifle light and familiar in his hands as both he and Jared leaped from the foxhole, bending on one knee to face their opponents.

"Stand down!" the soldier facing him shouted.

Will glanced at Jared who was just as shocked as he was. The man who had stumbled on Will's stomach got to his feet and stood behind the other men who were covering him. They were dirty, their uniforms rank with gas and filth. One of them had a bandage around his filthy, bloody hand, but he stood tall, his weapon at the ready. None of them moved, all of them frozen in place for what seemed like hours before Jared lowered his rifle an inch.

"You Brits?" he asked.

"American?" the British private asked.

"Canadian," Jared answered, straightening to his feet. "Kid's American though. We've been looking for you guys."

"The marines." Will licked his lips, tasting dirt. "Did they make it through the woods?"

"They got them cleared," the soldier answered. "Names?"

"Jared Cote, Will Garvin." Jared slapped Will in the chest and grinned at the groan it provoked.

"Peter Westcott." He held out his hand, and Jared grasped it.

"Want to tell me what in God's name you're doing out here all alone without a commanding officer? You on patrol or the like?" Peter asked as he stepped around Jared to shake Will's hand.

"We had a commanding officer." Jared's brow arced. "He was gunned down a few days ago. Sergeant John Young."

Peter's face grayed.

"I knew him. He was a good man."

"Better than most," Jared said as he ran his hand down his face.

"We were taken by some Germans but escaped into the woods. We've been digging in and trying to find our way for weeks," Will tried to explain.

"You're lucky then." Peter slapped his shoulder.

"Can you get us back to the front, Westcott?" Jared propped his rifle on his shoulder. "Can you get us back to our units?"

"I can certainly get you back to the front. A group of our wounded is being sent home. We can regroup and then my commanding officer can figure out where you both belong."

Peter started to move past him when Jared grabbed his sleeve.

"The kid and I come as a package," Jared said, his fist tightening until the circulation left his hand. "We get assigned to the same unit under the same officer."

"I can't make any promises, soldier." Peter's jaw tightened.

"Will and I stay together, or we find our own way back to the line."

Will looked back and forth between the two soldiers, watching the silence grow thicker between them. Suddenly Peter yanked out of Jared's grasp, his brow creasing with anger. He rubbed his shoulder before his head jerked up slightly.

"As you say. I didn't know there would be conditions to my rescuing you."

"We didn't need rescuing," Jared hissed, stepping close until he and Peter were nose to nose.

"Get out of my way." Peter shoved him.

"Enough." One of the soldiers in the group got between them. "Remember we are on the same side, boys. Now let's move."

Jared backed away, coming to his side as they took up the rear of the group.

"They're going to help us get home, Jared."

"I know."

"We will find a way to stick together."

"Just don't wander. Got it, kid?" Jared's whisper was right against his ear so no one else could hear. "I don't want to turn my back and have you disappear the next second."

"I'm not going to leave you. I promise that won't happen to me, Jared."

"See that you don't."

Jared strode a few feet ahead of him, keeping up with the group. Will watched him, hardly able to believe their good fortune. His heart lifted at the thought they would be headed back to the front, back to the fight, and maybe even back home if fortune favored them. He closed his eyes, picturing Christy's smile. He knew everything would be fine. Even if they sent him back into the fighting, he would be fighting with Jared. They would keep each other safe.

God please—I know I've doubted and I said I wouldn't do this, but I have no one else to turn to. Please, even if we are fighting side by side, please end this soon. Send us home. Keep us safe.

Will pulled in a long breath. They had made it this far. He was sure now that they would make it home.

Chapter Forty-One

Paris, France

"There now," Christy smiled, tucking the blanket close around the soldier's body. "Keep warm and safe. You'll be home before you know it."

She gave him another dose of morphine, his eyes beginning to grow heavy as two members of the Red Cross came to load him onto the truck that would take him to the ship. Christy smiled, stroking his hair once more before she gestured for the men to carry him away.

"Will you write to me?" He lifted his head, drowsy from the drugs. "To let me know you made it home too?"

"Yes, of course I will." Christy waved before walking away.

A part of her chest ached; she wanted to rush after him and get on that ship. She wanted to go home, she'd had enough, and she didn't know how Emma could stand to keep going. After they had lost Connor, she had gone silent. She didn't speak a word to anyone for three days. She whispered only to the wounded she tended, the ones she was sending home now.

Christy worried about her, wondering if this place had finally broken her soul. She knew that each and every soldier Emma tended broke her heart. But she always seemed to recover, to find her strength once again. After Connor, Christy didn't think Emma was going to bounce back.

"Christy." Emma seemed to appear out of nowhere.

Christy turned sharply, forcing a smile onto her lips as she faced her friend. She looked thinner, her skin gray and eyes dark with exhaustion. She wasn't sleeping or eating. Christy was frightened more than she cared to admit.

"We're being sent back to the line. You might want to prepare," Emma announced, shifting the rolls of bandages from one arm to the other.

"Are you well?" Christy asked, following her when she started walking away.

"Yes." Emma passed the bandages off to another nurse and picked up a crate of medicines.

"You haven't eaten since Connor."

"I don't want to talk about him," Emma snapped, turning on her. "I don't ever want to hear his name again, do you understand me?"

"Emma, you've always said talking about it is the best way to heal from it." Christy reached out to touch her shoulder, but Emma pulled away from the gesture of comfort.

"Just pack up." Emma circled around Christy, backing away toward one of the trucks. "We're heading out soon."

"All right," Christy whispered, watching her pass the crate up into the truck.

They'd be bringing supplies back to Walter on the front line, heading back into the heat of it. The hospital wouldn't last long Christy knew that. They would probably have just enough time to deliver supplies and give the soldiers some relief before they had to load them up and bring them to safety.

Christy crossed her arms, taking heavy steps around the trucks. Everyone was bustling about, hurrying around with the wounded, and shouting orders. No one but her seemed to stop for a moment, to observe, to think. There never seemed to be enough time to think about things and to just be ... silent. Just for a few minutes. To contemplate, to pray.

Christy arched her neck back, her eyes closed as she let the breeze bathe her. The longing in her heart pulled her away from the noise and the heaviness of war that surrounded this place. For a moment, she believed she could do it. For a moment, she believed she could walk away from here, from the wounded, even from Emma, and go home where she belonged.

She could leave easily. She could supervise the wounded aboard ship, see them safely back to a hospital in England, then from England she could go home to her family. To Will's family. To the home Will had found for them, where she'd lived for so short a time before this war pulled her into its net.

But every time she closed her eyes, she saw her husband. Every time she thought for a moment that she could leave this place without him, the guilt gnawed at her. The love she carried in her heart stopped her feet from moving forward. Emma had asked her if she'd given up hope for him, and she hadn't been honest.

Because she knew deep down that she hadn't. Whatever she did at this moment would change both their lives, she knew it.

"Christy!" Emma called, sitting behind the wheel of one of the trucks. "Are you coming?"

Christy hesitated. Her mouth opened to answer, but no sound came out. With a sigh she ran her fingers through her hair, dislodging the pins caught up in her locks. It was an impossible decision, but in her heart, she always knew what choice she'd make.

Without a word she rushed back to the truck and climbed inside.

Chapter Forty-Two

The Border of the Woods

With his gun still ready, Jared watched Will as he talked to one of the soldiers. It had been a long time since he'd been in the midst of a patrol with more than one man at his side to watch his back. After building a bond with only two men, he found it difficult to trust anyone else. He was sure these men would watch each other's backs before they watched his and Will's.

His eyes strayed to Westcott. He didn't know why, but something about the man set his teeth on edge. Maybe it was because he'd known John too. Maybe it was because he'd talked about him with so little emotion. He wasn't sure, but he didn't like him. He had a feeling the man wouldn't hesitate to tell his commanding officer to separate him and the kid.

That was something Jared wouldn't let happen. He'd disobey orders if he had to; he didn't care. After everything they'd been through together, there was no way Jared was finishing this war without making sure Will made it back home. Westcott turned to him, and Jared looked away quickly, pretending to scan the perimeter. They were preparing to leave the woods. After all this time, Jared could hardly believe it. They'd been found, they were headed back to the front—maybe even to home.

Westcott hadn't offered any progress on the war. He hadn't given him any hope that it was going to be over soon. But despite his initial feelings about the man, Jared could see the same grief and suffering in Westcott's eyes he was sure was in his own.

Jared crouched beside one of the trees, scooping his hand into the soft earth. Rubbing the dirt between his fingers, he frowned. He didn't want to think about how long he'd been fighting on foreign soil. He especially didn't want to think about how his best friend had died here, how he hadn't even had a proper burial but was left to fade away in the woods.

He shuddered, letting the dirt fall away between his fingers. He rubbed his hand along his chest, smearing the dirt in a long streak across his coat. Jared straightened again and looked up. An overwhelming feeling washed over him, the kind he always had when something terrible was about to happen. He had come to recognize that feeling and run from it, always searching with caution, his gun always ready.

It was different this time. Something was close, perhaps even closing in. He could sense it. He didn't know what it was, but he could feel the same sensation of loss washing over him just as it had when he'd left John behind.

"Hey!" Will's voice snapped him out of it. "You all right, Jared?"

"Yeah." He shook his head, blinking quickly.

"Then keep up!" Westcott snapped. "We're not waiting for you."

Jared glared but didn't answer. He simply raised his weapon and followed silently after them, watching Will's back and praying he was wrong.

Chapter Forty-Three

Lancashire, England
The Young Farm

"We're home!" Melody squealed, gripping George's hand as they raced up the path and through the front door.

Susan laughed; Beth forced a smile as she followed slowly behind her children. She almost stopped, unable to move any closer to the house where she had spent her happiest moments with the man she loved. She and John had built this life together; coming back without him was wrong in so many ways.

Beth inhaled deeply before stepping over the threshold. Melody had left the door wide open, not even stopping to close it before taking her little brother upstairs to their bedroom. As Beth placed her bag by the front door, her eyes were immediately drawn to the photograph she'd kept on the table. She picked it up, pressing it to her heart. The only family member missing in the photo was little George.

Beth had dreamed of the day John would come walking home to her. The first thing she would do was gather them together to take a new photograph of their complete family. In the photo, her husband would be able to hold his son, the son he'd yet to meet. John had missed his first four years. Beth's heart broke just thinking about it.

"Are you all right, sweetheart?" Susan asked.

Beth turned slightly, never lifting her eyes from his face. She traced her finger along the photograph, fighting the tears that wanted to flood her eyes. She started to answer when the patter of her children's feet signaled they were coming downstairs.

"Mum!" Melody rushed to her side. "Can George and I play outside?"

"Yes." Beth smiled again, stroking the top of her daughter's head. "But don't wander too far and stay away from the rooster."

"Yes, Mum." Melody skipped away, dragging her brother along.

Beth drew in a long breath of fresh air. She had missed that in London ... the fresh country air she had grown up with, the beautiful green fields rippling under a warm breeze. Everything that made up her home, she had missed. It had formed an ache in her heart that wouldn't go away.

Beth had prayed that coming home would ease her hurt, but it hadn't. It just made it worse. Now, standing in the middle of her kitchen, she looked down at the picture that would hold John's face for the rest of time.

"You can answer me now, Beth," Susan said.

Beth could feel her mother's eyes on her. She hugged the picture again, letting a single icy tear fall against her face. Coming home was supposed to be a wonderful thing. She should have felt the joy Melody did when she walked through the door. She should have felt the same thing her children felt as they ran in circles in the yard, their hands raised toward the sun, filling the air with squeals of joy.

But she couldn't. This place wasn't home anymore. This place would never be home again.

"No, Mum, I'm not all right," Beth gasped.

"Elizabeth ... it's not over yet." Susan took a step toward her.

"Yes, it is." Beth looked at her mother's face, distorted by her tears.

"There's still a chance ..."

"Empty words, Mother." Beth interrupted. Her chest ached.

She hugged the picture until the glass cracked, and she felt a shard pressing through the thin material of her dress. Pressure began in the hollow of her throat as she forced the words out.

"He's not coming home, is he?"

Susan bowed her head, her hands falling limp at her sides. Beth squeezed her eyes closed, plunging herself into darkness so she wouldn't see the pity on her mother's face. Her knees buckled, and she fell to the floor, her shoulder hitting the wood with a crack. Burning pain sliced through her, but she didn't care. It didn't compare with the pain she felt in her shattered heart.

Sobs wracked Beth's body. Susan rushed forward to gather her daughter in her arms. Beth felt as though half of her soul had been ripped away as her mind wrapped around her own words:

He's not coming home.

Chapter Forty-Four

France
The Western Front
Field Hospital

Will leaped out of the way as the truck sped by. Mud flew up, splattering his pants. Jared just shrugged before hurrying after West-cott through the camp. Will bent over to slap at the mud. When he lifted his hand again, rubbing the clumps between his fingers, he frowned and swallowed hard as he realized it wasn't water creating the mud but blood. He wiped the mud on his coat and hurried after Jared.

A sea of nurses, doctors and soldiers were hurrying about, load-ing wounded into trucks and shouting orders that they had to move out. The enemy had their location it would only be a matter of time before the bombing would start.

Will knew the Red Cross sign was like a beacon for the enemy. If the Germans could cut off the supply of medicines, if they could kill the nurses and doctors, then it wouldn't be long before the Allied Forces would fall. Without the help of these provisions and profes-sional medical care, none of them would make it out alive.

Just then, a body slammed into him, a small body carrying a bundle of bandages in her arms. The nurse looked up at him, fiery hair disheveled, her cap sitting at on odd angle on her head.

"Watch where you're going!" she snapped, glaring.

"I'm sorry. My friend—"

"Listen, this is no place to stand around like a fool. We need to get out of here now, so if you're looking for someone, stop. There's no point."

Without another word, she brushed past him, handing the bandages up into one of the trucks. Will puffed out a long sigh before he turned again. He could see Jared up ahead, arguing with Westcott about something, his hands flailing around in the air. He felt completely alone in this crowd of people. It felt like an eternity since he'd been around more than two people.

"Soldier." A raspy voice spoke behind him. "Please load this man into that truck."

He turned to address the feminine voice but she was already walking back into the tent. He looked back and forth before forcing himself to focus on the wounded soldier moaning on the stretcher. Will crouched beside him, hesitating before he lifted the corner of the bandage wrapped around the man's knee.

He drew back at the smell of rotten cheese and gas. The soldier's flesh was melting with an infection, the shine of white bone peeked out from the shrapnel that had cut through layers of skin. Will coughed, pressing the bandage back down onto the wound. The soldier's skin shifted beneath Will's palm.

"You can't tell me you've been fighting and have never seen something as bad as that before." The raspy voice returned, and Will looked up.

She was tall and blonde, her shoes caked in dirt and her entire apron stained with blood. Will cleared his throat, wondering for a moment if the nurses even had time to eat, considering how thin this one was.

"It's been a long time since I was on the front lines," he muttered.

"Grab that end." She pointed, crouching to take hold of the other end.

Will circled the stretcher, to stand behind the soldier's head. The nurse counted to three and they lifted. Will turned half a circle as the nurse backed toward the truck. She lifted with a heaving breath; the stretcher slammed onto the edge of the truck.

With her help, Will pushed, sliding the soldier all the way inside. He slapped the back of the truck before stepping back; the nurse beside him did the same.

"You look pretty worn out and filthy for someone who hasn't been on the front in a while," she commented. Scrunching her nose, she leaned close to his shoulder. "You smell like it too."

Will opened his mouth to say something.

"Em!" A soldier leaned out of the side of the truck behind the wheel. "We got room for one more?"

"No, that's all, Gabe. Get moving." She waved a hand and then turned on her heel. "You better get moving too, soldier. What usually happens next is never pretty."

Will growled under his breath as she disappeared into the tent once again. Not being able to defend himself and what he'd been through was frustrating. But he had seen something in her eyes he recognized all too well. As much as he'd suffered, she had suffered the same, maybe even more.

He knew he should go find Jared. Being separated in all this confusion could get them both into trouble, and they'd promised to stick together. But he only made it so far before the urge to turn back washed over him. He'd been running and hiding all this time. He'd lost his commanding officer and his friend. The least he could do was help that nurse pack up and get out of here before her life reached a different level of endangerment. Will turned around to do just that ... and stopped dead in his tracks.

Like an angel she stood before him, her golden hair in a thick braid over one shoulder and her blue eyes overflowing with tears. She had known it was him before he even turned, he could see it in her eyes. Her entire body trembled at the sight of him, her lily-white hands stained brown with old blood and her cheeks splotched with dust. But she had never looked more beautiful than in that moment in her light blue dress and filthy gray apron.

"It's you."

Her voice was music, lilting across the air to his ears in the most soothing tones he'd ever heard. He closed his eyes, not trusting it to be real.

"I can't believe it."

He opened them again and there she still stood.

"Christy!" He stumbled in his rush to her.

Then she was in his arms, her feet lifted right off the ground from the force of his embrace. He felt her sweet lips buried into his neck, her hair rustling against the side of his face. Her body was soft against his own, warm and welcoming as she tightened her arms around his shoulders.

Despite the dirt and dust, despite the rank odor of gas and infection, she still smelled like Christy. She still smelled like his wife.

"Don't let me go," she whispered against the side of his ear. "Please don't let me go."

"Never," he promised.

He smiled, lifting his eyes toward the heavens as a silent prayer of thanksgiving left his heart.

Christy felt him lowering her feet back to the ground. In a moment, he had her face in his hands, pressing her back so he could kiss her. She moaned, tangling her fingers in his filthy hair. His lips were cracked and bloodied, but her husband's kiss was still the most wonderful feeling in the world.

"Where have you been?" She gasped as he lowered her to the ground, both curling close to each other against the tent wall.

"Running mostly." Will couldn't seem to stop stroking her hair, his fingers catching in her braid. "I was cut off from my unit. We got trapped in the woods."

"We?" Christy asked, her eyes questioning.

"Me and two others. One was my friend's sergeant." Will shook his head. "Hush now. We don't need to talk about that."

He kissed her again, filling her heart with warmth and her body with heat from his long-awaited touch.

"What are you doing here?" He pulled back with a frown.

"I received a telegram." She touched her forehead to his and placed her palm against his face. "I came here to find you. I never believed for a moment you were dead then. But this place ... I should never have doubted. God has brought you back to me."

"You're no nurse, Christy." Will stroked his finger down her neck.

"I didn't come here as one." Christy laughed. "I came here for you and as someone searching for the story. But I have learned so much. I want you to meet Emma. She saved my life."

"I think I may have already." Will's brow waggled.

"There's so much to tell you." Christy sniffled, her eyes stinging. "I've missed you. I love you so much."

She grabbed him close, pressing her face into his neck to catch his scent. She pressed her hand to the back of his neck until they were flush against each other.

"I love you too."

"Hey."

Christy looked up at the sound of the voice. Walter stood over them, one of his eyebrow's twitching as he tapped the toe of his boot against the dirt.

"Walter, this—"

"It doesn't matter, Christy." Walter pinched the bridge of his nose. "Just come back inside and help me."

He walked around them quickly, heading back into the tent. Christy stood up hastily, taking Will's hands tightly in hers. He leaned in to kiss her again.

"I'll meet you back here," he whispered.

"Where are you going?" Her stomach dropped at the thought of letting him out of her sight.

"I need to find my friend. I can't leave here without him." Will kissed her once more. "Don't worry. I'll be right back I promise."

Will turned and hurried away, waving over his shoulder. Christy smiled. For the first time in months, she let herself believe everything was going to be all right. Then she ducked back into the tent.

Chapter Forty-Five

The Western Front
Field Hospital

"Where are you going?" Jared called after Westcott.

"Just, stay!" Westcott snapped. "I will be back."

Jared growled, both hands running through his hair as he turned away. He held his handgun in an iron fist as his eyes moved back and forth searching the camp. A few of the nurses eyed him warily, and he knew it was because of the weapon. But he wasn't ready to put it down yet. Not until they were off the front.

Where'd that kid get to?

He strode between the tents, one of which was quickly being taken down. He nearly doubled over at the sight of bowls of blood and human remains being moved about. One nurse tossed the contents of one of the bowls right out of the tent, thick red gore splattering on his boots. Jared closed his eyes, his chest heaving for breath, then moved on.

He had no idea what could have distracted Will so completely that he would lose him in this small crowd, but there was no way he was going to leave him behind. Jared certainly didn't trust that Westcott was searching for anyone to help them. He was almost sure the man was going to leave them behind to fend for themselves.

Perhaps that would be for the best. Perhaps if they returned to Paris, they would have an even better chance of regrouping with their divisions or being assigned elsewhere. Jared stopped by one of the trucks, stomping the side of his boots against the tire to dislodge some clumps of mud from the soles. He knew it was pointless, more dirt would cake onto them, but he did it anyway.

He kept his eyes on the ground, not on the men struggling for life as they were loaded into trucks, not on the frightened looks in the nurses' eyes as they rushed around, looking for a ride. He didn't want to see those things. He just wanted some peace. He wanted one moment of silence before he was thrown back into the fray.

"Hey, you!" Someone slapped his shoulder.

Jared reared back, gun ready. The soldier held up his hands.

"Easy there, mate." The soldier's English accent thickened at the sight of the weapon and Jared's narrowed eyes. "We need drivers and seeing as you're just standing around like an idiot, thought you might want to make yourself useful."

"Fine," Jared grunted. "Why not?"

"You got this one?" The soldier thumbed the truck Jared had wiped his boots on.

"Sure."

"I'll get one of the nurses to help me load it. Don't go anywhere."

Then he was gone, hurrying away toward one of the tents. Jared leaned back against the truck, stuffing his hand into his pocket for his last cigarette. He turned the small roll-up over and over again in his fingers. He had been holding onto this one. With a deep breath, he lit it.

The ominous feeling he'd had on the border of the woods had been growing all the way into the camp. He had tried to convince himself it was nothing, that he was overreacting. He tried to convince himself it was because they were so close to safety, so close to being where they belonged.

But instinct was something Jared had learned not to underestimate. He took another long draw on the cigarette, tilting his head back as the smoke drifted from his lips. It floated upwards, toward the clouds overhead beginning to flood the sky. He rolled the cigarette back and forth between his pointer and thumb. A grin split his mouth as he wondered what Emma would say if she saw him. She had never approved of smoking, had called it a disgusting habit. But

Jared hadn't thought twice when Ralph had offered him one their first night in the trenches.

Jared looked down at the cigarette before tossing it into the dirt, smashing it beneath his shoe. Taking a step forward, he stopped suddenly, blinking slowly. He swore he saw her, just now ducking into one of the tents. It had to be her. He would recognize her no matter where she was, no matter what she wore or how she did her hair. It had to be her.

Jared started forward, his heart racing. Was he losing his mind? Had the woods driven him to insanity or was this happening right now, here in this moment?

The tent flap swung back suddenly, and Jared came to a skidding halt. Their eyes met from across the field.

"Emma?"

"I need help loading another truck." The soldier jogged up to her where she knelt.

Emma stretched her neck back and forth before she ducked back into the tent. Her mind was racing with everything that still needed to be done, her ears were always tuned to that ominous whistle, the only warning signal before the bombs struck. With trembling hands, she reached for a bag of supplies. Emma couldn't remember the last time she'd eaten, but it didn't matter.

What mattered was getting out of here. She'd made her decision, as hard as it had been. She was going to take Walter's advice. She would get back to Paris, gather her things and Christy, and she would be on the next boat home. She had done enough; she had suffered enough.

Jared was gone.

Her heart nearly stopped. Forming that thought in her head hadn't been easy. Nothing here was easy. But she would never be able to do anyone any good again if she were to die here. If Jared was out there somewhere, he would find his way home to her. Of that Emma was certain. What good would it do if she wasn't at home waiting for him?

"Take him first." Emma pointed to one of the men just as the doctor passed his removed limb to one of the bowls. "Make sure his wound is wrapped tight before you move him, though. Too many of them bleed out during transportation."

"I'll meet you outside, Emma," Margie said before hurrying out with a box of supplies.

Emma reached for a bag with a faded red cross stitched across the front of it. She ran her palm over the symbol that had made her and her colleagues a target. She never thought one little symbol could cause so much trouble.

Shaking her head, she turned, stepping back out of the tent. Emma had taken only a few steps before she stopped. He was standing across the field, eyes piercing her. The bag of supplies fell from her shaking hands.

His hair had grown out again, curling slightly over his ears and his face was shadowed with coarse stubble. Her hands covered her mouth as hot tears threatened on the edges of her eyes. He was filthy from head to foot, but there was no sign of injury. No physical sign of sustained wounds. He was whole, he was breathing … he was standing not one hundred feet away from her. His lips formed her name, but she couldn't hear him over the rumbling of the trucks.

More than anything she wanted to go to him, but her feet wouldn't move. It was too much. Could it be real? Could this be happening? Emma gasped for breath, her lungs aching as her head swayed back and forth, disbelieving.

"Jared!"

The shout rang out from across the camp, and Emma jumped, her entire being startled at the sound of his name. Her husband turned slightly, looking over his shoulder at a young man running across the field toward him, his hand raised and waving back and forth to get his attention.

That was when she heard it.

The whistle. Emma's heart nearly stopped at the terrifying sound. She had heard too many times, that shrill sound, the one that made the world slow down. Jared's entire body tensed; she knew he heard it too.

His every move was slowed as his head swung back to her, his eyes widening in terror. Emma opened her mouth, but her throat was suddenly dry. No words would come; she couldn't shout for him to stop. Her feet finally moved, her mind willing herself forward toward the man she loved and refused to lose again.

"*Emma!*" Her name burst forth from his lips as he surged forward, one hand reaching for her as if to scale the distance and yank her to safety.

Then she was flying, her feet lifting right off the ground and her twisting body propelled back. She felt the heat of the fire, heard the screams of her friends before she thundered to the ground. Her body slammed into the mud as flames engulfed her shoulder.

Darkness closed around her, and suddenly, the pain ceased.

THE LOST GENERATION

Chapter Forty-Six

Location: Unknown

"Do you remember when we first met?"

Her voice was a song, filling his ears with music and his heart with joy. He turned to her, holding out his hand, beckoning her to his side. But she didn't move. She simply smiled, reaching out to him in return. Their fingers were so close but never touched.

"I didn't think much of you then. I was so stuck up." Her laughter sent a shiver down his spine. "I was too proud to admit I was in love with you. I regret that time we fought, the time we spent pretending we agreed with our parents."

"It didn't last long." He chuckled.

"No. But it was long enough."

She took a step closer to him, sun glittering behind her head, illuminating her body with light. But with that step, the distance just seemed to grow between them. He frowned, not understanding. She always seemed to be just out of his reach, just an inch too far away for him to hold her.

"I would give anything to go back to those days. To hold you in my arms and tell you how I really felt. I never dreamed I could love someone the way I loved you."

"It's not over yet."

She just smiled her blonde hair rippling as her head swayed back and forth. Her mouth opened but formed no words. He wanted to kiss her, to pull her close and press his lips to hers. They were full and glittered with moisture, the same way they had on their wedding day. Her thin figure was draped in that same light blue dress, the one the nurses wore beneath their bloodstained aprons.

"I will always love you. Every day until I see you again, I will be falling deeper in love with you," she whispered.

"That's what you said to me the day I left," he murmured. "Why are you saying this to me now? It's over; we found each other. We can go home now."

Her smile trembled. Her blue eyes swam with tears she would not shed. How could she be so strong? The tips of her fingers touched his, and he closed his eyes. How he'd missed her; how he loved her!

"Until I see you again, my love." Her whisper echoed across the space between them. "I will hold you in my heart."

Again, the words she had spoken to him that day left her lips. When he opened his eyes ... she was gone.

"Soldier?" The voice was unfamiliar, feminine and strained. His brow furrowed as the dream faded away into darkness. His eyes fluttered, giving him a moment of light, a glimpse of the nurse leaning over him.

"Doctor, he's waking up." Her voice sounded far away even as she sat beside him.

Will shifted his body on the uncomfortable cot. His sweat-soaked clothes made his skin itch. He moaned as sudden pain shot up from his wrist into his shoulder. A gentle hand pressed his shoulder, keeping him still.

"Don't move. You sustained a serious injury, soldier. You're much more fortunate than so many others." Her accent grew thick as she stroked his hair, soothing the tension from his entire body with her gentle touch.

Injury? What was she talking about? He wasn't injured. He would know if he was injured, wouldn't he? Will forced his eyes open. They felt bruised, stinging when he tried to focus on the woman.

She smiled at him, her cheeks flushed and her hair clinging to her forehead with sweat.

"There now," she murmured. "What a strong soldier you are. You'll be going home in the morning."

"Home?" he rasped.

"That's right, love."

"I don't understand … where's my wife?" He swung his head from side to side.

The tent was small, smaller than most. There weren't many cots. Perhaps, at the most, there were fifty injured, some of them nurses. But he didn't see the one he searched for, the only one he wanted to see right now.

"I'm sure she's waiting for you at home," the nurse cooed.

"No!" He shook his head. "She was nursing the wounded at the field hospital. She was here. Please, her name is Christy Garvin."

"Christy …" The nurse stood up slowly. "I'm sorry, soldier. I will try to find her. In all of the confusion, well, some of us were separated."

"Please, I …" He stopped, raising his right arm.

His eyes widened at the sight of the bloody bandage. His sleeve had been cut away, leaving his arm bare and cold. Will slowly lowered his arm again, his eyes never leaving his wound. The nurse knelt beside the cot again, pressing her palm to his forehead and grabbing up his left hand.

"I'm sorry. I was hoping … when the morphine is working, you'll feel just a dull pain. I wanted the doctor to come and tell you. It's never easy when you wake up different. I'm sorry."

"My … my hand!" he choked. "You took my hand?"

"Please, you must stay calm."

"No!" He shook his head, starting to sit up. "Where's Jared?"

"Jared?" She shook her head, confused. "Who's Jared?"

"There aren't enough people here." Will sat up, pushing against her hands as she tried to restrain him. "I don't see them … I need to find them!"

"Please, you must lie still." She pressed him back into the cot. "I will find your wife and your friend. But you must rest. You must let yourself begin to heal."

"Please hurry!" he gasped. "I need them, both of them. I need—"

A scream filled the tent suddenly, a female shriek that sent chills running up and down his spine. Will looked in the direction of the sound to see a woman, a nurse, struggling against the grip of another nurse. A doctor rushed over to help as the wounded woman thrashed on the cot.

His own nurse rushed away to assist. Will closed his eyes, pressing his left hand against his eyes. This had to be part of his dream; this couldn't be real. He wouldn't accept that it was going to end this way, he just wouldn't.

This was all a dream.

The first thing she saw was red. Emma blinked slowly, adjusting to the dim light in the tent. Her shoulder was on fire, a bandage wrapped tightly around her chest, holding her arm captive. Squinting up at Margie, she reached out her free hand to her friend.

"Oh, thank God!" Margie grabbed her hand, pressing her lips against Emma's knuckles. "You gave us quite a scare."

"What happened?"

"The hospital was hit. More casualties than we've suffered in a long time. You were hit in the shoulder." Margie reached down for something.

When she came back up, she was holding a shimmering piece of shrapnel. Emma reached for it, taking it between her fingers.

"We pulled this out of your shoulder," Margie said. "It's going to leave quite a scar, but no real damage was done, sweetheart. You're going to be just fine."

"Where's Jared?" Emma lifted her head, groaning as her temples throbbed.

"Lie back, dear." Margie stroked her hair. "You know Jared is somewhere on the front fighting. That's why you came here, remember?"

"No." Emma shook her head. "He was at the hospital; I saw him right before the explosion. He called my name. I saw him ..."

Margie removed her hand and sat back.

"Em, are you sure?" she whispered.

"Of course I'm sure." Emma closed her eyes, the effects of the morphine beginning to fade behind some semblance of clarity.

"But Em ... all of the survivors ..." Margie stopped, rubbing a hand against her chest.

"What?" Emma frowned, looking up at her again. "Margie what about the survivors?"

Her friend wouldn't look into her eyes. Margie shifted beside the cot, discomfort twisting her face.

"Tell me." Emma reached for her, and Margie took her hand.

"Emma ... as far as we could tell, all of the survivors are in this tent."

Emma blinked once, twice and then looked away, searching the bodies filling the tent. There had to be fifty cots set up, including hers and only a handful of nurses and doctors were wandering around between them. Walter was one of them, stopping to observe one of the wounded. But the others ... Emma shook her head, her eyes widening as she jerked back around to look at Margie.

"No!" She shook her head. "This ... this can't be everyone. Where's Christy?"

Margie bowed her head.

"Margie O'Brian, you look me in the eye." Emma sat up, grabbing Margie's arm in an iron grip. "Where's Christy?"

"Emma, I'm sorry." Margie sobbed, her shoulders arching forward. "She ... she was still in the tent when it happened. There was ... was nothing ..."

Margie sucked in a long breath, her hand circling Emma's wrist.

"There was nothing anyone could have done. The bomb hit the hospital so suddenly ... she couldn't have been in any pain."

"No!" Emma shook her head. "I … I promised her … no! No, no, *no*!"

Emma screamed falling back against the cot as the horrible truth washed over her. She shook from head to foot, struggling against Margie's hold, screaming until her lungs ached, until her body flailed with the pain of it all. This wasn't real! It couldn't be happening!

"Emma, stop!" Walter appeared at her other side.

"Do we have a sedative?" Margie's voice echoed in her ears. "Anything to calm her down?"

"Don't!" Emma clawed at Walter's shirt, pulling him down close to her. "I don't want anything. Do not take this pain away from me. I need to feel this."

"I won't." Walter grabbed her face in both hands. It was then she noticed that his neck was bandaged. Fresh blood seeping through the dirty cloth and his right eye was swollen, nearly shut. The explosion had left its mark on him. "But you have to lie still, or you'll open your wound. Can you do that? Can you let Margie share the burden?"

Emma's face crumbled, hot tears flowing down her cheeks. He kissed her forehead, and another hoarse scream rose up from the center of her chest. This wasn't how it was supposed to be, this wasn't how her life was supposed to end. Jared was supposed to be at her side. Christy was supposed to be on a boat safely on her way home.

This wasn't how it was supposed to be.

Emma quieted, her fingers groping at his shoulders, searching for comfort. He leaned back suddenly, putting space between them. Emma looked into his eyes as he rubbed away her tears, smoothing back her dirty hair.

"That's my girl," Walter soothed. He smiled, passing her to Margie. "Rest and heal. You're going home, Em."

The last piece of her soul broke as she fell limp into Margie's arms.

Chapter Forty-Seven

Aboard Ship

The ceiling was dripping.

Emma stared at the blackness overhead, the drip falling right past her temple into a puddle beside her cot. There were soldiers on either side of her, drowsy with drugs she had refused to take. The pain was horrible, but not unbearable. Nothing compared to the things she'd seen and the hurt she had attempted to ease.

She shifted and icy daggers stabbed her shoulder. Emma moaned, biting her lip hard to keep the sound at bay. The last thing she needed was for Margie to hear her in pain and come hurrying over with morphine.

She readjusted the bandage around her right arm. It was tight across her chest to keep her arm up and bent across her ribs to support her shoulder. Emma hadn't looked at the scar yet; she didn't want to. She didn't care how big it was, or how long it would take to fully heal once she returned home. None of that mattered.

What mattered was that she was going home empty. What mattered was that she was leaving and had achieved no peace of mind. There was nothing waiting for her back there, not even the possibility of hope.

For the thousandth time since she was loaded onto the ship, she asked herself why she had come here in the first place. She should never have made the journey, despite how much she wanted to find her husband. It had left her emptier than before she left. Perhaps staying at home would have been more bearable.

All Emma wanted to do now was die. She wished the explosion had killed her. She wished she hadn't seen him so she could pretend he was still out there. She could pretend they were forcing her to go home because of her injuries. She could pretend there was still a chance her husband would come home to her.

"Are you all right?" the soldier beside her asked.

Emma turned her head; her cheek pressed into the thin mattress. He didn't even look at her. He simply continued to stare at the ceiling as she had done. He wasn't wearing a shirt. A thin woolen blanket covered most of his bare torso. His right arm, stubbed at the wrist, was wrapped tight in bandages. He had been washed recently; the scent of soap was still fresh in his hair. It was a welcome change from the rank odors floating about below decks.

"Yes. You?" she replied.

"I lost my hand and my wife. So no, I'm not." He turned to look her in the eye.

"I ... I know you," she whispered, lifting her shoulders to rise up slightly. "You were the one who helped me load that truck at the hospital."

"Yeah, I remember."

"Did that happen in the explosion?" she asked, gesturing to the stub of his wrist.

"Yes."

"You said you lost your wife ...?"

"She was a nurse there." The young man closed his eyes, swallowing hard. "She shouldn't have been there in the first place. She should have been safe at home, away from the fighting. It's all my fault."

"You can't blame yourself," Emma rasped, fighting the tears. "I lost my husband too. I haven't seen him in four years, and just when I saw his face again for the first time ..."

He was staring at her, unblinking. Silence grew between them as Emma watched him in return.

Finally, she spoke. "You never told me your name."

He turned back to stare at the ceiling in silence, reaching with his remaining hand to catch one of the drips in his palm.

"Will," he answered quietly.

Emma's stomach dropped. Her throat dried out suddenly. When she spoke again, her voice squeaked, "Will? Will what?"

"Garvin. Why?" he asked, frowning at her.

Emma gasped, covering her mouth. He'd said he lost his wife. He'd said she'd been a nurse in the camp, and it was all his fault that she was there in the first place. Emma searched for air as more than just physical pain overwhelmed her.

Realization dawned in Will's eyes as he sat up, resting on his elbows, his face twisting.

"You're Emma aren't you?" he asked. "She mentioned your name right before … right before we separated."

"Yes." Emma was suddenly sick.

"She said you saved her life," Will murmured.

Emma shook her head. "No," she said. "No, I didn't … she saved mine."

Will turned onto his side, reaching out his left hand to her. Emma took it, letting him crush her fingers in his strong grip. Tears were falling from his lashes.

"I'm glad to meet you, Emma."

"I'm glad to meet you, Will," she replied.

They stayed like that, staring into each other's eyes. They didn't need to talk. There was no need for words. Emma knew everything she needed to know, just by looking at him. The person who stood between them would always be there, an ever-present thought, a ghost in their midst, an image in their eyes.

Christy's presence filled the space between them. Together they held onto her memory. Emma's eyes grew heavy, her heart rate slowing as she felt peace creeping up on her for the first time in what seemed a lifetime.

Together they fell asleep, and when Margie passed on her rounds, they slept peacefully hand in hand.

Will stood by the railing of the boat, leaning over to watch the foam splash up against the sides. He lifted his face to the sky. The salty air sprinkled his face with moisture, threatening to dislodge his hat. He wanted this moment to last forever. He didn't want to step off the ship. He didn't want to face his family.

How would he tell her parents? How would he explain that because their daughter loved a boy they disapproved of, she was now dead? How could he face life? Will reached for the bandage around his wrist, overwhelmed by the emptiness he felt there. Sometimes, when he closed his eyes, he could still feel his hand. The pain would wake him in the middle of the night, the feeling that he was bleeding out from his wrist turning his dreams into nightmares.

His heart continued its downward spiral, stabbing the inside of his chest with the shards. It would have been better if the explosion had ripped him apart and he had succumbed to his injuries or if he had fallen victim of infection and died on the trip home.

Will reached into his pocket for the packet of morphine he'd lifted off Nurse O'Brian. He licked his lips, wanting the sweet relief it offered. He licked his finger and stuck it into the package. He sucked the white powder off his finger, not caring if someone saw him. With a deep sigh, he returned the packet to its hiding place.

"Hey." Emma's voice brought him around. "How are you feeling?"

"Fine, nurse." The corner of his mouth curved up. "And you? How's your shoulder?"

"Healing." She adjusted her sling.

"What are you going to do?" He turned fully to her now, tilting his head to the side.

"What do you mean?" Emma stared down at the water, tracing her finger back and forth along the railing.

"When you get home ... what are you going to do?"

Emma was silent for a few moments. Her entire body rippled with trembling, but he knew she wasn't cold. It was the thought they were both getting closer to home that made her shudder. Will had never thought answering that question would be so hard. But if she were to turn around and ask him the same, he wasn't sure he'd be able to answer either.

"I suppose, I will try to pick up the pieces," Emma finally said. "I just ... I don't know how I will be able to step over the threshold of my house, the house my husband gave to me for our anniversary."

"I'm sorry." He bowed his head. "I shouldn't have pried."

"That's all right," she answered. "What about you? What are you going to do when you reach New York?"

Will looked down, his hand pressing the journal beneath his coat. Looking into Emma's eyes, he said, "I think ..." He hesitated, emotion threatening to stop his breath. "I think I'm going to write their story."

He turned to look out over the horizon. Blue waves glittered back at him as far as the eye could see.

"I'm going to tell the world ... everything."

THE LOST GENERATION

STAGE 5:
ACCEPTANCE

THE LOST GENERATION

Chapter Forty-Eight

Canada
November 1918

"She's been standing there for twenty minutes."

"Has she said anything at all?"

"Not a word. Not since we heard the news. It's worse than when she got back. I don't know what to do."

"Have you tried talking to her?"

"It sounds silly, but I'm almost afraid to. She just ... when Nathan came home with the news, she went white as a sheet and went to the window and has been standing there ever since."

Emma hugged her ribs as she listened to her sister and mother talking. They thought they were being so quiet, but she heard every word of concern flowing from their lips. Her shoulder throbbed. It always throbbed when she thought about the war, when every little reminder crept up on her. The stitches had healed nicely, and she hadn't been back to see a doctor in weeks. But the ache from her damaged muscles was going to take more than a few weeks to heal.

She shuddered, trying to tune out her relatives. They had all gathered around her when she returned home, offering their support and comfort. But Emma had wanted none of it. She had just wanted to be alone to grieve.

"She's still refusing to wear anything but black?" Her mother's voice was anything but a whisper in the next room.

"Yes." Laura was trying harder as she bounced her crying baby in her arms. "She said having a ceremony without a body is out of the question, but she's going to wear black for each and every person she lost."

"That could be …"

"Months? Years? I know. She just … she refuses to recover from it, Mother. She refuses to move on." Laura's heavy sigh vibrated in the air. "I don't know what to do. I've asked her if she wants to move back to America with me, to start again, but she hasn't given me an answer."

"That would probably be best," Grace agreed. "This house holds only bad memories for her now. This was not the way I wanted my daughter to start her life here. It's not the way I wanted either of your lives to turn out."

"I know," Laura said, her voice trembling. "It wasn't our plan either."

Emma stared out at the same thing she'd been looking at since hearing the news. The garden. She could picture it in the summertime, fresh green grass, and moist brown soil, her daffodils rising up out of the ground and reaching for the sun. Warmth filled her stomach at the thought but was quickly replaced with a weight she could not shake. He had spread daffodil petals on their bedroom floor. He had planted them out front because she loved them. He had placed her grandmother's rug in their living room, the first piece to enter the house.

He had given her his name and she would never, could never give it up for another. Emma turned swiftly away from the window, grabbing at the doorknob.

"Emma!"

She ignored her mother's call as she hurried down the steps. An icy breeze sliced into her skin.

She didn't care that her mother would scold her for going outside without a coat. She needed to get out of the house, away from them, away from the memories. They had had so little time together in that house, but what hurt the most were all the dreams she'd had for them in that house—dreams that would never come true.

Dreams she no longer wanted to come true, even if he were standing beside her right now. After what she'd seen, after what she was sure he had seen, how could either of them go back? But to face this alone … it was worse. To stand alone in the field where she'd dreamed their children would play—it was unbearable.

Emma sat down on the ground, hugging her knees to her chest. The rough material of her black dress itched her ankles. This was the dress she only wore to funerals; the one dress that was always buried in the closet, out of sight. Emma had experienced funerals only a handful of times in her life. She avoided them. Emma felt her grief so deeply, it could kill her. If she let it rule her life, then she would never get out of bed in the morning. That feeling was creeping up on her now.

She remembered the day she met Jared. The way he'd looked at her when she walked into the kitchen. That ridiculous grin and those sparkling eyes …

"What are you doing?" she'd asked, her hands on her hips.

"Fixing Mrs. Nickel's pipes," he'd replied. "What are you doing?" He was lying perfectly at ease on her mother's kitchen floor, his ankles crossed, his elbows propping up his shoulders.

"I happen to live here." Emma had scrunched her nose as his sweaty stench reached her sensitive nostrils. "You stink. You do realize that right?"

"Hmm, seeing as how Mrs. Nickels is such a nice lady, I would have thought she would raise her daughter with manners." He leaned his head back under the sink. "I guess I was wrong."

"What makes you think you have any right to speak to me that way?"

"What, you think you're something special because you live here, and I'm just the poor handyman?" His head popped out again.

"Maybe. But maybe you shouldn't judge someone before you get to know them."

"Now there's the pot calling the kettle black."

Emma threw her head back and laughed.

"What's that about?" His brow arched.

"Oh, nothing. That's just something my grandmother used to say. Where did you learn to talk like an old lady?"

"From my grandmother." He winked at her.

"But you're right," she said with a shrug. "I was rude. My name's Emma Nickels."

"Jared Cote." He leaped to his feet, holding out his dirty hand.

Emma hesitated before she shook it.

"Now, about getting to know you better ... " He leaned close to her until she could feel his breath on her face. "How about I take you into town to that new restaurant that just opened up?"

Emma had tapped her finger against her chin a few times before grinning.

"Let me think ... " Tilting her head she thought for a moment and then she skipped around him, turning quickly to back toward the kitchen door. "Absolutely not."

Then she'd run away.

"Emma?"

She lifted her head, sniffling. Laura appeared beside her, settling down in the tall grass close to her shoulder. Emma wiped away her tears, forcing a smile.

"I'm fine," she whispered.

"No, you're not." Laura clamped her arms around Emma's shoulders "Neither of us are. We won't be fine, my children won't be fine, ever again."

Emma bowed her head.

"Em, I don't know what you saw over there, and I won't force you to tell me."

"I appreciate that, Laura."

"But I do want to help you, even though you insist you don't need any." Laura's temple touched hers. "You were there for me when Eddie first left. I missed you so much when we received the news that he died, but I understood why you couldn't come home. Well, you're here now and so am I. It's my turn to help you."

"Laura, you don't have to—"

"Yes, I do." Laura pressed two fingers to Emma's chin, turning her face so she would look at her. "You're my little sister, Em, and I love you. I hate seeing you struggle like this. We used to defend each other and help each other through everything when we were kids."

"I remember." Emma gripped her hand.

"We need that bond to be stronger than ever now." Laura pulled her closer. "Please, let me help you."

Emma bowed her head.

"The war isn't over," she murmured.

"No, but the Germans have surrendered, the fighting has stopped, and the men are coming home. It won't be long before everything is settled." Laura scooted around on her knees until they were face to face. "When it is, I want you to come home with me. Come live with me in Boston until you have enough saved for your own place again. Please, Em? We need each other."

Emma hesitated, looking over her shoulder at the house, but all she could see was her husband standing in front of the door, swinging her around on their first anniversary. Emma closed her eyes as her head dropped.

"I'll make arrangements to sell the house tomorrow."

Chapter Forty-Nine

East Hampton, New York
November 1918

"Thank you for coming."

Will stood at the sound of Mrs. Simmons's voice. He was wearing his uniform, as he had been for the past few months since coming home. It was like a second skin to him now. He couldn't imagine going back to regular clothes. He'd worn this uniform during some of the most defining moments of his life, and it kept him close to the people he had lost.

"Is Mr. Simmons—?"

"No. He's not here." Mrs. Simmons sat down across from him on the settee.

Will hesitated before taking his seat again, tucking his arm against his ribs. The packet he always kept close crinkled beneath his coat, but Mrs. Simmons didn't seem to notice the unusual sound coming from beneath his coat buttons.

"William, I would like to apologize for my husband." Mrs. Simmons folded her hands in her lap, her black satin dress shimmering in the light coming through the open curtains. "He treated you horridly when last we spoke. You can understand his grief more than most, I'm sure, but to throw out a man who has lost so much and who our daughter loved more than life itself ... it was a cruel thing for him to do."

"Mrs. Simmons, you don't need to explain anything. I understand." Will spoke to the floor, his heel tapping rapidly against the thick red rug.

"But I don't." Her words drew his gaze upward once again. "You came here that day to explain something to us. You came to tell us how she died, but he wouldn't let you and I ..."

Her voice broke, her cheeks reddening with the sudden rush of tears.

"I need to know what happened, William. Please." She stood suddenly, hurrying over to the desk in the corner.

Will watched as she pulled a small pamphlet from the drawer, one that Will recognized all too well.

"Your uncle printed these." She returned with it. "These stories of the war. At the end, you told the story of a nurse, one who came home with you on the boat. That wasn't Christy."

"No."

"But she knew Christy."

"Yes."

"Please finish the story, Will. Tell me what happened." She held out the pamphlet to him.

Will took it, running his thumb in a circle over the front. He sighed. Inside were the personal accounts of John Young, the stories he had written in his journal and addressed to his wife, Beth. He'd asked him to write the story, to give it to the world, and Will had. Every last thing he'd seen and done he had written in that pamphlet. His uncle published some in his newspaper, others he turned into short novels, like the old dime novels Will's mother used to love to read.

He looked into his mother-in-law's eyes again. He didn't want to tell this story, the story he relived every night in his dreams. Every night he asked himself why he let her out of his sight, why when he'd finally seen her again did he let her go back into the tent, away from him? It didn't make sense, and he couldn't blame anyone but himself for what happened after that.

"She was so brave, Mrs. Simmons." He finally found his voice again, forcing the words past his lips. "She learned so much about healing so she could save my fellow soldiers. Emma, the one on the ship with me, told me that she had more courage than most."

Mrs. Simmons head rose, her chest swelling with pride.

"I saw her right before she died. She accomplished what she went there to do. She found me." Will looked away. "They were packing up the hospital. They knew the attack was coming because it had happened before. It always happened. That was when we separated."

"You separated." Mrs. Simmons repeated.

"Yes. She went back into the tent to finish gathering supplies, and I went to look for my friend, Jared." Will forced himself to look her in the eye. "If I had stayed with her, then maybe we would both be alive ... or maybe we would both be dead. Either of those choices would have been better than the actual outcome of my actions."

"Oh, William." Mrs. Simmons hunched over, pressing a handkerchief to her mouth. She fell to her knees suddenly, reaching up both hands to cup his face in her palms. "Don't ever say that." She smiled even as the tears flowed down her cheeks. "Christy would be devastated to hear such words. You lived to tell this story, and that is most important. God sent you back to me to give me peace."

Will's eyes widened; he couldn't understand.

"My daughter died helping people. She was a hero, my darling boy. A hero, just like her husband." Mrs. Simmons stroked his hair. "You have given me more peace than you can possibly know."

She stood then, running from the room, her weeping echoing back to him. Will sat there for a moment, stunned at the result of his honesty. He had expected her to scream, to lash out at him, to blame him as much as he blamed himself. Instead, she'd listened to his story and seen only the strong daughter she had raised, the selfless young girl she had nurtured and brought up under this roof.

Will shot to his feet, striding out of the parlor. The thump of his boots echoed on the marble floor as he hurried to the front door. He stopped for a moment, feeling a pair of eyes on his back. Turning, he saw Annie standing on the stairs. Her red hair was pulled back in a tight bun and her blue eyes pierced him like knives. Her skin looked doubly pale against the black chiffon dress draping her little body.

Will put on his hat, wanting more than anything to say something to her but he knew it wouldn't do any good. He could see in her eyes that her father had poisoned her against him, unlike her mother. It didn't matter. He never wanted to come back to this house ever again.

He stormed out of the foyer, slamming the large door behind him with a resounding crack. Sweat was dripping down his temples by the time he reached his car; he quickly climbed inside. Reaching into his breast pocket, he yanked on the packet so hard it almost ripped.

Gingerly he lifted the flap, gently placing the packet on his thigh. He raised his hand to his lips, licking his finger before sticking it into the powder. He sucked the morphine away, then leaned his head back and closed his eyes, waiting for it to take effect.

He took some more, seeking oblivion. But it was not to come. A rap reverberated off the car window, and he jumped, turning sharply as he tossed the packet to the car floor. Roger Bourke stood there, grinning that ridiculous gap-toothed grin Will knew all too well.

He opened the car door, letting it swing.

"Roger, what are you doing in East Hampton?" he asked.

"Looking for you, my friend. Heard you were heading out here today and thought I would follow you out and drop in on my girl on the way home." Roger handed him an envelope. "I believe this is what you've been waiting for."

Will's eyes expanded as he snatched it, ripping it open to pull the letter out.

"You found her," he whispered.

Roger winked. "I found her," he repeated.

Will fell back against his seat, crumpling the letter in his hand as Roger walked away whistling. Will scrambled suddenly for his packet. Half the contents had fallen out onto the floor of the car, but he didn't care. He folded the packet with what remained inside, stuffing it and the letter back into his breast pocket. A soft curse left his lips as he fumbled one-handed with the gears. It had taken him a long time to learn how to operate this infernal machine with only his left hand, but he'd been determined not to become dependent on others to take him where he needed to go. The automobile finally sputtered to a start, and he sped away from the Simmons mansion, dust clouding behind the wheels. He wheezed, the letter burning his chest where it rested.

There was one thing he had to do, one more thing that had been weighing on his mind since he came home. The contents of the letter would lead him to her and, hopefully, to peace.

Chapter Fifty

Canada

Emma wrung out the cloth, splashing water back into the bucket as she straightened again to polish the windows. Her knuckles were red from the hot water. Since receiving an offer on her house, she'd scrubbed it from top to bottom. Her mother had told her ten times that she could stop cleaning now, but she had to keep busy.

She was about to give up one of her most important dreams for the future. She was letting go in order to search for new dreams, and it was harder than she thought it would be. Emma dropped the rag into the bucket, splashing more water over the rim. Not bothering to mop it up, she went to the kitchen in search of a glass of water.

She leaned over the sink to fill a glass. The water was cool against her tongue—just what she needed.

"Emma."

She gasped, spinning around, spilling the rest of her water on the floor. No one was there, no owner to the whispered voice, the voice that sounded so much like Jared's.

Slamming the glass down into the sink, she pressed her fingers to her temples. How long would she hear his voice? How long would he haunt her? Looking up she could picture him standing there, as he had the day he'd come home in uniform. She could still hear the click of her scissors as she trimmed his hair, his brown locks falling silently to the floor around her shoes.

Her hands twined together, the memory of his soft hair still present on her fingertips. Closing her eyes, she swore she could feel it even now. The way his hair smoothed beneath her touch, dry and soft after a recent wash. His face, rough with a week's growth of stubble, a beard he never let grow too long before he would shave it again.

Emma's stomach fluttered. When she opened her eyes, she was still alone. She knew her memories wouldn't bring him back, but she still prayed that one day she would open her eyes and there he would stand, even though she knew it was impossible.

Both Margie and Walter had insisted there had been no more survivors from the explosion. It was just not possible for someone to have survived and not make it onto one of the trucks to safety.

Emma's eye caught the newspaper sitting on the kitchen table. It was covered with news of the German surrender. Laura insisted they should keep this issue which brought the first good news in four years. The fighting had stopped. The weapons had been laid down. Now all that remained was for the negotiations to be completed, and it would be truly over.

"Emma!" Laura called, hurrying into the house, her baby on her hip. She reached out her free arm to take hold of Emma. "Mother told me the house already sold."

"Yes," Emma replied as she returned Laura's embrace before taking the baby. "Hello, Jude."

She cuddled the child, breathing deeply the sweet scent of his baby-soft hair.

"I have three months to get my things together and prepare for the move. I need to figure out what to leave behind."

"Perhaps some of the living room furniture," Laura suggested. "I know a wonderful place in New York that sells furniture. You'd just love it, and we could send for a few things."

"If I'm staying with you, I won't have to worry about that until I can afford new things," Emma said.

"That's true." Laura looked her up and down. "Em … when are you going to stop wearing black?"

"When I start to forget." Emma handed her nephew back to Laura. "When I see the reason for it all. When I'm able to open my eyes in the morning and smile at the memory of my husband."

She turned away, straightening her apron as her eyes fell on the newspaper. She handed it over to her sister. "Get rid of this," she whispered. "I'm tired of looking at it."

"Emma—"

"I have to get back to work."

She turned on her heels and marched into the living room.

Emma stared up at the cross hanging on the back wall of the church. Her heart beat unevenly in her chest as tears streamed her cheeks. Once she had found comfort sitting here, in the pew she used to share with her husband. Once this place was a source of strength. But now she felt no peace in this place, no comfort or love. Her palm pressed into the empty space beside her, where Jared would've sat with her today.

The door to the church creaked behind her, but she didn't look. She knew it was the reverend, coming to prepare the church for the evening services. He was holding a special vigil to honor the men of their community who had given their lives for their country. Emma didn't want to come, but something had drawn her inside this afternoon as she passed, compelling her to enter.

"Emma?" Reverend Haywood's voice resounded in the empty church. She looked up at him, tilting her head. He looked older than when last she saw him, his hair whiter, his eyes circled by wrinkles. He stood there in his black coat and white collar, Bible clutched tightly in his hand.

Emma remembered her mother once telling her that he didn't go anywhere without his Bible. It was as though it was a part of him, attached to his hand, his shield against the world that would destroy his faith. Emma wished, for a moment, she had such a shield.

"Is something wrong, my dear?"

Emma didn't look at him as he cautiously sat down.

"I don't know why I'm here, Reverend," she whispered. "I didn't think I'd ever come back here again. I just ... don't see the point of it."

"Perhaps you were called here today," Reverend Haywood murmured, resting his hand on hers. "Perhaps God wanted you here."

"Just as He wanted my husband to fight a war that was not his own?" Emma looked at him now, staring into those dark, compassionate eyes. "Just as He wanted Jared to die and leave me all alone?"

"We're never alone, Emma. You know that." Reverend Haywood took her hand gently in his own. "You have suffered much for one so young, but God's greatest gift to us is that through the suffering, He makes us stronger. He shows us His grace."

"What grace was given me?" Emma asked, shaking her head. The sting of her tears was hot against her lashes. "What purpose was served, Reverend?"

"God has tested you, Emma. He has tested your faith, but remember, He never gives you more than you can bear."

"How can I believe that? How can I trust a God who would take my husband, take my *life*, away?"

"Your life is your own, Emma. It's up to you to decide how you live it now." Reverend Haywood smiled, defining the crinkles at the corners of his eyes. "God has offered you a chance. Your faith has been stolen from you, but He holds it out to you once more. That is why you are here, isn't it? Inside, in your heart, you long for the faith you once had."

"I long for the peace my husband gave me. He is the one who nurtured my faith, he is the one who kept me strong." Emma gasped, fighting the tears that overflowed down her cheeks.

"You can have it again, Emma," Reverend Haywood gently replied as he stood. "If you cannot find comfort in my words, then think of this. What would Jared wish for you now? What would he tell you to do?"

Emma closed her eyes, bowing her head. When she looked again, the reverend had left, but on the bench beside her sat his Bible.

Turning back, she looked up at the cross again, a flicker of warmth igniting in her heart, a flame that had long been extinguished.

"Once you're saved, there's no undoing it." Jared's voice whispered in her ear. *"Jesus will just keep coming back to save you over and over again, no matter what, and you'll run right back into His arms because it's in your heart to do so. So we don't have to worry, Emma. There's nothing we can do about it. He's chosen you and me. He's chosen all of us."*

Emma picked up the reverend's Bible and pressed it to her heart.

Chapter Fifty-One

Lancashire, England
The Young Farm
November 1918

Beth looked up from stirring the stew simmering on the top of her stove. Frowning, she set the spoon aside and moved to the kitchen window. Leaning as far as she could over the counter, she called, "Melody! Button your brother's coat, please!" Her breath steamed in the cold air.

"Yes, Mama!" Melody waved before catching up with her brother, pulling him around to face her. George wiggled in her hold as Melody ordered him to stand still while she struggled with the buttons.

Beth shook her head, watching them for a few minutes more before she returned to her dinner. Melody was still yelling at George; she could hear her from across the yard. It wouldn't be long now until the ground was covered with a layer of pure white snow, sprinkling from the heavens to announce the first days of Christmas.

John loved the way their fields looked, covered in snow. He would chop their own tree to bring into the house, filling each room with strong pine scent, while she did her best to combat the smell with fresh baked cookies.

Beth rubbed the ache in her chest, trying to smooth out the knot there. Ever since her mother's last visit before returning to London to be with Ruth, Beth had been struggling to hold her own. She remained strong for her children, though nights had consisted of soaking her pillows with her grief. Each day was a battle, but she was fighting it. She had to ... for her little ones.

The Germans had surrendered—cause for celebration. The war was finally coming to an end. But still no word from her husband, or anyone who had possibly been with him during the fighting. If he was alive, he would have contacted her by now. If he was alive, he would be coming home to her.

Beth looked at the picture again. She'd had the frame replaced after cracking the glass in the first one. She looked away, not wanting to go to that place again. She couldn't let her children see such a scene nor could she let them see, or even sense, her devastation.

The stew bubbled in the pot. Beth moved it to the back of the stove, dipping her spoon into the liquid to test it. It burned her tongue, and she winced, but then she smacked her lips, the strong herbs filling her mouth with delight. Happy with her dinner, she smiled then turned to set the table.

She was about to call to her daughter when Melody came barreling through the front door. "Mama there's a man outside!" she announced. "He's wearing a uniform like Daddy's!"

Beth's head snapped up, her heart leaping against her chest. She found herself suddenly frozen in place, unable to do anything but stare at John's picture. It had been so long since she'd seen him. Could Melody have mistaken her father for a stranger? Was it John standing outside, coming back to her?

Beth was terrified. She couldn't look out the door; she couldn't even move her feet in that direction. Melody and George were tugging on her dress, urging her to come outside.

"Come on, Mum. He's waiting!" Melody insisted.

"What wrong, Mama?" George's chubby cheeks formed red apples when he smiled.

"Nothing, darling." Beth picked him up, holding onto him as though her life depended on it. "I'm fine."

"Come *on*, Mum!" Melody yanked once more on her dress before running back outside.

Beth gasped for breath, her feet shuffling against the floor as she made her way to the door. Keeping her head down, she stepped out the door after her daughter. But when she looked up, her hopes were shattered, and a different kind of fear swallowed her heart. The soldier removed his hat as soon as she met his gaze, tucking it beneath his right arm ... the sleeve that was cuffed and pinned where his hand used to be. Beth hid her disappointment as best she could, quickly closing the distance between them.

"Can I help you?" she asked.

"You're Elizabeth Young?" He swallowed loudly. "I'm at the right house, aren't I?"

"You are. What can I do for you?" Beth hugged her son closer, not letting him down even when he wiggled.

"My name is Will Garvin." He held out his left hand.

Beth took it carefully, forcing her eyes to remain on his face and not on his opposite wrist.

"Will Garvin ..." she said hoarsely, the vision of a beautiful blonde-haired girl, cuddling close to her in Ruth's basement flashing past her eyes.

"I've come here to give you something." Will reached into his breast pocket but didn't reveal what he clutched there. Beth just stared at him, unable to speak, unable to tell him she already knew who he was. "First, let me start by saying that I ... I knew John."

Beth stiffened at the sound of his name. Will's hand came out of his pocket empty again, forming a fist at his side.

"He and I went missing together with another private in his unit, Jared Cote."

The familiar name rang in her ears. That was the private she'd been searching for, the one whose wife she'd written to, to give the young woman hope.

"You went missing ..." Beth repeated, her throat suddenly parched. "But you're here ... and he's not."

Will bowed his head.

"You've come to tell me what happened," Beth whispered.

She lowered her son to the ground, letting him run away to play with his sister. Will was watching her children, the pain in his eyes mirroring her own when he looked at them. Beth wiped her sweaty palms against each other, forcing air into her lungs.

"Why don't you come inside?" She gestured toward the door.

Before he could answer, she turned and hurried back into her house. She heard him following her, the sound of his boots thumping the walk almost ominous. She stopped in the doorway, motioning for him to step past her and take a seat. Will cleared his throat, tapping his hand against the table.

"Now." Beth sat down across from him, folding her hands on the table. "You came here to tell me what happened to my husband."

"Yes." Will nodded, refusing to look her in the eye.

"I'm ready, Mr. Garvin. Please don't make me wait any longer. I've waited these past two years to hear from him, to find out what happened to him."

Will shifted in his chair and then leaned in, both arms on her table. He didn't start until he gathered the courage to look her in the eye again.

"We were fighting in the trenches together the day we went missing ..."

Her face was stained with tears. Tears he had caused. Will was sweating, his nerves stretched thin. His body ached from tension as he finished his story. Beth simply stared at him, not a sound slipping from her lips. Silent tears continued to flow down her face.

Will had never seen anyone so strong as the woman sitting before him. She seemed to stare right through him. No hysterical weeping. No screams of rage or grief. Just tears, pure and clear teardrops making her fair skin glitter like crystals.

"I can't tell you he wasn't in pain. That would be a lie," Will said softly, reaching for her hand. "But I can tell you that courage is stronger than anything else out there, even morphine. John was the bravest man I knew. Even with his pain, he was strong."

Beth bowed her head.

"I know it doesn't comfort you for me to tell you he was a hero. He wasn't supposed to be my hero; he was supposed to be yours."

"He was." Beth looked up at him, a small smile teasing the corners of her lips. "He was my hero long before he left. He will be my hero until the day I die."

She pressed his hand between both of hers.

"Thank you for coming so far from your home to tell me this. Thank you for giving me peace."

Will lowered his gaze.

"I wanted to, for you and your children. But I wanted to do it also for John ... and for me. I know it was selfish, but I wanted you to know. I don't sleep. Every time I turn around I see him and Jared and ... and my Christy."

Beth gasped, the first sound of grief she'd made since he started his story. She bent over the table, her hand pressed to her mouth. Will tugged the journal loose, placing it on the tabletop. He slid it across to her, keeping his palm pressed against it a moment longer.

"Everything he wrote in this journal he wrote to you. He asked me to share it with the world." Will tapped it. "Every entry is addressed to you. I have kept my promise to him. I have shared this story with the world. He would want you to have this now. There are things in this journal that are for your eyes alone."

He stood suddenly.

"You're leaving?" She looked up at him, surprise widening her eyes.

"You should be alone when you open it." He put on his hat. "I've done what I came here to do. I've brought enough grief to your house."

He turned and made his way toward the door when her hand clamped around his sleeve. Gently, she reached up on tiptoe to kiss his cheek.

"You've brought me closure," she whispered in his ear. "For that, I will be forever grateful, Will Garvin."

His eyes shuttered closed and then he pulled away, rushing out of the house, unable to bear another moment in this sea of memories. He had brought peace to Christy's mother and now to John's wife—peace to everyone but himself.

The packet of morphine burned in his pocket as the desire to relieve his pain grew once more. Will crushed the packet in his palm, aching for the oblivion it offered as he strode down the lane and out of sight of John Young's home.

Beth watched him go. She could see the pain in his stance, the way he walked. She wished she could have helped him better. She wished she could have eased his hurt the way he had eased hers. Knowing what had happened to her husband, knowing he had been left with no choice but to give himself for his friends … somehow it helped. It hadn't been for nothing; it had not been in vain.

She returned to the table, that worn black book screaming at her in the silence. Beth sat down, her trembling hands reached for the cover. Her breath grew shallow as she quickly turned over the cover, staring down at the first page.

Dearest Beth,

I had not thought to write anything in this book. I did not want to put down on paper the torture of war, the grief. But I find myself trapped in the woods, unaware of my surroundings, lost in a sea of trees with two men. One man has fought beside me for the past three years, the other is young and inexperienced in war.

I will do whatever it takes to keep them alive, my love. I will do whatever I must to see that they make it home to their loved ones, as I intend to make it home to you. The woods grow dark now, Beth, and I cannot help but remember how afraid Melody was of the dark. I am sure by now you have taught her there is nothing to fear in the shadows. That the Lord is with her and will chase away the demons that feed her terror.

I wish you were here to tell me the same, my darling. For the first time since my childhood, I fear the monsters that lurk in the dark …

A single teardrop soaked into the page, smearing one of the words. Beth sat back with a sigh, pressing the journal to her heart. Her neck arched back; her tears fell down her temples and into her hair. Her heart slowed, anxiety and fear subsiding behind the truth of what had happened.

She finally had her answers. She finally knew what happened to her husband. John had left her one last gift that she could carry for the rest of her life. His thoughts and prayers, his last words before he was taken from this world. His unwavering faith in God which he poured onto the pages of this little book. Beth smiled, staring up at the ceiling.

Outside her children laughed, reminding her why she got out of bed every morning without him, and that John had left her more than just his words. He'd left her his legacy, two little images of himself to fill her life. Beth would never be without him.

He was in her and their children, and he always would be. She hadn't lost him when he left. John promised her that he would always be with her, even when he was gone. She had spoken those words and forgotten.

What she hadn't realized these past years was that he'd kept his promise. Until this moment, she hadn't realized that he had been ever present in her life. Joy filled her as she hugged the journal tighter to her chest, her lips forming the words that were bursting from her heart.

"Thank you, my love."

THE LOST GENERATION

Chapter Fifty-Two

Canada

The post office. It used to be one of her favorite places. As Emma stepped inside, she couldn't help feeling that things had changed. Because if she was honest with herself, this was where it all began. The fear, the not knowing. She used to come here to visit with Miss Stein where she sat in her place behind the counter. She used to have long conversations with Mr. Rose. Emma was one of the only people he would talk to, one of the few he didn't just grunt at when he passed them on the street.

Her mind raced back to that horrible day, a day that seemed so long ago now, when Miss Stein had handed her that telegram. She remembered how afraid her mother was of telegrams, how they terrified her even to this day. She hadn't understood her mother's fear then, but she understood it now.

Emma looked around the small room now, where thousands of letters exchanged hands every week. She used to love this place. She watched Mrs. Johnson, smiling as she handed a pie to Miss Stein in exchange for her morning mail. She caught sight of Mr. Rose in the corner, skimming through the morning paper and puffing smoke rings from his pipe. Emma and Miss Stein's eyes collided, and the woman smiled. It was a smile Emma had come to recognize, not the usual smile Miss Stein gave her in days past. This smile mirrored the pity she saw in the eyes of every friend she passed on the street.

Emma turned, tempted to leave, her hand trembling as she pressed it to the doorknob. She heard the click of the telegraph, bringing urgent news to some poor family in town. Emma's eyes fluttered closed, and she reached for her shoulder, feeling the pain slice through her flesh. As she gripped it, she reminded herself that this moment was real. Her wound throbbed beneath the pressure of her thumb, and relief washed through her. Pain was the only thing she understood these days. Pain was the only thing that made sense.

God, I know You're there. Give me the strength to face the day.

Drawing her sweater tighter around her waist, she turned back, holding her head up as she took a step closer to the counter. This was where her world had crumbled all around her. But she would face it; she would draw strength from the memory; she would not let their pity weaken her.

Emma stepped right up to the counter, resting her hands atop it and forcing a smile.

"Do you have anything for me this morning, Miss Stein?" She asked, tilting her head, letting her braid fall against her collarbone.

"Yes, Emma, I believe I do." Miss Stein reached beneath the counter, pulling out a small stack of letters. "You must have made many friends in France."

"Why do you say that?" Emma accepted the mail, looking down without really reading the script on the front of each envelope.

"Some of those are postmarked from overseas … Ireland, England … all of them look like feminine handwriting, and I didn't want to pry, but I'm sure they are from some of your nurse friends."

"You're probably right." Emma tapped the letters on the counter, straightening them in her hands. "Thank you, Miss Stein. I will see you next week."

She turned to go.

"Emma, dear." Mr. Rose stopped her.

Emma closed her eyes for a moment, wishing she had gone unnoticed by the man. Of all the days for him not to be engrossed with his paper, it would have to be today. It would have to be on her first visit to the post office since receiving the telegram.

"Yes, Mr. Rose," she said as she released the breath she was holding. She turned to him with yet another forced smile.

"I hear you're leaving us." He shifted, leaning back into the wall.

"I am. My sister asked me to move back to America with her, and I agreed. The house has already been sold."

"That is a shame." Mrs. Johnson joined the conversation. "We will miss you. You were a great help to the hospital I hear."

"Some things just have to come to an end." Emma's chest tightened at her own words. "Some things aren't meant to be, I suppose."

"You are certainly right about that, my dear." Mrs. Johnson touched her arm as she passed. "We will see you before you leave, won't we?"

Emma turned and watched the woman leave before she even had a chance to answer. The scent of fresh blueberry pie filled the post office in Mrs. Johnson's wake making Emma's mouth water. She licked her lips, closing her eyes for a moment. Mr. Rose's hand on her shoulder brought her back around.

"Not all things have to come to an end, my girl," he commented, waving his pipe at her.

"Sometimes we don't have a choice in the matter, Mr. Rose." Emma's voice dropped to a whisper.

"That's true, but it doesn't mean you have to give up hope."

"I have held onto hope for too long, Mr. Rose. It's time to move on."

"I suppose you're right, Emma." He pinched her chin between finger and thumb. "Take care of yourself, dear."

"You do the same, sir." She kissed his wrinkled cheek.

Emma hurried out of the post office before anyone else could say something to keep her there. She gulped in the fresh air, desperate for relief from the horrible tightness in her stomach. Emma's stitches stretched against her skin, pulling until it ached. She rubbed them again. Laura had been such a wonderful help during her healing, massaging her wound every day and helping her exercise her shoulder.

Her warm breath turned into a white cloud before her face, the cold air threatening snow. Emma rubbed her arms, her letters crumbling slightly between her fingers as she hurried down the street. Her heels clicked loudly in her ears as she quickened her pace toward home. Laura had told her that walking to town was a bad idea in this weather, but Emma didn't care. She enjoyed the cold. She enjoyed the way it stabbed her skin and reddened her cheeks.

Emma's blonde hair fell loose about her shoulders. She hadn't bothered to pull it back this morning. Instead, her hair fell in waves down her back to her waist, the way Jared liked it. Emma shuddered. She could almost feel his hands even now, stroking her tresses and whispering in her ear how much he loved her soft hair.

"Emma!" Rosie's voice rang out down the street. "Emma, wait for me!"

She stopped, turning slowly to face her friend. Rosie slammed right into her, her small arms reaching around Emma to hug her. Emma returned the embrace, a sharp sigh slipping from between her lips at the warmth Rosie's hug provided.

"I've missed you! I thought you'd come back to the hospital when you came home." Rosie stepped back, bracing Emma's shoulders in her hands.

"I've been so busy, Rosie."

"But you've been home for months. You've only been preparing to move for two weeks."

"I know." Emma stepped back away from her. "Things change, Rosie. They can never be the way they were before."

"I still think moving to America is a mistake." Rosie eyed her, worried.

"Maybe so. But I have to try. I can't stay here in that house, Rosie. It's just … too painful. Even if Jared was alive out there … I couldn't stay here." Emma backed away. "I'm sorry."

"Emma …"

But she turned her back, hurrying away. Leaving behind her friends and her home wasn't going to be easy. There was nothing easy about walking away from the place a person grew up. But Emma was willing to find the courage to do so. Her sister would be at her side, and she would never have to be alone again.

She turned the corner and stopped at the sight of a man in uniform, his back to her. Her heart thundered in her ears, blocking out every other sound. He was tall; his brown hair curled at the nape of his neck beneath his hat. His hands gestured wildly as he spoke to his companion. Then he turned.

Emma didn't know him. She didn't recognize him at all. But for a moment, just one moment ...

He looked like Jared.

Emma pushed against her wound again, thankful for the pain. It always brought her back to reality, it always kept her sane. She moved on, heading for her home. Gray clouds, threatening either rain or snow, shadowed the blue sky overhead. Emma prayed for snow. She wanted to see a blanket of white covering the field behind her house one more time before she left it forever.

Emma passed the first house on her street, looking down at her mail as she went. If she looked preoccupied, perhaps she wouldn't be stopped today. Perhaps no one would call out to her and tell her again how sorry they were that she was all alone and that she was moving away. She couldn't bear to hear it again, not from anyone.

One of the letters caught her eye, and she ripped it open, tugging the contents of the envelope loose. She smiled, running her fingers over Margie's neat handwriting. Her friend had followed her to England and from there they'd separated, Margie heading back to her homeland in Ireland to live with her grandmother.

Emma skimmed the letter, her heart gladdened when she read how good Margie was doing. Her friend had filled the pages with her recovery from their experience overseas. Ireland sounded wonderful from Margie's description, her life with her grandmother filled with the sort of happiness Emma had desired for herself when she returned from France.

Pressing the letter to her heart, Emma smiled, pausing for a moment on the road.

"Oh, how I miss you, Margie," she whispered, her breath turning to fog before her face.

Her thoughts then turned to a blue-eyed, blonde-haired girl, the one she had held on the streets of France when she was frightened, the one she'd promised to protect, the one she had failed.

Emma shivered, rubbing her arms to warm herself as she started out again. The warmth was quickly slipping from her body as she rushed down the road. She hoped her sister had their dinner waiting on the stove.

Her white fence was in sight up ahead when she opened another letter. One of these should have been from Christy. Emma would give anything to see her face one more time, to have just one moment to tell her what she had meant to her during that horrific time.

A light snow began to fall as she pushed open the gate, her heels clacking against the stone path. As she turned to close the gate, she ran her hand over it. How she would miss this place. Every little part of this fence, this path, and this house, her husband had touched. He had finished it all for her in preparation for their anniversary.

Emma shook her head, turning quickly ... and stopped. Her mail fluttered to her feet. The blood drained from her face. Emma gasped, her chest heaving as she stared at the figure standing on her porch steps.

Snow was sticking to his shoulders and hat as he pulled it off, tucking it beneath his arm. He stood before her like a statue, his back straight, and his hair, glistening with moisture from a recent bath, combed to the side. She could smell Bay Rum wafting toward her. It was a scent she knew well. It still clung to their bed sheets, and she drowned in it every night. His uniform fit his body perfectly, framing his broad shoulders and wide back. It stretched across his chest beautifully, fitted all the way to his waist.

When he moved, her breath completely left her. Her body swayed, her head suddenly light. For a moment, she thought she would faint. Emma shook her head; she couldn't believe this. How could this be real? It was impossible ... she knew it was impossible. This was just one of her many dreams.

Emma closed her eyes, knowing when she opened them he would be gone.

"Emma." His voice bathed her in warmth, the cold wind fading away.

Air pulled into her lungs as she opened her eyes. There he was, his beautiful eyes caressing every inch of her face. Snow caught in his hair, glistening against his brown locks as he leaned in. Her tears started to freeze on her cheeks when his brow touched hers.

"You're real," she rasped. Her hands slid up his arms, grabbing the front of his coat.

"I'm real." He laughed, his lips brushing against hers. "I'm here, Em, and I will never leave you ever again."

"Promise?"

The snowflakes sprinkled around them, bathing them in white splendor as he brushed his nose against hers. Emma felt her future beginning. She sensed the whole world shifting in that moment as his solid chest pressed into her palms and she felt his heartbeat thunder against her wrist.

This was Jared. This was her husband.

He's come back to me.

"I promise."

Then he sealed his promise with a kiss. Emma knew this was a moment she would hold in her heart forever. This was an oath that would last a lifetime.

Epilogue

The day Jared came home was the day my life began. I was saved, rescued from the despair that clamped around my heart the day Margie O'Brian had looked down and told me that my husband was dead. Finding him waiting for me in front of our house had been God's final act to save my soul. For the first time in those four longest years of my life, my heart was at peace once more.

Yet our losses would return to haunt us. Two years after Jared returned, we received a telegram from an attorney in New York, informing us that William Garvin—my friend Christy's husband and the man who had fought beside Jared—had died. I knew there were some wounds that could never heal, some things even morphine could not numb. Will had discovered that as he tried to live those last two years without Christy. The morphine ended his pain once and for all.

I had thought never to return to France after those horrible weeks there, but our friend's last wishes were clear. He trusted only Jared to return his ashes to that one field, the place where he saw Christy for the last time. The place she had never left. We spread his ashes over that field and finally put both their memories to rest.

In the days that followed Jared's return home, he rarely spoke about the time he was missing in action. He had sustained an injury in the explosion that separated us on that field in France, leaving him permanently deaf in his left ear. He did not speak to me about his escape or how he managed to find his way home, and I did not ask. I understood the pain and would not force him to explain the measures he had to take to finally come home to me.

It took three years, not long after our move to America, before he could speak about his time in the woods and five more years before he told me about John Young, the man who had saved his life. I suppose, in the end, Sergeant John Hanover Young saved us both.

I will never forget the day I met Beth Young. I knew what I intended to say to her when I met her. I would say I was sorry and that her husband was a hero. I would say that God had intervened in both our lives and given us John to bring us all home. But the day I faced her, I could not speak at all. Neither did Jared have any words. But what I never expected was her tears. Beth Young embraced me, and we shared tears of grief for her loss.

Parting with her had been the most difficult moment of my life. But we would meet again. In the months that followed our meeting, Jared and I asked Beth to come to America. It was with great joy that she accepted our offer to lay the memories of her life with John to rest and begin anew.

I never met a woman as courageous as Beth. The First World War had taken her husband ... the Second World War took both our sons. And we held hands as we received the news that our children would not be returning home. We would place them to rest together, side by side.

War tears husbands from their wives and sons from their mothers. But through this war, we found our courage. Through this war, we found honor. Beth and I remained close long after I lost my Jared in the summer of 1980, and I would hold her hand when she was called home to finally be with John again.

This is a story of what World War I took from me and of what it gave back. I reminded my children of the sacrifice, and they passed it to their children, and so it would go on.

This was their legacy; this was the reason. Their sacrifices would live on. In me, in my children and in their children.

The Lost Generation would live ... in hearts and memory. For as long as our hearts beat ... they will be there.

Author's Note

Dear Reader,

Thank you so much for reading *The Lost Generation*! I hope you enjoyed the story and characters as much as I enjoyed writing about them. While many of the settings in my book are based on historical events, the story itself is fictional. My characters live in my imagination alone to serve the purpose of reminding us of the great sacrifice that comes with war.

When I first wrote *The Lost Generation*, I was inspired by something my father once said. I can't remember the full conversation, but I do recall my father, in a fit of emotion, lamented that one day no one would remember the lost generation of 1914. In that moment, a story of loss was born in my mind. The first character to emerge was Emma Cote. I didn't know her name then, but she came alive in my imagination all the same. I became determined to write a story that would remind us all what war can do; what war can take from innocent families and that we should cherish the memories of those young men who fought and died for us so long ago.

If you enjoyed *The Lost Generation*, then I encourage you to pass it along! Spread the word about my debut novel so this story can reach the hearts of many more people. As Emma says at the end of the story, let's let the Lost Generation live again in our hearts and memories.

For as long as our hearts beat ...

Blessings,

Erica Marie Hogan

About the Author

From as far back as she can remember, Erica Marie Hogan loved to write. When she was a little girl, she adored make believe, but gradually her imagination became too big to restrict it to playtime and so, she wrote.

Erica was born and raised for nine years on Orient Point, Long Island, New York. After that she moved with her family to Virginia and, finally, to Texas where she now lives. She was homeschooled, is an avid reader, and a member of American Christian Fiction Writers. She lives to plot new stories, enjoys a good tear-jerker, and chocolate is her cure for any ailment. Once a month, Erica publishes a post on her blog, "By the Book: Diary of a Bookaholic," where she shares her experiences with writing and, occasionally, a book review.

Only twenty-four-years-old, Erica's wish is to continue to write stories that not only drop her readers into the middle of historical time periods, but also show the ability to rise up out of adversity and tragedy in hope, faith, love, and strength. When it comes to genre, she has no limits.

The Lost Generation is Erica's debut novel. You can learn more about her on her blog or Facebook page.

Erica's Blog: www.booksaholic.wordpress.com